# GUIDED

## BOOK ONE

Also by the author:

WASTED
MIDNIGHT SHERBET
DEAD FINE

This book may contain mature scenes,
including bullying, peer pressure, suicide,
and references to sex.

Suitable for older readers.

# GUIDED

GUIDED

ISBN – 9798816851145

emmasmithbooks.com

for Sana, Bridget, Isobel,
Ada, Christina, Hannah,
Hannah and Martha-May

# PART ONE

Dear diary,

My name is Macey Collins, and I am a murderer.

Yes, you read that right. A murderer, defined online as a person (or persons) who causes the death of another human, due to malice or lack of care. In some American states, my actions still receive the death penalty. In England, I've just ruined my life.

Lekie McCoy. So young and innocent, so sweet and happy, content. She didn't deserve to die. She was so young, had so much life ahead of her. Why? Why did I do it? Why?

Because I was selfish. The last two years, I've thought of nobody but myself. Two years of ignoring the truth, of letting events run away with themselves, of pretending everything was fine when Lekie's small life was spiralling out of control. I watched her unravel, her mind trampled on by those four trolls. Lucy, Chloe, Kayleigh and Orla. Such nice little girls... and Lekie's very own wicked witches of the west.

I watched as things got worse, watched as my own mind sagged beneath the weight of Lekie's demise. I clutched her bloody fingers under the flickering bathroom lights as she sobbed, then went back home to my nice warm bedroom in my nice warm house, forgetting all about the storm waging inside the McCoys' own home.

Why didn't I say anything? Why didn't I stop the bullying, the teasing? Why didn't I make things better? Was I really that oblivious, that cruel?

Yes. Yes, I was.

But it's fine, don't worry.

I got what I deserved.

# 1

The funeral is terrible.

I don't know what I was expecting. When a twelve-year-old girl dies, it's hardly cause for celebration... The room is small, too cramped for the turn-out, family members spilling around the door and towards the refreshments as a herd.

Lexie's parents are gathered around the door. They're welcoming guests (guests, mourners?), shaking hands and faking smiles, clad in cheap black and making small talk as though it's somehow relevant. *Hello, Vera – so nice of you to come! Traffic was a nightmare on the way, was it? You're missing your yoga class to be here today? We're... We're so sorry, Saturday was the only day the crematorium had free –*

I don't want to stare, but my eyes keep wandering. Mr and Mrs McCoy look like the kind of people to eat every last morsel of their Sunday roast, with crumble and custard and glasses of Baileys for afters, so undoubtedly chose the funeral spread. Mini rolls (off-brand); packets of After Eights; paper plates filled with classic church biscuits: bourbons, custard creams, and soggy pink wafers. It's kids' party food. Cheap and cheerful, neither here nor there.

Lexie's dad is shaking hands with an older man, nodding his head so vigorously that the rolls in his neck open and close like blubbery lips. Her mum is crying as she straddles a cluster of cousins, tears smudging her mascara. Lexie's younger brother – Daniel, I think – isn't talking. He looks angry. Angry at the way his parents are acting, and probably angry at the fact he's even here, at his sister's funeral. It alarms me, that determination, steely eyes staring straight ahead and unmoving.

It's the exact expression Lexie used to wear.

I tear my eyes from them, flitting back to the coffin. It's shiny – too shiny – I can almost see my face in it. But it's not my face. It's too plump, rounded, not slim enough. I watch my eyes, distorted and grotesque, blue turned mouldy green against the wood.

She's in there. Lexie. Watching, blaming, laughing. Basking in all the attention, no doubt – maybe even jealous of the biscuits and chocolate.

They said she'd sustained several head injuries when she was found. I imagine her unsmiling face, bruised and broken beneath the coffin, lids swollen round glassy grey eyes. I imagine her fingers, still clutching onto that rock, tearing at the grass as the current ripped her away. I imagine them now, clawing at the lid as she tries to drag herself out to join the party...

I pick a bourbon from the nearest table. Tease it apart, so that the cream falls onto my palm in one long, rectangular slab. When I was younger, I'd nibble off the biscuit and lick out the chocolate cream, until Mum said it was a dirty habit, that I wasn't to tear apart my food like a wild animal.

If she had it her way, I'd be banned from eating bourbons completely, confined to avocado and boiled egg salads.

She's in here somewhere, mingling. I wasn't sure why she bothered coming at first, but she slipped a pile of business cards into her pocket before we left home, which made an awful lot of sense.

I bite down on the biscuit. It sticks to the roof of my

mouth, hard to swallow. There's orange juice at the end of the table – off-brand, again – and red plastic cups, the kind we use at house parties... I wonder if Mrs McCoy knows that. Yellow liquid swills around the bottom, a featureless smiley face. I pour a cup. It's sickly sweet.

Footsteps, heard on the ground behind me, moving through the crowds. A pair of trainers, squeaking on the polished floor, the low hum of some eighties banger reverberating from lips. Jenna taps me on the shoulder before I have the chance to turn around, swiping the nearest plate and sinking her teeth into a jammy dodger.

"Don't let Lisa catch you with that," she warns. She eyes the bourbon, before switching her gaze to my cup and wrinkling her nose. *"Pure sugar, Macey, it'll rot your teeth right out of those gumsies!"*

Her impression of Mum is infuriatingly spot-on, but I don't think my sister realises this isn't the place to be laughing.

"Funerals are weird," she continues, raising her eyes to gaze around the room. She stops on Lexie's family, who are now stood around a table in silence. This time, I can't stare. I'm forced to tear my eyes away, stomach clenching. The breath catches in my throat and I go to cough...

*You caused this.*

*You caused this.*

*It's all your fault –*

I withdraw my hand from my face, straightening up and wiping my wet eyes. With my pinky, I remove the crumbs from either side of my mouth.

"You okay?" Jenna asks, one eyebrow arched. "Need some fresh air?"

I take a deep breath and reach for a napkin, trying to

smile.

"I'm fine."

Her sympathy isn't real. Jenna doesn't usually like me, or show much interest. She thinks I'm boring; as far as siblings go, we're polar opposites. We stand in stilted silence, Jenna still absently humming as she picks at a pink wafer with her electric blue nails. They're not very Jenna. They're too bright, too cheerful. Too blue.

The venue murmurs around us, filled with the quiet, reverent tones of those attempting to sound respectful. Is it *dis*respectful of me to assume they're loving it? Cousins and aunties and family friends, reconnecting for the first time in months, catching up and enjoying a break from their hectic lives. *You're missing your yoga class, Vera? Such a shame.* They smile, hug, kiss blotchy cheeks and painted lips. Pass around biscuits, throwing aside post-pregnancy diets and supping juice from a never-ending supply of cartons.

Munch, munch.

Slurp.

I spot Lexie's grandparents out of the corner of my eye, sat across a table with unreadable expressions and hands clutched round cups. I force myself to look at them, look at them directly. Her granddad is staring at a digestive in his palm, eyes moist, other hand wrapped round his wife's. Staring, staring. Staring. Unstaring.

"Hey!" Jenna waves a hand in front of my face, a flash of blue acrylic. "Wake up, dopey. It's not your funeral."

As if I hadn't noticed.

There's a sudden flurry of gasps and the clip-clop of heels behind me, the sound of someone pushing themselves through the crowd towards us. I hear an angry "Watch out!" as liquid slish-sloshes over the edge of its plastic cup and splatters across the floor.

"I'm so sorry!" a woman is saying, voice clipped and professional. "I don't have a tissue… but I do have some business cards here. I don't know if they'll help, but they might soak up the juice. Let me just try…"

Pivoting, I turn to face my mum.

She's dabbing at a man's shirt with one of her stone-grey cards, one that reads "Lisa Collins Estate Agency" in fancy cursive writing. Her lips are pursed, a tidy blush colour she undoubtedly spent a fortune on, and her hair's in its trademark tortoiseshell clip, the one that says she put no effort into her hair when realistically it took fifteen minutes to perfect in the bathroom mirror.

Glancing up to meet the man's gaze, she runs a fingernail across his chest and retreats with her sodden business card. He's not an attractive man – his eyes are too far apart – but that hardly seems to matter.

I think I recognise him from somewhere… maybe. A school run, or girl guiding event. That being said, Lexie's family all have those trademark mouths, turned down at the corners, and stone grey eyes, just like her brother.

"Again, I'm so sorry for the inconvenience." Mum's expression is plastic, cheeks carved into an unmoving beam. "Keep the card, honey."

She pushes it straight into the pocket of his trousers, fingers lingering before she turns away. Jenna mimes vomiting behind me and I try to stay calm, composed, but my fingers are trembling and I have to clutch them into balls by my sides.

This day is about *Lexie*. Why is no one taking that seriously?

"Macey!"

Mum's voice is saturated with sympathy as she drops an arm round my shoulder. My nostrils fill with pungent rose as I breathe in her familiar perfumey scent.

"This must be so tough, Macey," she's saying, voice an octave too high. She wants people to hear. She wants them to realise what a good mother she is… or isn't, evidently.

I don't say anything. Jenna's face is stubborn, mouth a thin line as she glares at her talons.

Lexie's grandparents are watching us now. Their grief has been disturbed by the commotion and they're staring with narrowed eyes, disapproving expressions. Mum doesn't seem to notice, continuing to talk to my ear as I zone out. I've caught the eye of Lexie's grandma, and we hold our gazes steady. I don't know if she knows who I am. Would Lexie's dad have pointed me out? Would he have really felt the need to tell her that *I was there* when Lexie died?

Five, four, three, two, one…

As though in slow-motion, the talking around us seems to stop. The man who spilt his juice shuffles away in his too-long trousers, and the floor becomes clear as the crowd shifts.

I tear my gaze from Lexie's grandma, her pale eyes echoing in my vision as I try to shake them away.

"Hello, Macey."

It's Lexie's dad.

I recognise his voice from… from that day. The anxiety, the stress. The raw emotion, trying to comfort his howling wife, speaking to the police, suddenly breaking down in tears –

I can't face him. I can't.

*Pull yourself together*, the voice in my head screams. *He deserves to speak to you!*

Mr McCoy stands with his wife in one hand and his son in

the other, smiling beneath a stiff collar. His eyes are storm grey, too – that must be where the kids get it from. Mrs McCoy's aren't. They're blue. Too blue, like Jenna's nails. A horrible shade of summer sky that might seem cheerful in August, but just plain cold past September.

"Hi," I try to say. It comes out like more of a croak, and Lexie's brother frowns at me from behind his dad's back.

Mr McCoy's eyebrows are knitted together, trapped in a thick, slug-like log. He holds out a hand. Grasps at my own. It's sweaty – mine, that is.

"Thank you for coming," he says, but it's a regimented line, one he knows he's supposed to recite. It's an unspoken rule at funerals, one I don't really understand. Why *wouldn't* I come? It's my fault we're here. It's my fault her grandparents are nursing their cups, unsure of what to do with themselves. It's my fault –

"You seem to be holding up well," Mrs McCoy adds. It's supposed to sound like praise, but the look on her face is anything but appreciative. I can't hold her gaze. Her eyes narrow at me, scrutinising, wondering. Blaming.

I don't know what to say.

"We're really grateful for the help you gave the police," Mr McCoy adds. "You've been… well, vital."

Vital.

It's a dig, I know it is, but I force a smile and nod my head. It's what they want to see, and I'm well-practised in compliance.

"I just want to find out what happened."

That's what everyone says. The McCoys, Jenna, the people at school… even Mum the other day, waltzing round the kitchen with a cucumber in hand, murmured absent-mindedly, "If only those poor parents knew how it happened... At least then they'd get some peace."

"We all do," she adds now, smiling at Mr McCoy and squeezing my shoulder gently. I'd almost forgotten she was there. Her nails dig in, making indentations in my shirt. "They'll get to the bottom of it soon. You needn't worry yourselves. Lexie wouldn't want that."

Wouldn't she? Lexie *liked* being the centre of attention. She liked people talking about her, people caring, crying, loving, in a way they rarely did when she was alive. She wouldn't want them to forget.

The silence is awkward, hanging around us. I daren't breathe. Mrs McCoy is still watching me, those blue eyes watery and piercing mine.

She knows.

I know she knows.

She knows I know *exactly* what happened to Lexie.

# 2

The car is silent on the way home. I stare out of the passenger window, eyes fixed on the blur of houses, lit up with the blue of televisions and pumpkin-orange streetlights.

Jenna's music bursts from her headphones, pulsing a beat around her. Mum never listens to the radio as she drives – she's too easily distracted – so there's no escape from the drone. When the rain starts, splatters of neon on the windscreen, it's a relief.

The house is in darkness, the way we left it. I hate it. I hate that so much can happen in a day, yet nothing's really *changed*. Lexie's family will go back to their modest semi with its leather sofas and electric fire, just to sit in silence, as they have done for the last two weeks, one seat empty. And here we are, still complete, sliding up the drive to a house we scarcely inhabit.

Mum drops her keys on the telephone table, kicking off her heels and reaching down to rub her sore ankles. I hover near the door, wringing my hands together, unsure of what to do with myself.

My phone buzzes in my pocket, but I don't want to look at it.

"Could you help with tea, girls?" Mum asks. She slips on her slippers and pads down the corridor towards the kitchen. "We have salad stuff in the fridge, and there's a can of chickpeas on the carousel…"

I shiver. My hair's still damp from the rain, tendrils curling round my ears, and there's nothing I want less than limp lettuce and tomato. I kick my own shoes off, listening to them hit the skirting board with a crack.

"Not a chance, Lisa," Jenna fires back, as Mum winces at the use of her first name. "I'll order pizza." Jenna looks at me then, lip curled slightly, and asks, as an afterthought, "You want some, Macey?"

I shake my head.

Despite everything, I don't want to upset my mother today.

We end up eating together, a mismatch of legs and fluffy socks on the sofa, *Countdown* on the telly. Jenna's pizza steams from across the chair, warm and greasy against her lap, and I try not to breathe in for the sake of stopping my mouth watering. Her calves are heavy in my lap, the result of too many takeaways and not enough exercise.

Mum is stroking my foot, hand absently trailing my ankle. It's cosy… probably the closest moment we've had as a family since Dad left. I can't enjoy it. I *won't* enjoy it. How can I?

I keep picturing the McCoys, sat around a dining room table with four places set, one dish steaming to itself. Mrs McCoy's eyes are bloodshot and watering, staring at her food like it's poisonous. Lexie's brother pushes it round his plate with his fork. He has no appetite, now. That childish innocence and desperation for food has disappeared; he seems to have aged years. Mr McCoy sits at the head of the table, trying to stay strong. His hand curls beside him, where a smaller fist once clutched his.

I focus on the TV, to where the presenter's making a joke Mum finds hilarious, but it blurs before me and I reach up quickly to wipe my eyes. *Don't cry. You're not pathetic.*

I'm worse than just pathetic.

I have a shower later, for lack of anything else to do. Jenna locks herself in her room again, painting something "abstract", and Mum goes back to work in her office. I bolt the bathroom door and slip out of my clothes, leaving them in a jumbled pile beside the toilet, turn the knob to fire up the water. My legs are white, deathly white. The hairs on my legs stand up straight on goosebumps.

I haven't shaved since Lexie died. I wonder what the girls at school would say? And Tyler... he wouldn't be impressed. He said so before, sometime before we started dating, that girls should look after themselves, make themselves presentable. It's dirty, he said. Dirty to let unwanted hair grow, to let your hair go greasy, your skin oily. It's unhygienic, unhealthy, unattractive.

At least I don't have to see him for a few more days. I shiver, twisting my hands tight between my knees before stepping into the flow.

The water's hot, the tiles cool. It slides through my hair, my fingers, my toes, dripping onto the mat and filling the bathroom with steam. I revel in it, the heat and smog and endless downpour, let it fill me with numb nothingness. My memories are in the condensation, the scent of lavender, the hair sliding down my back towards my waist...

Through closed eyes, my vision is white. Hazy blank spaces fizzle and expand, swimming to touch every corner of my head, curling round my thoughts. I reach to grab the shampoo and my fingers clasp cold metal, and suddenly I'm back there, clutching onto the silver harness with river water stinging my eyes and wind battering my face –

I twist the knob, shocking myself back into reality.

The bathroom's cold. I think the window's open, just a

crack, but I can't reach up to close it.

It's the simple things that do it. Send me hurtling towards the edge again, wracked with guilt. The fact that Lexie will never experience a steaming shower, never scrub her teeth with her pink electric toothbrush in their damp family bathroom. That the last thing she felt was gushing icy water, filling her mouth and frothing in her strangled scream. The rush of a heavy current, dragging her hands from the rock –

I squeeze my eyes shut, shaking my head, trying to block it out. I perch on the edge of the toilet. Pull a towel from the rack and wrap it round my shoulders, letting it envelop me and provide a moment of comfort I know I don't deserve.

My phone, perched on top of my trousers where I left it, buzzes quietly to itself. I reach to pluck it from the floor with trembling fingers. I'm freezing, still bare from my shower beneath the towel, and it feels like ice beneath my hands. I press the screen, watching it fizz to life.

One Snapchat notification, from Tyler. Two random Instagram likes. An event reminder from Facebook, telling me it's Lexie's funeral today and that *I don't want to miss it*.

There's nothing from my friends. Not one message; no interaction in the group chat. Silence.

I tap down on Tyler's name, waiting for the screen to flash yellow.

**gud day? xx**

I blink at how insensitive the question seems. Good day? It was Lexie's *funeral*. My fingers hover above the keyboard, unsure of what to say. How can I answer that? Can't I just… ignore him?

As if hearing my thoughts, Tyler's icon bursts into view,

announcing his arrival in the chat. It's all there: his tousled hair with its bleached quiff, big brown eyes and bushy brows, plain t-shirt, stretched across his torso. I hold my breath as he types, fingers clutching the phone tight above my naked thighs. The three dots appear and reappear, dodging in and out of view before he vanishes, and I let out a strangled breath through my nose.

He doesn't understand what I'm going through, that's all. No one does. It's not his fault.

The floorboards are warm but the corridor is icy. I cross the landing to my bedroom still shivering beneath my towel. It's properly dark now, rain hurling itself at the windows and crashing into the side of the house. The covers envelop me, dragging me under and cocooning me in pink velvet. It's soft against my bare skin, but I hate it, I hate it, I *hate* it –

Lexie loved pink. She was wearing pink wellies that day, over her pyjama bottoms. Her sleeping bag was pink too, half-hanging out of the tent flap, where it was found a day later, sopping wet. She was a girly-girl, the funeral celebrant said. He didn't really *need* to say that, though. Anyone who knew her was already well aware.

I curl up into a ball, squeezing my eyes shut. It just hurts. All of it. The constant reminders, the guilt, the overbearing sense of fear…

The worry is perhaps the worst part. The part that keeps me on edge at all times, unable to sleep, to eat, to do *anything* properly. It's the same now as it was at the start, when they first found her body. Terrified that it'd give something away, some minor detail which would link me directly to the cause of death, confirm that I was there that night, by the river. But it didn't. It hasn't. Nobody knows, and *nobody is going to find out.*

I try to go to sleep. Switching off and stretching under the covers, I turn onto my side and try to breathe naturally, in and out, in and out, but my mind won't stop whirring.

It doesn't matter if I sleep or not – there's no escape from her, even then.

Tonight's no different to any other.

The minute I fall asleep, I dream about Lexie.

3

I was fifteen when I first met Lexie. She was ten. Chubby for her age, perhaps, with very small, inward-bending teeth. Her hair was still wispy and stuck to her cheeks and forehead, those stormy eyes little more than rainclouds.

She stood by the door, clutching a stuffed unicorn. It didn't look expensive, and seemed to have been dragged severely through a hedge; it was missing one eye, poor mouth half unpicked. She hugged it to her chest as though she couldn't let it go, twisting on the spot.

Her uniform was second-hand, too. The red and blue had faded, the faint "guides" logo peeling round the edges. She caught my eye and smiled hesitantly, but I'd already started walking over.

"Hey," I said. That was the first thing I ever said to her. A small, pathetic, "Hey." No doubt I was a little shy, awkward, and that definitely came across in the delivery.

"Hi," she replied, wrinkling her nose. "I'm Lexie."

I knew that, of course. Sharon had shown me the list of new starters earlier, and Lexie McCoy's name was written amongst the carnage. She'd never been part of girl guiding before, and was new to the area, Sharon explained. She needed to make friends.

I was a young leader there, helping Sharon on Tuesday evenings, organising activities and games. One hour a week away from studying would be good for me, she insisted. It wasn't exactly *fun*, but volunteering would look great on my university applications.

Lexie was still watching me.

"I'm Macey," I told her. My voice was faintly patronising, an octave higher than usual. That always happened when I met new kids; they unnerved me. With teens, you start off on an even playing field, battling to make the best first impression. Children see straight through you. "Do you know anybody here?"

Lexie just stared at me, raising one eyebrow as though I'd asked a stupid question.

"I'm new," she said, squeezing the unicorn tight. "I don't know *any* of these people."

"Okay." I flushed. Nodding my head, I turned to gaze around the room. "Let me see…"

There was a cluster of girls in the corner of the room, smaller than the rest, a collection of newbies. There were four girls; one was tiny, hidden in the middle and clutching something tight between her hands. The others seemed entranced by it, peering over her shoulders and making faces of wonderment.

"Come on." I gestured for Lexie to follow me.

The girls didn't notice us approaching, giggling and reaching into the circle to touch whatever the smallest girl was holding. Lexie stayed close behind me as I stood over them, hands on hips, before clearing my throat.

They spun around at once, jumping and staring back in guilt, pushing away the object. The tiny girl thrust her hands behind her back and blushed, taking a few steps back and quivering her bottom lip.

"I'm sorry," she burst out, green eyes wide. It was amusing, almost, the hold I seemed to have over them as the older girl. They thought I was scary, despite the fact that I was probably more intimidated by *them*. "We weren't doing anything wrong, we were just talking and –"

"What's behind your back?"

"Nothing, I –"

"Show me."

The girl, now with tears in her eyes and her front teeth firmly latched over her trembling lip, held out her hands. Prising her fingers open, I tried not to let a smile take over my face; for there, in her palm, was a phone. It was more of a starter phone, really, the old-fashioned kind they give kids before letting them have a proper one. She'd decorated it with stickers and Sharpie, and the screen was alight with the building blocks of a tacky game.

"You do realise you're supposed to leave technology at home?" I checked, biting the inside of my cheeks to keep from laughing. "I'm sure your parents wouldn't be impressed if your... *phone* was stolen."

The girl shook her head solemnly, gazing up at me in terror. "Please don't take it away. My dad would kill me."

Faking a frown, I asked her, "What's your name?"

"Lucy." Her green eyes were big and apologetic, the fear on her face almost endearing. I'd been exactly like that, once. Simpering, anxious, eager-to-please.

Raising an eyebrow, I turned and gestured for Lexie to come forward. She'd been watching the exchange, unicorn now hanging by her side and eyes fixed on the girls.

"This is Lexie," I explained, placing my hand on her back and pushing her forward. "She's new."

The other girls took her in cautiously, the sniffing of wolves checking out a new member of the pack. The tallest girl, a slim blonde with a narrow face and sharp freckles, wrinkled her nose at the unicorn dangling from her hand.

"I like your teddy," she said, smiling at Lexie, expression like plastic. "It's really cute."

There was no way on earth Lexie's drooping unicorn could be considered cute, but her eyes lit up and a smile burst onto her face.

"Thanks! His name is Mr Sparkles – I've had him since I was a baby."

The girl, clearly trying to suppress a smirk, grinned again and eyed it warily. "Mr Sparkles." Exchanging a look with one of the other girls, her lips twitched as she added, "What an original name."

I hated the expression on Lexie's face, one of excitement and hope. She thought she'd made a new friend, one who shared her love for the bedraggled unicorn with its pathetic name. She thought she was fitting in. That's one thing kids still share with teens, one thing I don't think you ever truly grow out of... A desire to please people, to blend into the background. She wanted to join this group, to be "one of them".

I could hardly blame her.

I turned back to Lucy, fixing that severe frown back onto my face.

"I'll let you keep the phone," I promised, slipping it into the pocket of her hoody. "But only on one condition."

Lucy nodded, pushing her hands into her pocket and squeezing it tight.

"Anything," she insisted, moving her head vigorously. "I just don't want my dad to kill me..."

"He won't." I glanced from Lucy to Lexie, then back to Lucy, a smile creeping onto my face. "Look after Lexie for tonight. Make her feel welcome... and Mr Sparkles, of course." Lexie grinned at me then, all teeth and dimples. "Got it?"

Lucy nodded, turning to Lexie with a huge beam. "Of *course*. You can be friends with us, Lexie… and Mr Sparkles!"

The four others nodded and giggled, cheeks flushed pink as they took in Lexie. The tallest girl didn't seem so pleased, but smiled down her long nose. Lexie's expression was one of pure joy, chubby fingers clutched around Mr Sparkles' hoof.

"Thank you," she whispered, reaching onto her tiptoes in ecstasy and holding her arms out to embrace the group.

Lucy smiled back. "We're going to be the *best* of friends!"

# 4

I wake to a racing heart and a body drenched in sweat. Lexie's face is still clear in my mind, grey eyes wide and full of joy. Mr Sparkles' lopsided expression is vinegary sharp.

*We're going to be the best of friends.*

Lucy couldn't have been more wrong.

Feeling for my phone, I pull it under the sheets with me and feel it buzz to life. There are eighteen messages, all of which are from the group chat at last. My friends have been discussing outfits and hair combinations since Jaye first woke at six, no doubt for her early morning run.

Of course. Today is shopping day.

The tradition started at the beginning of last year, before we started sixth form. Rosie declared our wardrobes "tragic" and insisted on organising an end-of-August shopping spree in the city, and the idea stuck. It's a monthly thing now, despite the fact it's early September and we've technically missed the deadline. I'm in dire need of new clothes, but the thought of travelling to the city to spend an obscene amount of money and sip iced coffees through a straw the day after *Lexie's funeral* just seems… weird.

Soraya thinks that going out will make me feel better.

I disagree.

I crawl out of bed, shivering in the pale light. I never bothered to get dressed last night, so I reach to grab my robe and wrap it around me. The hall outside is empty, dappled yellow filtering through the skylight and dotting the floorboards with vanilla.

Mum's door is at the end of the corridor. I knock. Silence. When there's no reply, I push down on the handle.

It's a tip, as usual. Her clothes are in a pile on the floor, slippers in disarray, lacy underwear dotted across her rug. The curtains haven't been shut properly and let in a sliver of light, pouring round the edges and filling the room with a golden glow.

That's when I notice a hairy ankle poking out from under the covers, attached to a taut, pale leg. I'm about to retreat, blushing furiously, when Mum's head emerges by the headboard and she lets out a breathy gasp.

"Macey!" she exclaims, voice hoarse and hair in a wild clump at the top of her head. "Did you sleep well, dear?"

I blink, nodding my head and feeling my face flush even more as a second head pushes its way from beneath the duvet. Our eyes meet for a brief second and I can't help letting out a horrified, "What the fu–"

"Do you remember Doyle, Macey?" Mum asks, beaming and turning to him. "I spilt orange juice all over him at the funeral!"

I don't want to look at him again, but I almost can't help it. Doyle, the man with eyes too far apart and trousers which trailed along the floor, stares back at me with equal apprehension. He quickly retracts his hairy foot from the end of the bed and pulls the covers up around himself, as though to hide his bare shoulders and pretend, even for a moment, that he isn't naked under there.

I can't stop my cheeks from turning red.

"I just wanted to tell you I'm going out today," I say, beginning to retreat. "Sorry to interrupt…"

"With Tyler, dear?" It's painful, how eager she is for me to say yes. Her adoration towards Tyler has always faintly annoyed me. Most girls would *die* for their parents' approval of their boyfriends... but most girls don't have Lisa Collins for a mother.

"No." I take another step back until I'm completely hidden by the door, so I don't have to see her face fall. "With Rosie, Soraya and Jaye. I'll be back later. Bye!"

Then I slam it closed behind me.

I don't know how she does it. I don't know *why* she does it. It's not the first time I've walked in on Mum with a guy, but it's not something you get used to. Jenna doesn't understand how she lasted all that time with just Dad for company. She says she's making up for those lost years now, the years spent arguing and screaming and slamming doors before they divorced.

It could be worse; at least today I was prepared. Last time, the guy walked into the kitchen in his boxers while Rosie and I were watching Netflix and eating pancakes, and threw himself down on the sofa opposite with pretty much everything on show. Despite the fact Rosie *thinks* she knows everything about me, I don't think either of us were quite ready for that.

I don't bother with breakfast, heading back to my room to pick a pair of leggings and a hoody. I'm preened, dressed and waiting by ten, stood at the bottom of the drive with my phone clutched beneath my fingers. It's cold out, September settling in properly and the air alive with a chill. My heart's pounding as Jaye's battered old car swings onto our road, racing down the street and screeching to a stop before me.

"Macey!" Rosie yells, hanging out of the window with a huge grin and holding a hand up to salute me. "Your ride is here!"

Soraya pushes the door open for me, brown eyes wide and welcoming. She doesn't say anything as I step forward, but offers a smile and pushes a packet of Haribo my way.

"How was the funeral?" she asks, as I take a gummy heart and bite down on it, hard. Climbing into the back seat and slamming the door shut, Rosie and Jaye turn round to look at me.

I'd assumed they'd have forgotten all about it. I'm not sure whether that would've been better or worse.

"It was a funeral." I frown, reaching for another sweet. I'm not sure what I'm supposed to say. How *was* the funeral? Pretty shit, but I don't think that's what they're expecting. "It was sad. But it was good to finally say goodbye, you know?"

The others tut-tut, nodding like they understand. Goodbye? I don't even know where that came from. I didn't want to say *goodbye*, and still don't. Saying goodbye would be forgetting and moving on, and I don't want that, don't need that. I don't deserve that. *Lexie* doesn't deserve that.

"It must have been so hard," Soraya says, shaking her head sadly. "You're so brave, Macey."

The others nod in agreement, sympathetic and unsmiling.

Brave.

I'm the opposite of brave.

The conversation in the car is odd, stilted, very unlike us. Rosie hardly stops talking, trying to fill the gaps with meaningless gossip and chatter. A girl from her maths class slept with one of the fairground boys on the Dodgems, apparently, when they were moving; Mr Roberts, the head of sixth form, snogged a student in the ball cupboard during a meeting about sports apprenticeships; Tyler's older brother does drugs, so should we try to get hold of some, just to try?

It's trivial chatter, and Jaye contributes every now and then with a nod or a short "mmhmm", while trying to steer the car and stick to the speed limits.

The city centre is bursting with back-to-school shoppers, hauling kids by shirt sleeves and sticky hands, dodging in and out of shops to find shoes, trousers, blazers. Clipped tags and sweet wrappers cluster along the pavements, and harassed grandparents hurry along with sticky fingers in hand. It's oddly nostalgic, the clamour for school uniform. Mum used to take us the week before the return to school, when all the supermarkets had run out of most sizes and the shoes were sweaty from being taken on and off summery feet. She'd try to fit us into shirts that were far too small, cramming into one dressing room to squeeze our arms into miniscule cardigans that hugged our armpits and barely came down to our wrists. It's not like she couldn't *afford* proper clothes for us. She just couldn't be bothered.

I try not to think about the fact that Lexie will never wear her woollen tights and Velcro shoes again, won't beg Mrs McCoy for a new bag or shiny water bottle. The fact she won't ever go back to school, won't ever walk those corridors or wave at me from across the playground –

I'm dragged out of my daydream as someone tugs on my palm, and the cobbled street reformulates before me.

"Shall we get a Starbucks?" Soraya's asking, as she links an arm through mine. It forces me to smile, and I nod my enthusiasm.

"Coconut milk iced latte?"

We end up drinking outside, sat around a table nursing plastic cups with our names scribbled in black marker. It's cold for September, but not enough that the drinks can't be enjoyed. There's a breeze drifting through the square, and we sup in amicable silence, interrupted every now and then by a burst of chatter or hazy remark. Rosie's eyes are fixed on the barista, who Jaye claims is far too "boarding school vibes" for any of us, and Soraya scrolls through her phone with a smile, smile not meant for any of us.

It's nice, the simple distraction. I wasn't expecting it. Talking to my friends feels like going back in time. Despite the guilty feeling curdling in the pit of my stomach, I'm almost... *enjoying* myself.

I take a sip from my drink, the coffee sharp and sweet against my tongue. I can do this. Maybe now the funeral's over, now that everything's behind me and I can finally process it, I'll be okay. I won't forget her, but at least I can *live* with the pain.

I'm smiling now, relief flooding through my body, revelling in the realisation that I can enjoy myself without feeling selfish.

I can *cope*.

I can.

Until Soraya looks at me and says, "I bet Tyler's been so supportive during all of this."

I'm brought back down to earth with a crash, left to nod and simper, to blindly navigate their conversation as if I agree with what they're saying. It's just another thing to think about, an extra worry weighing down on my mind.

I don't know if it's normal to feel this way about your boyfriend. He's by far the best-looking guy in our year, and dating him has only been perfect so far. We've been together for almost eleven months – not that Tyler knows that, or has been keeping count. But I love him. Who wouldn't?

I still haven't answered his message. Even thinking about doing so fills me with unease.

"You're so frickin' lucky," Rosie's saying, but I glance up to see Jaye jab her in the ribs and shake her head warningly. "Oh – I don't mean lucky in that way, obviously. It sucks about Lexie. I only mean… at least you have Tyler."

"He's amazing," Jaye agrees.

"Yeah," Soraya echoes, but the smile doesn't quite reach her eyes this time, and an extra layer of paranoia settles in my gut.

"He's been great." Maybe he *has* been great, and I simply haven't noticed. We've only spoken a handful of times since Lexie died. I swirl my straw through the drink, watching it spiral through the liquid. My stomach churns.

"I mean, how do you even *get* a boyfriend?" Jaye ponders as we continue to sup in silence. I welcome the change of topic as Rosie and I meet eyes, a look passing between us.

We've talked about it before, Jaye's lack of experience. The most she's ever done with a boy was snog Rhys Carter at prom. She said his hand went up her dress, but, knowing Rhys Carter, that's probably a lie. Rosie puts it down to her scrawny frame and flat nose. Boys don't want abs, she says. Jaye's pretty much *all* abs. She's not conceited, but spends an extraordinarily long time exercising each day, and feeds herself leaves and strange pulses she calls "food". We only recently got her into clothes which weren't meant for the gym.

I stay quiet, smiling at Jaye sympathetically.

"Boys are complicated," Soraya continues, wrinkling her nose. "You can *never* tell what they're thinking."

"How would you know?" Jaye responds. There's a hint of resentment in her voice as she pouts. "You're not even allowed to talk to guys. Your parents would go berserk!"

"You don't know everything about me – and neither do

they!" Soraya argues, while the rest of us raise our eyebrows in a simultaneous smirk. "I *do* talk to boys, you know I do. Just because I don't give you a running commentary…"

That's undoubtedly aimed at Rosie, who just grins and flicks her hair behind her shoulder. "At least I have action to relay, Virgo."

But Soraya just tilts her chin and goes back to her phone, acrylics tip-tapping on the screen insistently. The three of us are all thinking the same thing, I'm sure: that we need to find out *exactly* who she's talking to.

We dip into shops for the rest of the afternoon, splashing our earnings on clothes, new bags, stationary, food. Soraya buys a dress for her older sister's wedding and we crowd into the dressing room to watch her try it on, snapping selfies and making all the right noises. It's gorgeous, a gentle teal covered in gemstones and tiny beads, and costs a fortune, but Soraya's family isn't short of cash, and the arranged marriage of their eldest daughter isn't taken lightly.

"I hope you guys will make it, too!" Soraya gushes, though I know I'd never afford something grand enough, and that we'd stick out like sore thumbs.

We try on make-up at one counter, swooshing silvery eyeshadow and mascara over Jaye and experimenting with lipstick on the palms of our hands. It's childish, the sort of thing Rosie and I did when we were kids and would take the bus into town, but it's nice, all the same.

As long as I don't think about Lexie.

There's a queue for McDonald's. We cluster in the line as we wait for it to cease. Rosie's showing us a new top she's bought for the party next Saturday, one that dips to her belly-button and looks three sizes too small, and we "ooo" and "ahh" in appreciation as she twirls around with it held to her front.

"I don't know if it's too much," she queries, pushing her chest upwards with an expression of distaste. "Maybe with the right bra. Thank God I was blessed with these beauties, or I'd be a lost cause…"

I'm clutching my own bag, holding it tight in my hand, and smiling and nodding along to the conversation.

That's when I see her.

A girl, not much older than eleven, stands with her parents clutching a Happy Meal and a big cup of cola. She has wispy brown hair and huge, beseeching eyes and is looking right at us, smiling, laughing, as Rosie spins in and out of the queue with her sparkly top.

I feel a lump rise to my throat. Tears spring to my eyes as I watch her, the spitting image of Lexie, still here, still breathing, still *living*.

She's eating her chicken nuggets and enjoying the hustle and bustle, while the real version's ashes fly through the air…

Free, lost, gone.

I can't stop the wail from escaping my mouth, bags dropping to the floor and eyes squeezed shut against her. I faintly hear Soraya's voice in one ear, Rosie's in the other, hands clutching my back and pulling me away from the queue.

*It's your fault, it's your fault, it's your fault –*

This time, I don't try to silence the voice.

# 5

It really *was* my fault, right from the beginning. All of it. The run-up to Lexie's death, the trauma, the chaos... I blame myself for every single shred of pain.

It took a few months for me to notice something was going on with Lexie. By that time, it was far too late. She'd been well and truly integrated with Lucy and her pals, part of their group, their *crowd*.

But although she was one of them, she was never really a *friend*.

The first indications were small, subtle. She was never involved in the carshares, perhaps because the other mums were already well-acquainted; Mrs McCoy was just as much an outsider as Lexie. She'd turn up late each week, Mr Sparkles the unicorn clutched in hand, and trundle over to the group in her glittery trainers with an anxious smile on her face, eyes wide and worried.

The girls – Lucy, Chloe, Kayleigh and Orla – would grin and embrace her, hugging with their elbows flush to their ribs and heads held back from hers. Chloe, long face held taut and mouth carved into a grimace, would prod her jeans, pluck at her leggings, point to her shoes.

"Do you *like* your outfit?" she'd ask, voice faintly patronising, horribly reminiscent of my own. "Do you think it looks... *good*?"

And Lexie would shrug and flush, holding the cheap

material between her fingers and clutching Mr Sparkles with a forlorn expression. "I thought they were cool," she'd say, glancing down at her feet. "They were a Christmas present from Mum."

Chloe and Kayleigh, a dumpy girl with limp brown hair and too-thick eyebrows, would exchange amused glances and put Lexie down with a plastic smile, patting her as though she were a dog – something to poke fun at and enjoy when convenient, then put back in its cage when bored.

They didn't *dis*like her, I don't think. Their feelings weren't strong enough for that. But they didn't exactly *like* her, only enough to keep her dangling on the edges, wanting more, craving involvement in their group. It was good for Chloe's image, four tag-alongs instead of three. It made her look desirable, the kind of girl everyone should want to be. The group revolved around her, rotating from favourite to favourite, friends to fake.

The fact they were a five didn't seem to help, either. Five isn't a number of harmony and content. Five isn't a number which *works*. It's the number of pairs, of even numbers, one poor odd.

More often than not, the odd-one-out was Lexie.

Lucy and Orla were close, and Kayleigh was Chloe's biggest fan. She'd offer her lifts every night and gush about her hair, her makeup, her clothes. But Lexie was just there. They'd line up in couples, fingers latched together, while Lexie hovered behind with her unicorn hooked beneath her elbow.

I often think about that now. How easy it would've been to find another little girl to pair her with, someone who didn't have many friends. I think about how easily I could have torn Lexie from the group, from the sharp freckles of

Chloe, Kayleigh's glaring eyebrows.

But I didn't.

I just watched it unfold, right before my eyes.

Lucy would turn around first, noticing Lexie stood by herself and tugging on her shirt sleeve.

"We can be a three," she'd suggest, green eyes wide and kind. Orla would nod too, stepping back as if to let her between them. But Lexie didn't want to group with Lucy and Orla.

"Chloe?" she'd ask anxiously, ringing her hands in front of her. "Can I join your group?"

It was always, always Chloe.

\*\*\*

Chloe Alize was your typical ten-year-old poster-girl. Shiny, blonde hair that always smelt of strawberries; a constellation of dark freckles across her pointed face; skinny arms and legs, which she'd fold menacingly, perfectly level to her brown eyes. They were almost black, those eyes, like bullet holes in her face.

Her mum owns a cosmetic company, I think. I vaguely remember seeing her at the funeral, though not for long, as the girls weren't allowed to stay for the wake. Hair and nails, she said. Acrylics, gels, false sets… you name it, she does it.

That must be where Chloe gets her love for glitz and glamour from.

The first time she turned up to a guides' session wearing makeup, Sharon was appalled. She hauled me over to one side with eyebrows practically at her hairline and jabbed a finger in Chloe's direction, mouth opening and closing like a goldfish.

"Eyeshadow!" she spat, shaking her head in disbelief. "On a ten-year-old, I ask you!"

That was only the beginning.

She started experimenting the year they all turned eleven, twisting her hair into space buns, plaits, complicated braids, messy topknots. She'd use beads and feathers, morphing them into shape to fit whatever style she was going for, later ditching the craft equipment for delicate hair grips and silken flowers, clipping them into place beside her long, pale face.

The other girls loved it. Kayleigh teased her straggly hair raw trying to cram it into fishtail plaits, and Lucy resorted to Pritt stick and Hama beads to achieve the desired effect. Orla, a quiet girl with thick-rimmed glasses and permanently pursed lips, was "persuaded" to slice her hair into a bob using squiggly scissors in the toilets. I found them there one evening, hissing and screeching with laughter, trying to flush her beautiful brown locks by jamming them down with a toilet brush.

Lexie tried harder than any of them, desperate to get into Chloe's good books, eager to please. Mrs McCoy would spend hours attempting elaborate hairstyles which never quite turned out right, creating one plait that was significantly smaller than the rest, or leaving baby hairs smattered around her face and neck. It just gave Chloe even more to make fun of. She was never *explicit* with her teasing. She never told Lexie her hair looked bad, or that the tight ponytail made her forehead stretch too far.

That somehow made it worse.

"Did you realise one bun's smaller than the other, Lex?" she'd ask, frowning in sympathy. Or, "Yes, I heard the off-centre look is *totally* on trend right now."

And Lexie would beam and shake her newly-styled head,

while the other girls exchanged sneaky glances and smug smiles.

It didn't surprise me, the way they clustered around Chloe as though she was the sun and they were dwarf planets. I would've done the same when I was their age. I remember latching onto Rosie, the South African new kid, viewed as exotic and exciting by the other girls in our class. I loved her bold sense of style, her confidence, her curly hair and wide smile. I wanted to be just like her, too.

It was harmless, I thought. Kids like to work out who's boss, to establish a hierarchy between themselves. What could be so wrong with that? It wasn't hurting anyone. Lexie was growing more confident by the day, boasting new outfits, trying out dance classes, flicking soft eyeshadow across her lids and blinking ecstatically in the bathroom mirror at her new image.

Kids – girls, in particular – like to look the same, to fit in. I know that better than most.

If you look the part, just enough to blend into the background, they won't notice you. You won't be involved in drama, fallings-out, trouble. Teachers forget you're there; sisters won't start arguments.

You can be invisible, if you fit in.

I've mastered the art of being invisible.

# 6

The days before my return to sixth form seem to all blend into one. Wake up, eat, think about Lexie, sleep, repeat. It's an unbreakable cycle, one of lying in bed and munching through packets of digestives, staring at my laptop screen until chemistry equations blur into one big blob.

It's not just school I dread returning to, however. That part's fairly manageable.

It's the next guides' session, one held by Sharon on Tuesday evening, to commemorate Lexie. I can't *not* go. She wants me to speak, to say something about how wonderful and friendly and adventurous Lexie was, how she was the model girl guide, how what happened was so terribly tragic.

She's inviting parents, too, which doesn't surprise me. A girl *died* in our care, and she wants to reassure them that it won't happen again, that Lexie was a one-off.

My stomach churns just thinking about it, as I turn onto my side. How can I stand there and face them all, knowing full-well that it could've been *any* of the girls that night? How can I stand there and say it was an accident, when Lexie's death was all my fault?

Sharon sends me a Facebook link to a post on public speaking, but I flick through it without reading properly. The words all blur together before my eyes. There's a tiny diagram of a girl with criss-crossed red lines across her cheeks, clutching a mic, water trickling from between her legs.

I'm not *nervous*.

I'm only worried that I won't be able to keep up the pretence.

Tyler tries to message me again, on Sunday evening. I watch as the "typing" notification pops up on screen, a tiny threat above my glossy Instagram feed. There's a photo of Rosie, Soraya, Jaye and I, smiling and angling our Starbucks' cups, expressions deliberate.

### can't wait to cu tomrw xx

I stare at the message, just a sliver of impersonal pixels lit up on my phone. I don't know why I find it so infuriating. He's being nice. He "can't wait" to see me. I'm very lucky to have a boyfriend like him – that's what the girls are always saying.

The message I send back is short and sweet, no room for speculation, argument, debate, pettiness. It's simple, like my life used to be, before Lexie. If I were being selfish, I'd say it's the way I want my life to be again, one day. Filled with messages and pixelated hearts, the biggest source of stress, contempt. I wait for a reply, heart racing beneath my chest.

### lemme c ur face, missin u xx

The sky is dark outside, the velvety navy of early autumnal evenings, bright blue fading into darkness. My bedroom is dark, the sheets soft and reminiscent of fur against my legs, violet LEDs filling the ceiling with a purple glow. I stare at the screen. It's bright, illuminating me completely.

Flicking onto the camera, I hold it further from me and lean back into my headboard. Shoulder bare and cold, I snap the photo, eyes wide and lips slightly parted, then drop it to my lap and shudder. It's simple, basic, hardly risqué. It hesitates before disappearing from my phone, lost forever to the internet's sneaky depths.

**ur so beatifull xx**

**lower the camera xx**

I stare back at the screen in faint disbelief. A few months ago – a few *weeks* ago – I'd have flushed at the sight of such a message, filled with excitement. I'd have crawled out of bed to perch in front of the mirror, weak summer sun still leaking through the window, to snap and smile as he'd screenshot the photos to remember, praising me on how "fit" I was, how pretty and perfect and fun.

Now it fills me with dread, staring at those misspelt words filling the phone. His sleazy icon seems to wink at me, all big brown eyes and shivering quiff.

**Sorry, I'm with Rosie atm x**

The lie doesn't bother me as much as it should. It's ridiculously insensitive of him to even *ask* at a time like this... isn't it? I place my phone face down on the sheets, pulling them up to my chin and staring obstinately at the wall opposite.

Maybe I'm overreacting. He doesn't understand.

How could he, when nobody really does?

***

The road leading up to the secondary school is rammed on Monday morning. Cars speed through the town with kids and ties and crunchy new rucksacks hanging out of windows, zips still stiff and hair jammed into spiky pigtails. Boys run fingers through quiffs and girls roll up their skirts, sick of the uniform already and craving their holiday-outfits, shorts and sliders and tacky anklets spelling "Tenerife" in beaded letters.

The smokers cluster outside the gates, cigarettes held at chapped lips. One girl glares at me as I pass, eyes hooded by thick false lashes. She puffs a tendril of smoke in my direction.

Usually, I'd press my lips inwards and frown back, determined not to inhale the poisonous fumes. My granddad died of lung cancer a few months before I was born; I know smoking's a disease, a nasty habit intended to induce yellowed fingers and stained teeth. It repulses me, as a rule. I wouldn't go near Rosie when she tried a ciggie at a party last year.

But today's different. I breathe in, letting the fumes fill my mouth, my throat, my lungs, my already-blackened insides. It's warm and stale, the smoke of somebody else's pleasure, not designed for me. I'm ready to gag by the time I reach the playground, swilling contaminated saliva and trying hard not to swallow.

The school is packed. Kids run round with laces untied and bad makeup smudged over acne, screaming and shouting, pointing fingers. The stench of sausage rolls and strawberry milk swills from the canteen window towards me.

There's a wind picking up, bustling beneath skirts and eager baggy trousers. I tug my coat further around me, frowning up at the building. The school is loud, life creeping through the gates for the first time in seven weeks. Something has changed, altered. The sliding doors are squeaky with fresh oil, and windows gleam in the weak sunlight. The walls are stained black, dirty and moss-covered. They're no longer hopeful, inspiring. They just look very… sad.

"Yeah… I hope we get Mr Browne this year…"

I freeze, something picking up in the back of my ear: a tiny voice, a little broken, from just behind me. I glance around for somewhere to hide but I'm in the middle of the playground, surrounded by tarmac and yellow painted lines –

Behind me, Lucy and Orla clutch new school bags and shiny lunchboxes with anxious, pale faces. Lucy's eyes are puffy, like she's been crying, and Orla's arm latches through hers protectively.

I kid myself for a second, hoping they haven't spotted me, until my eyes meet Orla's and her expression pops with surprise. She elbows Lucy, who whirls around to gaze at me with twin green eyes and her mouth open wide.

"Macey!" is what I think she cries, but it's only a second before she jumps at me and latches on with her tiny hands and patent shoes, squeezing so tight I almost squeal. "Oh my God, Macey! We've really missed you!"

She pulls back and I gasp for air, trying for a smile but failing miserably. Orla watches from behind her thick-rimmed glasses, shuffling from foot to foot.

"I missed you guys too," I say, but it sounds wrong, cold. The playground is chaos around us, but our bubble feels awkward, stilted in time. We stare at each other, cheeks flushed and silent, the expressions of those caught unaware. "How – how – how are you feeling?"

Lucy looks down at her feet then, puffy eyes screwed up. "It's just weird." She glances sidewards at Orla, then says, "It feels wrong to be here without Lexie. We still can't believe it, Macey."

I shiver, goosebumps rising on my arms. I shake them

desperately in an attempt to disperse the guilt.

"Yeah." I don't know what else to say. *I'm sorry for your loss?* That doesn't seem to cover it. *I'm sorry it was Lexie who died that night, rather than one of you?* Hardly acceptable.

"Well… we'll see you tomorrow, I guess," Lucy's saying. "You know… at Lexie's event."

I drag myself back, nodding and taking a step away.

"Yeah," I say, voice flat. "Tomorrow."

"Bye, Macey." Lucy gives a little wave, and Orla smiles weakly. "See you tomorrow!

"See you."

I watch as they wander into the crowds, shaking school bags and beaming at friends and teachers. They're just innocent year eight girls, twelve-year-olds with their lives stretched ahead in a long, promising line. They don't deserve this. I don't think I even realised the world could be so cruel when I was their age.

That's another reason I'm dreading the commemoration evening. Bringing light to what happened makes it so much more *real*, like what happened that night stole all of their childhoods, not just Lexie's.

Two younger girls wobble past, tottering on baby heels. They're smiling, mascara brushed over lashes and onto their lids, lipsticked-teeth bright. The girl to the left has huge, storm-grey eyes, and wispy brown hair…

And I still hate it. Tears spring to my eyes as she goes to laugh, mouth open wide in a lively cackle, and I hate it, I hate it, I *hate* it. It's not fair. None of this is fucking *fair*.

"Macey!"

Clutching the lining of my sleeves tight, I turn to face my boyfriend. Tyler walks towards me with a huge, animated smile, brown quiff quivering, stark against the grey-white sky.

He's much more tanned than when I last saw him – his family holidayed in Italy this year, I think – and freckles stand out on his nose and cheeks. I'm rooted to the spot, watching carefully as he approaches, shivering and smiling.

"… Hi."

Tyler's arms go around me, strong and solid and *there*, and suddenly I'm back in that place, all those months ago, when Tyler was the only thing I cared or thought about.

I'm not really there, though.

I pull away, startled at how close our faces seem to be, how smooth and shiny the skin of his forehead is before mine. He leans in to kiss me and I jerk to the side, smashing my nose against his and wincing. His hands are still on my back, though they've loosened, and he's now staring at me as if he doesn't know who I am.

"Mace?" he murmurs, frowning. "You smell like smoke…"

I don't say anything. We stand, cloaked in silence, as the playground screeches around us and the school begins to buzz with life.

"You okay?" he checks. There's no recognition on his face, no emotion, no connection. It's like there's a wedge between us, blocking out the familiarity of last summer. It's awkward, cold. He goes to stand back and I almost fall, alarmed at how tight he must've been holding me.

"I'm just going to…" He gestures helplessly behind him, towards the building. I nod. "Me and the lads are having a catch up. I'll see you at lunch? We can go out, maybe grab a Subway or something…"

So I smile and shrug, as if it sounds as appealing as it once would have done.

It doesn't.

# 7

The assembly hall is silent. Jaye is picking at her nails to my left, and Rosie is drawing on her hand with a purple gel pen. Beyond her, Soraya is still tapping away on her phone, completely engrossed, head angled away from us.

Mr Roberts clears his throat from the front, stood on the stage by the projector with a sheaf of papers in his hands. He glances around the audience, taking in the sixth form as though preparing himself for battle. The room smells of cheap perfume and face powder, faintly nauseating. It's the stench of drugstores and toiletry aisles, that fusty sweetness.

"Good morning, everyone!" he announces, voice echoing around the hall. "Welcome back to Vibbington Sixth Form!"

To the side of the room, a teacher raises her hands to clap. Noting the silent, unmoving bodies and flushing, she lowers them back to her lap and nods at Mr Roberts, who smiles back tensely.

"Thank you, Miss Marian."

Jaye and I exchange glances. The impulse to laugh is slightly alien, so I swallow and try to focus on the screen.

"Well, Vibbington. It's certainly been a summer to remember. Last year's year thirteen students gained the highest grades this county's seen in six years, and we had three students go off to Oxbridge! No pressure, guys, but we're expecting good things from you!"

No pressure, indeed.

"We're also welcoming one-hundred-and-six year twelves into the sixth form this year, so be kind." He glances round eagerly, eyes falling on the first rows. "Any year twelves in the room, raise your hands!"

From the front of the room, a group of speccy, nerdy boys raise their hands, beaming and glancing round excitedly. Just a year younger than us, they have the enthusiasm of baby Labradors. It's more than just irritating.

"Come on, Vibbington! There must be more of you than that!"

A couple more hands slowly dart upwards, but it's hardly a full house. Admitting defeat, Mr Roberts clears his throat again, consulting the first sheet of paper. His collar is too constrictive, digging into his neck so that flesh bulges over the sides. He must've shaved for the first day back. The rash on his skin is red-raw.

"Aside from exam results, this summer was life-changing for… well, *other reasons*." He doesn't need to continue – we all know what he means. He does anyway, of course, stumbling over his words to string them together coherently. "As you may already know, a young student from Vibbington sadly passed away several weeks back, as the result of a tragic accident which took place not far from here."

The room is silent now. Every breath feels like a sin. Around me, hundreds of eyes point my way, unsubtle glances from beneath false lashes and fringes. I focus on my hands between my knees, cheeks filling with colour.

"Lexie McCoy was a tribute to the school, a burst of positivity and enthusiasm, and will be greatly missed by students and staff alike. We would've welcomed her into the sixth form as she grew older, nurturing her into the wonderful young women she now sadly won't have the chance to become. Taken from us too early, I'm sure we can all sympathise with those around her, those who've been so deeply affected by such a terrible loss."

My heart's pounding, the lump returning to my throat.

It's an attack, and I feel a dozen eyes on me as I shrivel further into my chair. They're not blaming *me* – they have no idea of the extent of my involvement. But maybe they should.

"May we now take a minute of silence to remember Lexie, and say a prayer for her family and friends."

The hall's already filled with quiet, thick and dense and gloopy, but a spluttering sneeze from one corner breaks the barrier. Soraya's hands are clasped on her lap, long lashes sweeping her cheeks in solemn prayer. Rosie looks at me and smiles in reassurance. I can't smile back.

I count the seconds away, on my fingers. *One Mississippi, two Mississippi, three Mississippi.* Miss Marian's eyes are wide and shiny, filled with unshed tears. *Twenty-one Mississippi, twenty-two Mississippi, twenty-three Mississippi.* Mr Roberts has loosened his tie and is looking slightly purple now, shuffling his papers. *Thirty-six Mississippi, thirty-seven Mississippi, thirty-eight –*

Mr Roberts clears his throat and glances back out over the audience.

He didn't even last forty seconds.

"Thank you, all." His eyes float across the room until they land on our row. They skim each of our faces, coming to a stop on me, and I take a deep breath. "The headteacher has also asked me to say a special thank you to Macey Collins. She was a huge help to the police and was a *wonderful* role model to Lexie before she died. We all feel for her at this extremely difficult time."

There's a pause. It doesn't last long enough.

"Thank you, everybody. Have a great first week back!" Mr Roberts lifts a hand into the air, before stepping back into the shadows of the stage.

I shiver, glancing round at my friends. Tyler, just a way off, is muttering to his mates, head down. He catches my eye and nudges his mate Rhys, calling, "To Macey, everybody!"

"To Macey!" Rosie calls, grabbing my hand and forcing it upwards. Jaye reaches up to clasp it and the people around us begin to laugh, grinning in our direction. I try for another smile. My mouth aches.

"To Macey," Soraya repeats, eyes meeting mine, expression lopsided.

To me.

\*\*\*

We crowd into the canteen after the assembly, burbling with giggles and gossip and observations.

"Did you see that Darcie's dyed her hair green?"

"I know, it looks so *shit*."

"… I quite like it, she looks really different…"

"Oh, give over, Soraya, you wouldn't say anything bad about her if she broke out in purple spots!"

"I just don't see why it's any of our business what she does with her hair…"

I'm silent. I tiptoe behind them with my hands in my pockets, cold and distant. All I can think about is tomorrow night. Lexie's commemoration event. I don't want it to be anything like this morning, full of sympathy and praise and deceit. I can't stand there and tell everyone what a tragic accident it was, how sad it is, how unfortunate. I'm terrified that one more crack will push me over the edge.

I can't lie for much longer – it's not right, not fair.

But then none of this is *fair*.

The common room is warm and busy, and Rosie leads us to a table at the back, by the window. I perch next to Soraya but she immediately budges up, back pressed against the wall with her phone angled away from me.

"Who are you messaging *now*?" Jaye asks, one eyebrow raised.

Soraya doesn't respond.

Rosie fetches us cartons of popcorn chicken and a big box of fries, placing them in the centre of the table and digging in. She's dressed in a leopard print top that dips at the front, artfully leaning forward with her elbows on the surface. I don't have to turn around to figure there's a group of boys on the table behind us.

"Macey," Jaye murmurs, jerking her head to the side, but I don't have time to react before a pair of sweaty paws slide over my eyes and submerge me in darkness.

"Tyler!" I dart forward, reaching up to push his hands away and turning to stare at him. My boyfriend stands behind me, eyebrows raised. His hair is tousled from the wind, cheeks pink with cold, and my heart jumps despite itself. "You… surprised me."

"That was the point." His smile is smooth and clear as he nudges me and climbs onto the bench between Soraya and I, curling an arm around my shoulder. He reeks of aftershave, the overpriced kind, the type you can't get in the supermarket. He doesn't look at me, instead turning away with wide, eager eyes. "Blimey, they look top-notch, Soraya!"

Soraya blushes as he dives into the paper bag on her lap, pulling out a carefully wrapped sweet. It's jewel-bright and crackles as he unwraps it, revealing a square of pastel green, crumbly goodness. My mouth waters as he places the *barfi* between his lips. Soraya's mum is a whizz when it comes to cooking, and has been making sweet treats daily since the announcement of her eldest daughter's wedding.

"Don't be getting any ideas, Mace." Tyler grins at me, swallowing it with a gulp. "You know you need to keep your figure for... Well, you know."

I flush at how much he sounds like my mother, but remain silent. Has he always said things like that to me?

Tyler licks his bottom lip, grumbling in appreciation. My stomach churns. "These for the wedding, Soraya?"

She nods, eyes huge. She flaps his hand away as he delves in for another piece, pushing the bag behind her back and letting out a squeal. "Don't you dare! Mama gave me all the new flavours to try, and you've completely wasted the pistachio!"

Tyler just laughs, shaking his head at her. "Aw, man. If it helps, it tasted bloody *epic*."

Soraya frowns, unwrapping a tiny blue square and biting into it. She's trying not to smile, cheeks still pink.

"So..." Tyler leans back and turns to me. There are still *barfi* crumbs around his mouth, green and sticky against his lips. "I guess I now have a famous girlfriend, right?"

I blink, unsure of what he means.

"The assembly?" he prompts.

More silence.

Nobody wants to acknowledge what he's trying to say, to encourage him, but he does it anyway. "That Lexie girl's made you pretty popular..."

"Tyler..." Soraya gasps, hand over her mouth. "Just ignore him, Macey, he didn't mean it like that –"

But I can't breathe, throat constricted and eyes wide,

staring at him in disbelief. I don't have the words straight away and open my mouth, waiting for something coherent to come out.

Silence stretches out across the table.

"Lexie died, and it made me *popular*?" I finally manage to croak. My voice is higher than usual, almost a screech. Tyler is staring at me with one eyebrow raised.

"Chill out, Mace, it's not that big of a deal..."

I stand up then, fists curled into balls by my sides. It's the only way I can stop my hands from shaking.

"Macey, come on –"

"You're a dick, Tyler." It comes out more like a spit, and he gazes back in confusion. I don't know where that came from – until I look at Rosie, and realise she said it. She's glaring back with furious dark eyes, hands resting on the surface of the table.

"Macey, you're just upset..." Jaye tries to tug on my arm to get me to sit once again, but I shake her off, tears once again filling my eyes.

*Don't cry.*

Not here, not now.

That's when Rosie takes her cue again and stands up, reaching towards me and placing a hand on the small of my back. "We just need a second, okay? Come on, Mace. Let's go outside."

I let her lead me forward, vision blurred and hands shaking violently. We cross the common room, all eyes on us. Rosie's curls tickle my face as I turn towards her, hiding my head on her shoulder as we wander out into the sun.

There's a breeze still, drifting towards us, though weak rays flit through the clouds.

I rub my arms, goosebumps rising.

"Tyler didn't mean to say that, you know," Rosie says, pushing me forward to face her. "You know he doesn't think before speaking sometimes, Mace, but he never meant to hurt you. He's just... a bit of a dick."

I nod. It's easier than disagreeing.

"We know how hard this is for you, Macey," she continues, patting my shoulder. "It must feel horrible..."

But she doesn't know how hard it is for me. No one does.

And isn't that exactly what I want?

8

You may be wondering how I ended up with a boyfriend like Tyler Campbell... but things with Ty weren't always like that. There was a time when things were different, better. A time when we didn't feel like strangers, when he knew exactly what to say, how to act around me. But that was the part he was good at, what he'd had plenty of practice at – the *before*. After we started dating, things began to change.

He was in my maths class. I sat in front, him behind, shoes resting on the back of my chair, tip-tapping away to get my attention. I don't know why. It's not as if I'm anything special. Those first few weeks, he kept a stash of flashcards in his pockets and would drag them out to write love notes... or sometimes just notes. They weren't anything particularly riveting, just the odd "ur beatifull", followed by a cartoon drawn in crude highlighter. I found it faintly irritating at first, and more than just embarrassing. It felt like he was doing it on purpose to draw attention to me.

Soraya loved it, of course, though Jaye found it cheesy. Rosie was sceptical. He didn't have a good reputation, she claimed, and was trying *way* too hard.

I just wished he'd never noticed me.

Tyler was one of the "popular" boys, the kind everyone knew but didn't necessarily *like*. Rumour had it he lost his virginity to Darcie Carlton on a bus in year nine, and that he had a tattoo on his ribcage of a gun (later investigated –

definitely not true), and got high on the school trip to Paris. He scared me, more than anything. He was just so effortlessly cool. Cool in a way we all tried to be, yet never quite achieved.

I responded with caution at first, telling him to leave me alone, that I was flattered but uninterested. He took that as an instruction to continue, though now with much more force. He wasn't used to losing, Rosie said. He *always* got what he wanted.

It was October before he asked me on a date. The sky was clear and blue, not a cloud in sight, and leaves swirled from the trees in all shades of orange. We were stood by the gates, waiting for the bus, and he slipped one of his infamous flashcards into my hand. It had been ripped in half so the edge was all jagged, and my hands shook as I fingered it.


## MOVIES ON SUNDAY NITE? x


Tyler – *the* Tyler Campbell – was asking me out. I stared at it, eyes wide, like it would evaporate before me. A few steps away, he let out a small sigh, as though he was waiting and losing patience.

I looked at him then – I couldn't help it – and his eyes latched onto mine. They were the kind of eyes I could've lost myself in back then, deep brown and fanned with long lashes. Tiny dark freckles sprinkled his nose, hair turned up in the wind. As much as I wanted to hide, there was a different feeling inside me this time, something stronger, something I hadn't really felt before, writhing in my stomach like a long, black snake.

"So... is it a yes?" he breathed, watching me intently. I couldn't move, let alone speak, stuck to the spot before him.

That was when he kissed me.

\*\*\*

Lexie and the others found out straight away. They'd just started at Vibbington Secondary, bright-eyed and fresh-faced, and one of Chloe's cronies spotted Tyler kissing me at the bus stop. Word travels fast when you're eleven-years-old and boy-mad, and guys like Tyler are kind of infamous.

"You have a boyfriend!" Lucy shrieked, rushing into the chapel one Tuesday with her guide's uniform all rumpled and hair spilling out of its pigtails. "Oh my God, Macey, why didn't you *tell* us?"

I flushed and smiled. As embarrassing as it was, I quite liked the feeling it gave me, the feeling of pride and satisfaction. Everyone likes praise, I suppose, and dating Tyler certainly felt like an achievement.

The girls buzzed around me like flies that night, crowing for information and tugging on my arms and legs as they followed me down the corridor to the bathroom, away from the chaos. Our guides' sessions have always been held in the local chapel, in a soggy backroom they've only recently renovated. Back then, it was laced with spiders hanging from each beam, and mould crowded on notice boards and around the doors. The tiny two-cubicle bathroom always smelt faintly of tinned peas, like a nursing home.

Crammed into the far-left cell, I pushed my back against the door and sank to the floor. I could hear the girls scrabbling outside, giggling and whispering, and couldn't help but smile. The floor was damp beneath me, water seeping from the base of the toilet in a faint, brown trickle.

"Macey, come out!" Lucy crowed, rapping with her tiny fist. The others were giggling and whispering, the sound buzzing through the crack. "You need to tell us *everything*!"

Even though I didn't necessarily want the attention – even though it was awkward and part of me wanted to shrivel up and hide – I liked feeling interesting, wanted.

It made a change.

I teased open the door, peering round the edge at the girls clustered outside. Lucy was staring up with her green eyes wide and expression eager, and Orla and Kayleigh clutched each other's sleeves in anticipation. Chloe stood by the radiator, arms folded across her chest and disinterest splayed across her features, glittery eyeshadow decorating her lids. She pursed her lips at me and turned her long face away, pretending to be preoccupied with picking paint from the wall.

Lexie cowered by the sinks, eyes unfocused. She'd tried some fancy topknot and the skin around her forehead had stretched to reach it. Mr Sparkles shivered in her pocket.

"Do you love him?" Lucy burst immediately, hopping up and down in excitement. "Macey's in love, you guys! With *Tyler*!"

Kayleigh went on to make an "ooo" noise and Orla flushed behind her glasses. Chloe just shook her head sourly, with the look of someone far too old for her age, far too experienced. "She's not in *love*. They've only been dating a week. It's basic attraction."

Lucy glanced at me as if hoping I'd disprove her statement, clearly crestfallen.

"You *do* love him, don't you, Macey?" she asked. "Because if you don't, I don't think you should be with him!"

I smiled, meeting Chloe's eyes. "Of course I do, Luce. Not everything Chloe says is true."

That was when Lexie glanced up, brow creased and pale face. She was watching Chloe with a steady expression, grey eyes transfixed, confused. It was that intense stare she had, one which could twist up your insides and make you feel all kinds of uncomfortable, even if you didn't know why.

"What would you know, anyway?" I think the words flying out of her mouth shocked Lexie more than anyone else, for she clapped a hand over it quickly, as if to take them back. Chloe narrowed her eyes and continued to stare back, face pinched in the harsh LEDs.

No one moved. We were frozen in time, watching to see what Chloe would do, would say.

"What do you *mean*, Lexie?" Her tone was slightly accusatory, acidic round the edges. Lexie was even paler now, skin white and waxy. Lucy and Orla had shrunk back, eyeing each other nervously. "I said, *what do you mean*, Lexie?"

"I just meant…" Lexie glanced down at the floor, to where her sparkly trainers were poking inwards, toes touching. "Your parents are divorced, aren't they? So you can't know enough about love to lecture Macey on how she feels."

The atmosphere in the room was frosty, the only sound coming from a dripping skylight. Drops of water fell from the ceiling like slow, sly gurgles of laughter, creating a puddle on the floor beside us. I watched as Lexie swallowed, glancing back towards the door as if hoping, *praying* that Sharon would come through it at any moment, clutching her notepad and beaming a huge, toothy smile.

"Did you really just say that?" Chloe breathed, taking one step closer so that their faces were just centimetres apart, freckles stark and angry on her blue-tinged cheeks. "I think you're going to regret saying that, Lexie. You and your perfect little family, thinking you know everything..."

She glanced at me for confirmation then, as if expecting me to back her up. I opened and closed my mouth, eyes flitting from Chloe to Lexie, then back to Chloe.

"I don't think Lexie meant to be rude, Chloe. She just meant –"

"My parents still love each other!" Her fists were trembling and eyes were furious, so dark they almost looked black. She couldn't keep her eyes off Lexie, glaring down with her thin arms hung by her sides and ankles raised. "You don't know them, you don't understand! The divorce was a mistake. They're going to get back together, they promised!"

Lexie's bottom lip was trembling, staring at Chloe with guilt. She didn't say anything. They were still waiting for me to break the ice, to diffuse the situation.

"Chloe..." I didn't know what to say, in that moment. But staring at her, a mixed-up eleven-year-old with smudged sparkly makeup and a broken home, I knew *exactly* what someone should've told me when I was in her position all those years ago. When my parents were breaking up, all I did was blame myself. It took a long, long time to be able to look back and accept that they just weren't right for each other.

"People fall out of love, Chlo. It's just life."

Her expression was on fire, mouth carved into a cruel, thin line, eyes full of hurt and anger and *pain*. It wasn't directed at me, though, not in the slightest.

Every ounce of hatred was directed straight at Lexie.

9

It was subtle at first. A shiny shoe stuck out at the door, designed to trip Lexie up; a spilt pot of PVA, all over her lap; gum in her floppy pigtail, stuck deep between the pleats. But bullies are always subtle at first – that's how they get away with it. If it builds up slowly, you begin to think it's normal.

And when you think something's *normal*, you start to accept it.

I passed it off as an accident, the first time. Chloe was apologetic, wiping Lexie down, linking an arm through hers to steer her to the toilet and help clean her grazed knee. She'd pull out the craft scissors and snip away at the gum-ridden spot until Lexie's hair laid in tufts across the floor. Kayleigh would follow behind with the dustpan and brush, snorting with laughter and cheeks turned red.

Lexie didn't seem to notice either, at first. She shook her head at Chloe's apologies, smiling and batting away helping hands. She was unperturbed, sat in the corner of the chapel's hall with Mr Sparkles on her lap, picking at her pink nail polish with a distracted, far-off look in her eyes.

It was easy to ignore the signs, and so we did. Looking back, it seems so obvious. It's different when you're right there, living this reality, watching things go wrong.

If you don't *want* to notice something, you… don't. And we didn't want to notice. Awkward conversations, tellings-off, staring into Chloe's bullet-hole eyes and right into her skull.

No one wanted to deal with that. There was no time, no need.

Chloe's twelfth birthday party was the tipping point. It was almost a year ago now, around the time I got with Tyler. It was Christmastime, and Chloe was planning to go ice skating. Her mum had hired out the whole rink, she said. They'd have good music on the loudspeakers, disco lights in pink, purple and blue, and *plenty* of male guests.

"Where are you going to find all of these boys?" Lucy asked, eyes wide, but Chloe just tilted her head with a smile.

She sent out the invitations on lilac paper, decorated with tiny gold stars her mum had glued on individually, one by one by one. They were folded up in her bag when she got to the chapel that night, wrapped up in tissue paper and tied with a hair-bobble.

"Help me give them out," she instructed, thrusting a pile onto Kayleigh's lap and making her jump. "I've got loads..."

Most girls received one, including some of the older girls, who raised their eyebrows as though uninterested, only persuaded by the mention of sausage rolls and boys. The very youngest girls, just recent newbies, were handed pale pink cards with earlier leaving times, slightly demoralising yet stared at with googly eyes. It seemed like *everyone* wanted to be a part of Chloe's celebrations.

As the last of the invitations were handed out, I glanced round the room. Everyone was smiling, admiring the décor and talking excitedly about who would be there, which boys they'd try and skate with, what they were going to wear. Lucy was gushing about a sequinned crop-top she'd bought from Primark, as Orla smiled solemnly and nodded along, caught up in the magic of it all.

That was when I got a tap on the back.

"Macey?" It was Sharon, stood behind me with an anxious

expression, forehead creased. She was sporting a fresh trim, the kind of hairstyle middle-aged women seem to love; shaped around her face and gripped into place, roots shining through in eager grey. "Have you seen Lexie?"

"Lexie?"

Glancing around the room again, my eyes skimmed Lucy and Orla, Kayleigh, the younger girls with their pink paper, the older girls tapping away on their phones.

Then Chloe, stood by the door, a spiky smile on her face and dark eyes fixed on the room before her.

"No," I replied, feeling my stomach sink. "No, I haven't seen Lexie."

"I don't think she got an invitation," Sharon was saying, though I wasn't really listening.

Of *course* she hadn't gotten an invitation.

I think I'd known that the moment Chloe took them from her bag.

"Can you find her, Macey?" Sharon continued, eyes brimming with sympathy. "Poor love, she must be feeling pretty left out…"

*Left out?* I wanted to scream at the understatement, twisting my fists into balls and staring around the room in fury. Chloe was still stood by the door, a smug smile on her face, one eye still latched onto the corridor, head cocked as though she was listening for something.

"I… I think I know where she is."

Slipping past Chloe and refusing to meet her eye, I paced down the corridor to the crooked bathroom door. The light was flickering, casting a speckled glow on the cubicles. One door was shut, mouldy hinges flush against the surface. I rapped my knuckles against it – once, twice – then listened, ear to the wood.

There was muffled sobbing coming from the toilet beyond, the sound of someone trying to subdue their tears against a sleeve.

"Lexie?" I hissed, mouth against the gap. "Lexie, it's Macey."

Silence. A stifled snort sounded, just audible above the chatter from outside.

"Lexie, can you open up, please?"

Again, no sound.

I pushed against the door so that the latch rattled, but it wouldn't budge, trembling very slightly beneath my hands.

"Lex, I just want to talk to you. Chloe's... well, a bit of a bitch, but I think we both know that. Can you let me in?"

Slowly, I heard the bolt sliding back through its holder. The ancient wood creaked and the hinges gasped for air as it swung back into the cubicle, bottom hissing at the linoleum floor.

My stomach dropped.

Lexie was sat on the toilet seat, legs crossed, sparkly trainers tucked underneath her and Mr Sparkles folded into her lap. Her face was blotchy and tear-stained, grey eyes red and glossy, protruding from her face as though on antennas. She'd clearly been sobbing for a while, for her sleeves were wet and slick with snot, a layer of slime covering the rim thick enough to coat her entire face.

And her hands...

Her nails were red and raw, bleeding from the cuticles, like she'd been scratching ferociously. Fleshy and purple and swollen, they hardly looked like hands anymore. Two swollen hearts, arteries elongated and dripping. I noticed the wall. The paint was peeling and patches had been torn off completely, exposing bare brickwork and mould-infested concrete. A collection of tiny grey woodlice hurtled from the hole, diving towards the floor and disappearing behind the toilet.

"Lexie…"

I didn't know what to say. I just stood there, frozen, staring at her wet face before me.

"I'm sorry," she whispered, eyes creasing and a tear sliding down her cheek. "I'm just so unlikeable, I don't know what happened, I just lost control and –"

As if suddenly bolting into gear, I pushed forwards into the cubicle and dropped to the floor in front of her. Squeezing her hands, we watched each other in silence, grey eyes latched onto mine and leaking salty tears. Her fingers were wet, but I didn't dare look at them.

"I'm sorry," she repeated, quieter this time, more calm. "I don't know what's wrong with me, Macey. Why does no one like me?"

"I like you," I said, but my words were meaningless. She didn't really care if I liked her, if her family liked her, if Sharon or her teachers liked her. That wasn't important.

She just wanted Chloe and the girls to like her.

"I'm not so awful," she continued, voice hoarse, "am I, Macey?"

"You're not, Lex." I squeezed her bloodied fingers gently with a smile. "You're not at all."

"But they all think I'm weird," she murmured. "And I'm not, I know I'm not…"

"Lexie, you're not weird. You're just you, and that's pretty awesome."

She hung her head, eyes filling with tears once again and hands pulled out of mine. She crushed them beneath her thighs, despite the fact it must've hurt, and stared back with that steely grey expression. "I didn't mean to say that thing about Chloe, Macey. The thing about... about her parents. Mum was just talking about the divorce and I didn't think..."

"I know." There was nothing else to say, not really. "I know."

The bathroom door creaked open, a whining screech behind us. I stood, peering round the edge of the cubicle to find Sharon at the sinks with a cup of squash in one hand and a bourbon in the other.

"Is she in there?" she mouthed. I nodded, and stepped back to let her in.

"Lexie!" was what she cried, hurrying forward with a horrified expression and squash spilling over her wrists. "Lexie, what on earth happened?"

Yes, Lexie. What happened?

She wouldn't tell her, of course. I knew that already. Mr Sparkles was propped against the wall and her hands were firmly wedged in her pockets, away from Sharon's watchful eyes. Her lips were zipped.

I wouldn't say anything, either. Why would I? It wasn't any of my business...

Was it?

\*\*\*

Two weeks later, I arrived at the chapel to find it in darkness. The lights were off; the corridor shrouded in black; the LEDs sprung to life as I entered the hall, crumbs crunching underfoot and floorboards creaking.

Sharon must be late, I thought. That was the most logical explanation.

I checked my phone, frowning. 7:30pm. I was right on

time, but the building was silent.

Behind me, the door burst open and a harassed Mrs McCoy flew over the threshold, dragging Lexie by the hand. They were both soaking from the rain and held an umbrella above them, which dripped onto the welcome mat. Her thin fringe stuck to her forehead, blue eyes beady and cold behind her glasses. She shook the water off her like a wet dog.

"I'm just dropping Lexie off," she said, throwing me a waxy smile and pushing her daughter forward. "I'm late for my Zumba class, and this little so-and-so didn't want to get out of the car…"

Lexie looked like she was about to cry. Her bottom lip was trembling and her grey eyes were huge and glassy.

"I'll be back at nine, Lex." Mrs McCoy bent down to plant a kiss on her daughter's forehead, then turned to leave. "Be good!"

As the door shut behind her, the building once again lapsed into quiet. I glanced at Lexie, trying for a smile, but something felt off.

"Do you know where everyone else is, Lex?"

She shook her head obstinately, though her mouth was still trembling. She was lying; I wasn't stupid. Frowning, I dug into my pocket for my phone, dragging it out once again and clicking onto my emails.

**Hey guys! Sorry for the late notice, but seeing as it's Chloe's birthday party tonight and most of you will be there, I decided not to host a session this week. See you next week for festive biscuit decorating! Sharon**

I pushed it back into my pocket, glancing back up to Lexie.

"You knew it was Chloe's party today," I said slowly.

"Didn't you?"

She nodded, expression terrified. "I didn't want Mum to know I hadn't been invited, so I deleted the email from her phone," she whispered. "I'm sorry, Macey…"

In that moment, I swear I hated Chloe Alize.

# 10

The house is quiet when I return from school, the TV on low, casting blue light out into the hallway. Jenna is curled up with a bowl of popcorn on her lap, eyes partly closed, feet under a blanket and stomach bulging over her joggers. Her face is puffy, like she's been crying, and one hand hovers by her mouth with an unpopped kernel.

"You okay?" I hesitate in the doorway. My sister glances up to face me, mascara smudged across her cheeks, electric blue and blotchy. It matches her nails – that's the first thing I notice, though I shake the thought when a tear slips from her eye and down to her nose.

"Fuck off, Mace," she murmurs. Her eyes flit back to the TV, expression wobbling. "Please, just fuck off."

"What's up?" I cross the threshold and near the sofa, crouching on the edge. There's a significant gap between us, as usual, big enough to park a canoe. Her phone is spread across the blanket, screen black. "You've been crying, Jen."

"You're a genius, aren't you?" My sister scowls, pushing the kernel into her mouth and crunching down, hard. She swallows, then glances back with a slightly mournful look in her eyes, opening and closing her mouth, as if trying to figure out what to say. "Megan dumped me. I don't know why I'm so surprised." She throws another piece between her lips to stop them trembling, and clutches the bowl hard.

I'm silent for a moment, unsure of how to react. She and

Megan have been together for the last month or so – not long, but enough for Jenna to become attached, as usual. Megan was her type in every way. Wildly unsuitable, covered in tattoos and piercings, and desperate for her tongue to be split, which was "so *ridiculously* cool" according to my sister.

"That sucks," I say at last, pulling the best sympathetic face I can. "But there are other fish in the sea –"

Jenna rolls her eyes. "Oh, don't be so dense, Mace. Around here? Everyone's dead from the neck up. It's okay for you – there are plenty of mindless football goons for you to pull. Yorkshire's hardly roaming with gay activity."

I flush, picking at the blanket.

"I… I wouldn't know." There's a short silence, interrupted by a burble of laughter from the TV. It's *Countdown* again. She doesn't even like *Countdown*. "Maybe if you'd gone to university, you'd have found someone there…"

"Not you as well." She throws another two pieces onto her tongue and crunches furiously, head turned away from me. "I didn't want to go to uni, Macey. It's all a con – I don't need to spend twenty-seven thousand pounds to learn how to paint."

"You could've done maths," I say, although I already know what she's going to say. It's not an uncommon conversation in our household. I've overheard it a dozen times from the top of the stairs, listening to Mum screeching from the kitchen as she throws packets of lentils in Jenna's direction, yelling obstinately about her future and success, and how her "abstract" paintings are trashy and will never bring her any money.

"Anyone can throw paint at a canvas and call it art!" she'll scream, mingled with swear-words and fury. "Go and get a job like the rest of us, for God's sake! You think you're entitled to sit around here all day just because I've always provided for you..."

"You're beginning to sound like Lisa," Jenna growls now. She pushes the bowl away from her and drags her legs up to her chin, frowning. "I hate maths, Macey. You know I want to be a *painter*."

Because no matter how Mum tries to persuade her, that's the point they always come back to.

"I know," I say. And I do know. I know that's what Jenna wants, but because I'd rather not get on the wrong side of my sister today, I don't tell her what I really think of her grand schemes. "Do you really think you'll ever be successful, Jen?"

Jenna looks at me then, eyes narrowed.

"Successful?" she repeats. "What does having success even *mean*?"

"Money?" I reply, though the word tastes metallic in my mouth. "A nice house?"

"That's where we're different." She smiles flatly. "I just want to paint – that's all I can ever see myself doing. I can't get a degree, become an accountant, do something dull and repetitive and blah. It'd literally kill me."

"But that's just how life works," I counter. I can feel myself becoming increasingly exasperated, as I always do whenever Jenna starts on a spiel about her purpose and the meaning of life, the thing we always seem to disagree on. She doesn't get it. She doesn't understand how boring *real life* has to be, for society to work. Not everyone can just paint and create, the way she wants to. "You have to work. Someone needs to do those jobs –"

"Yeah – someone like *you*."

Our eyes meet again and I feel myself flush.

*Someone like you.*

"What's that supposed to mean?"

"You don't have a passion, Mace." She raises an eyebrow as I open my mouth to object, cutting in and continuing, "Don't. You know I'm right. You don't wake up with a burning desire to create, to play sport, to… well, do anything." I know I must look offended, because she smiles lightly and adds, "That's not a bad thing. What you want from life is just different to what I want."

"What *do* I want?" I press, though there's an edge of sarcasm in my voice and I don't know if I want to hear the answer.

Jenna frowns. "I guess…" Sighing, she picks up the bowl again and delves around, electric nails scraping the bottom. "Look, do you want me to be harsh, or what?"

I shudder. "Go for it."

"Well… I'd say you just want to get through life. Am I right? No drama, no hurt, no trouble… stable friends, stable boyfriend, average grades, normal job."

I don't say anything.

There's no point.

"It's okay, you know," she perseveres. "You've been like this since primary school, around about the time Dad left. I guess it just affected us in different ways – you wanted to disappear, I wanted to be noticed."

Still, I say nothing. The TV drones on in the background, the edge of her blanket tickling my knee.

"I guess that's why Lexie's accident hit you so hard."

The TV has switched to some tacky newsreel now, edged in blue, shiny writing. Somewhere in the top corner, the time reads 5:04pm. Mum should be home from work soon – she'll want me to help her cook, no doubt.

"I guess it was a disruption," Jenna's saying, though I'm trying not to listen. What do we have in the fridge? Smoked salmon, I think, and some leftover tuna pasta... "You probably didn't expect to have all eyes on you quite so much. It must be... well, a bit of a shock to the system. *I'm* usually the one in trouble, not you."

*You're not in trouble. You're not. Lexie's death was an accident – that's what everyone thinks. No one knows it was you.*

"I know it wasn't your fault, but you must be feeling that a little, right?" Jenna's trying to understand, read between the lines, invade my privacy. She's doing what she always does best: get inside my head and over-analyse everything. "I know people have been saying stuff, Mace – I saw the way Mrs McCoy looked at you at the funeral. She thinks you didn't take care of Lexie well enough that night, or something."

She stops talking, and goes to turn off the TV. The room once again descends into darkness, no light peeking through the drawn curtains, the blinking red light on the cabinet opposite glaring.

"Your life before was perfect, Macey." Jenna's voice is bitter, interrupted by the steady crunch of popcorn between her teeth. "You had everything you wanted, right? And this... I'm not stupid. I know it changed everything."

But Jenna has no idea of just how much it's changed.

"You'll be okay though, Macey." In the dark, I feel her reach for my hand and squeeze, tight. Her fingers are sticky and damp, and curl around mine beneath the blanket.

*I'll be okay. I'll be fine.*

*I'll be absolutely fine.*

\*\*\*

The screen is blank. The dull white glow lights up my face and the surrounding sheets, illuminating the keys.

**My name is Macey Collins, and I was there the night Lexie died.**

It's hardly an appropriate way to start my speech.

I hit the delete key over and over, until the little black mark jumping up and down screams at me to stop.

Once again, the screen fades into a thick blank canvas, ready to paint with my lies. No one knows what happened that night. No one but me. I have the power in my hands to create whichever picture I want.

**Lexie's accident was terribly tragic, and we're so sorry for the pain and hurt it caused her family.**

I can't apologise, though.

That's too much like admitting it was my fault.

I nestle further into the sheets, pink velvet meeting flesh. My legs are still dotted with bleach-blonde hairs, like the ones on my head, just finer, the kind no one but Tyler would notice. I imagine him now, beneath the duvet with me, scrutinising every inch of my unkempt body. It's enough to make me shudder.

**Sadly, Lexie McCoy passed away three weeks ago, as the result of a terrible accident. Our thoughts are with her family and friends, and we hope to provide reassurance and support throughout tonight's session.**

That's better. I sound sympathetic, kind, welcoming, like I agree that what happened was a terrible accident and there was nothing we could do to prevent it. I sound distant from the event, not really a part of it. It all lines up, that way. It confirms that I was tucked away in my tent when Lexie died. It suggests, as well, that her death was some sort of shock to me. That I heard of her passing the way everyone else did, when her body was found.

**I knew Lexie well. She was a good friend of mine, and her death hit me hard, as it did everyone. She was a joyous, beautiful girl who loved life and had such a zest for everything – including guiding and camping, which is why I'm so glad her last day was spent doing something she loved.**

But there's a huge difference between masking the truth and blatantly lying.

Lexie wasn't happy that day. She wasn't joyous. She didn't love life. She *hated* life.

I click on the tiny red cross in the upper corner, watching the screen revert to home. There's a photo of the four of us splayed before me: Rosie, Jaye, Soraya. Rosie's leaning to the side, bum deliberately outstretched and visible in its tight skirt. Jaye is grinning and holding up a bottle of vodka, which she's undoubtedly about to take a swig from. Soraya is sat beside me in the middle, a mint-green scarf on her head, brown eyes smiling.

I'm laughing, hair dipping over one shoulder and stomach creased above my jeans. I look happy.

I'm not happy.

I push down the lid and slide my laptop onto the floor, dipping below the covers until I'm completely submerged.

I was once the girl in that photo, a girl who laughed and smiled and had *fun*.

So was Lexie.

# 11

Lexie's downfall was fast. Too fast. Unlike the bullying, which built up slowly out of nowhere, it was impossible *not* to notice the change.

It was the January of this year that she officially stopped tugging Mr Sparkles to our guides' sessions. Long gone was his bedraggled expression and missing eye, his unpicked mouth and grubby horn. Without him clutched beneath her fingers, it was like she'd lost a limb. Her presence was halved, hands swinging emptily by her sides.

"Thank goodness you've finally thrown away that grotty unicorn, Lex," Chloe sniffed unsavourily. "You *have* binned it, haven't you? It's not rotting away in your bedroom?"

Lexie flushed, shaking her head. "Of course I have. He's… he's probably in landfill right now."

It was the makeup next, gifts from her family at Christmas. Thick foundation, two shades too dark and slightly orange-y. Clumpy mascara that stuck to her lids, creating a pattern of black. Sticky pink lip-gloss which seemed to permanently overlap her chin and Cupid's bow, refusing to stay within the lines. Her face was smeared in the stuff, waxy skin hidden beneath a tower of bronzer and blush.

She tried hard to get it right, evidently. She'd push heavy eyeshadow across her lids and brush her wispy hair desperately throughout the night, tugging on it to make it stay and scooshing the baby hairs back with hairspray and clips. Extravagant styles were no longer "cool". In order to keep up with the girls, Mrs McCoy's hairstylist skills were left in the dust.

The others had resorted to straightening by now. Chloe's pale blonde hair was long and thin and fell past her shoulders in clean lines, so Lucy, Kayleigh and Orla followed suit, dragging out every last curl and wave. Ringlets and baby hairs suddenly carried the plague. They were to be avoided at all costs, chopped and squashed from view.

"What *does* she look like?" they'd whisper, pointing to one of the younger girls, who sported a head full of neatly packed curls. They were glossy and red, the kind of hair you'd find in a shampoo commercial. "It's like she's never heard of straighteners. *Any* sort of treatment would do…"

It's not unusual for girls to feel like this, especially at that age. The make-up, hair, and Mr Sparkles' fate were all fairly normal. It's part of growing up. I remember Mum buying me my first pallet of eyeshadow, taking me to get my ears pierced, chucking away my old teddies… I wanted to be sparkly and new, a sophisticated version of my old self, someone who wouldn't stand out as "different". Blending in means looking the same as everybody else, losing your identity. It's a small price to pay for happiness.

The physical change in Lexie was minute, seen as a good thing. Mrs McCoy was loving it. Every mother wants a daughter they can dress up and paint, someone to parade in front of the other mums, someone to be *proud* of.

The sadness was never supposed to be a part of that.

It seeped through Lexie like the plague, turning her skin waxy and pale behind its mask, drip-dropping circles of darkness beneath her eyes and in the hollows of her face. Halloween was long behind us, but Lexie was permanently in costume, the ghost of a girl painted bright orange for the cameras.

That was the worst part. She wasn't herself anymore, not even close. In growing up and developing into a whole new person, it was like the old Lexie had died, leaving an empty shell. She was cold, fleshy, lifeless, leered at by Chloe and Kayleigh for her terrible makeup skills, the grease in her hair, her failed outfit attempts. Even Lucy and Orla were wary, eager to help and yet afraid of Chloe's ridiculing.

"Are you trying to copy me?" she mocked one day, when Lexie arrived at the door in a space-themed crop-top and black jeans – a variant of Chloe's outfit a week earlier. "Oh gosh, are those shoes *knock-offs*?"

And so it continued.

None of the girls would wear their guides' uniform anymore, which irritated Sharon no end. It was "uncool", apparently, to follow the rules and dress in the fusty red-and-blue shirt with its sagging hoody. They weren't at school, and so they weren't going to be told what clothes to wear.

"It makes me look like a bloody Union Jack," Chloe complained, peeling it off and dropping it by the coat racks.

"Yeah," Kayleigh sneered, eagerly doing the same. "A Union Jack!"

Patriotism was one of many things they now thought to be "lame".

The weeks dragged as darkness spread throughout Lexie. We watched with wary eyes, unable to interrupt, not sure of what to say or do, if anything.

She was just lonely, we decided, shrugging it off. She didn't have many friends, but loads of kids struggle, especially at that age. People assume kids can't be depressed. The very *idea* is seen as ludicrous. But looking back, there's no other word that would have fitted Lexie's state so well.

Chloe would call her miserable. She'd tug on her wispy hair and snort with laughter, saying she needed to lighten up, that she brought down the mood.

"What's wrong with you?" she'd ask, frowning and poking her face. "Can't you just *smile*, Lexie?"

But Lexie couldn't smile. With each passing week, the raincloud above her head expanded, casting a shadow over every positive thought she once possessed.

Sharon noticed the change, too. She started pulling Lexie to one side to question her on not joining in with games or activities, to ask why she'd spent so long in the toilets, whether it was appropriate to wear such heavy makeup to a guides' session.

"I'm worried," she hissed at me, walking back over and shaking her head. "Something's going on with that girl, Macey. Do you know if everything's all right at home?

Things weren't fine in the McCoys' house, either. Her parents were worried stiff, dropping Lexie off right by the door with anxious expressions and fresh wrinkles on foreheads, eyes wide and concerned as they watched their shadow of a daughter slink inside. They knew something was happening, of course. It was so obvious. They just didn't know *what*.

But with the bullying so subtle, the whispers and giggles, hidden behind glassy smiles and perky framed photos of their friendship group, what was there to notice? Lexie wouldn't say anything. I wouldn't say anything. Sharon had no idea that Lexie's downfall was occurring under her very nose.

She blamed some outside force, another stormy sea battering against her door. The stormy sea, however, was right inside her. It was causing havoc against her soul, ripping it to shreds, a continuous battle to survive.

Because although Lexie died in August, I think we lost her months before that.

# 12

I can't think about anything else. My mind is fixed on the commemoration event, counting down the hours, fingers crossed and heart racing. My speech is tucked in my bag, tied with a pink hair-bobble – the kind Lexie would've snapped round her wrist when she was nervous – and I twang it beneath my desk as the maths class persists, Tyler's foot tip-tapping on my chair, teacher droning, air hot and sticky, stifling –

"If you could start packing up now, year thirteen..."

I rush from the room as the bell goes, belting it out of the building and onto the playground. Kids fizzle across the concrete with satchels and rucksacks and handbags swung over limbs, skirts too short and trousers too tight, illegal gum stretched across tongues, cigarette-stained teeth grinning at the blue, cloudless sky. The sun's too hot for September, contrasting with the bleak weather of the last few days. My coat is sticking to my skin.

"You're fine," I murmur, completely to myself. "You're fine, you're fine, you're *fine*..."

There's a girl to my left watching me curiously, and I flush. Why can't I just take a hold of myself and just be... well, normal?

I duck my head as the path winds through the school, fresh leaves crunching underfoot, the first to fall. Younger kids slip around me like tadpoles, yelling with laugher, eyes open wide and hands clutched eagerly around bag straps.

The common room is quiet. People dot the tables here and there, the sofas empty. I buy a panini to give me something to do, taking it from the rack without reading the label. It's cold, the cheese waxy against wet bread, slivers of what looks like onion dotting the surface amid snotty clumps of dough.

"Carb overload, Mace." It's Jaye. She slides onto the sofa beside me with a grin, poking at the panini and shuddering. "God, is that even food? It looks *dead*."

"I don't think any food from the canteen is actually *edible*, Jaye." Rosie slips round the other side of me, falling into my shoulder with her curls in disarray and glittery eyeshadow swept across her lids. "What's up, Macey? You ready for tonight?"

*You ready for tonight?* I greet my friends amicably, shifting over to let them in, though my hands are trembling and I want to scream. I hate the way she says it, like it's a social event I should be ready for, something to excite over, something I've been *waiting for*.

Am I ready? I don't think I ever really will be. I just want to get it over with.

"I managed to get the night off work…" Jaye is saying as I tune back in. "Big Gav wasn't too pleased, but apparently he knows Lexie's dad, so that sweetened the blow. It's on, Macey. We're coming with you!"

I blink, surprised.

"You are?" My eyes flit backwards and forwards between them in disbelief, but they're both grinning, eyes lit up and shining.

"We thought you might need some support!" Rosie beams. "Soraya asked Tyler to go too, so that'll be nice…"

"Soraya asked him?" I try to keep my voice light, but there's a tremor of doubt there, just audible.

I don't know why it still makes me feel so uneasy. Can't Soraya and Tyler be friends without my approval? Is that weird?

"Yeah... I think they discussed it in sociology yesterday." Rosie shares a glance with Jaye, a subtle frown I'm supposed to not notice.

Unease ripples through me.

I never thought I'd be the kind of girlfriend to be controlling. I thought people like that were petty, that it showed a lack of trust. Tyler's only interested in me, I know that. I should trust him.

I should trust *Soraya*.

"Well..." I glance down at the panini in my hands. I've been squeezing it so hard that plasticky cheese pushes from its soggy base and hangs limply over the edge. I don't want to eat it. I don't know why I bought it. I pick at a piece of onion and push it between my teeth, but it's slimy on my tongue, like the underside of a toenail.

"Don't, Mace, I'll barf." Rosie plucks it from my hands and throws it in a perfect arch towards the bin. It lands with a thud among bits of fried chicken and blue paper towel. "There. Let's go out – Soraya's got psychology now, but we can grab some food, right?"

"I don't know..." I begin to say, but Jaye jumps up and grabs my hands, pulling me from my seat.

"Don't be daft!" She swings her bag over her shoulder. "You need to have some fun before tonight – and so do we!" She and Rosie exchange glances, eyebrows raised. "We're not taking no for an answer, Macey."

"I'm not hungry..." I continue, but Rosie tugs on my arm

and drags us in the direction of the door, shaking her head.

"Then just get a drink!" she says. The two exchange another glance, one of eye rolls and exasperation, one which questions where their old best friend has gone. "Come on, Mace – you need to get back to normal. You can't be miserable forever!"

I don't really have a choice.

***

We get a pizza to share, pepperoni with low-fat cheese and a wholemeal base. Jaye says she only wants one slice yet ends up taking three, and Rosie orders a pot of ketchup, dipping and munching and smearing red all round her mouth like blood.

"This pizza is so *good*," she mumbles, licking her lips and smacking them together. "I swear there's no better food on earth…"

The pub is quiet around us, the odd table filled and sunlight shining through latticed windows. The middle of the day on a Tuesday isn't exactly the most popular time, which is why we love it so much; the peace and quiet, the choice of the best tables, food that hasn't been rushed and is still crisp from the oven. Another group of students sit a little way off, Darcie Carlton at the head of the table in the shortest skirt possible, green hair tumbling over her shoulders.

"God, who does she think she is?" Rosie murmurs, noticing me watching her. "Look at her, sticking her boobs in Bob's face. What a *tart*."

The three of us glance her way again, wrinkling noses and shaking heads. Darcie's a loud-mouth, the centre of attention, and today's no different. Rosie is still staring at her in disgust, and finally says, "Does she not have an off button?"

"Probably not," Jaye adds. " I don't have a clue what Tyler saw in her…"

I feel myself flush. The pizza sticks to the top of my mouth, greasy and wet. I don't know why I'm so hypersensitive to conversation about Tyler today, but the thought of him still makes me uncomfortable. Talking about his history with other girls isn't exactly *helping*.

"Apparently she only slept with him to get back at her ex, you know. That's what Soraya was saying…"

"Soraya?" Rosie asks, glancing up with one eyebrow arched. "How does *she* know? She hates gossip."

"Maybe someone told her?" Jaye suggests. "She talks to Tyler in sociology. Maybe he mentioned it?"

But Rosie and I exchange confused looks, and she shakes her head. "He's hardly going to talk about losing his virginity in a sociology lesson, Jaye." My best friend picks up another slice and lifts it to her teeth, cocking her head thoughtfully. "Not to Soraya, anyway… and he's never mentioned that to you, has he, Mace?"

I shake my head. Tyler doesn't exactly talk about Darcie Carlton, or about what happened on that bus journey in year nine. Even when we first slept together over summer, he didn't exactly disclose his past experiences. We had a mutual understanding. He had experience and I didn't, so he was *firmly* in charge.

"Who knows," Jaye says, but when silence settles over the table, we're all wondering the same sequence of things.

Rosie and I order chocolate brownies afterwards, with clotted cream and diet cokes. Jaye says something about missing the gym and sticks to her water, but she picks up an extra fork and tucks into mine the minute it arrives.

We eat in amicable silence as the pub buzzes to life

around us and lunchtime hits, the bar glowing soft orange in the corner and the scent of garlic and chip spice wafts from the kitchen. It's still hot outside, golden light flittering onto the table and a light breeze blowing through the cracks. My foots taps restlessly on the floor. Here now, watching as the clock ticks past twelve and afternoon falls upon us, my heart's in my throat and my mind's working overtime. It's getting closer, closer –

"Nervous?" Rosie asks, dragging me from my daydream. The look on my face tells her everything, and she grins and taps her fork against my hand. "You'll be fine, honestly. Have you written a speech already?"

I nod, stomach churning, and she holds out a hand. Pulling it from my bag, I pass it over. She unfolds the sheet and frowns. Jaye glances over her shoulder, pulling a face and cocking her head as she reads.

"It's two paragraphs, Macey," she says after a moment, stating the obvious. "You know it'll have to be more than that, right?"

Flushing, I stab at the remaining brownie with my fork. "I… I was just going to wing it."

Rosie and Jaye turn to each other in despair before Rosie pushes the sheet down onto the table and pulls a pen from her jacket pocket. She scribbles something above the speech and sketches two loopy hearts in one corner, then swivels it round and pushes it towards me.

"There," she says, grinning. "We're adding to it. Go on."

I pick up the pen. Stare at the piece of paper before me. Then I glance back up at them, wrinkling my nose and shaking my head.

"I can't," I say. The white blurs before me, greying and creased from my bag. "I can't put it into words."

"You'll be ten times worse tonight," Rosie reasons.

"I might not be…"

"You'll be nervous, Mace, you can't just make it up on the spot. Just a few prompts, that's all you need."

"What you gonna talk about?" Jaye cuts in, reaching to steal a forkful of brownie. "What she was like, how close you were… or what happened that night? Will you talk about it? About the… accident?"

I stop chewing. Swallow. Pretend to be preoccupied with glancing around the pub, to where Darcie Carlton's laughing and practically sitting on Bob's lap, chest popping from her shirt.

"Mace?" Rosie adds. "What are you planning to talk about, Macey?"

I frown. The brownie's centre is oozing out over the plate, colliding with the cream. It's almost unappetising. The room's too hot all of a sudden, the air blasting through the window sticky and warm.

"I… I don't know," I say. "I don't think it's really appropriate to talk about the night she… you know. It seems insensitive."

"But that's the reason they're hosting it, right?" Jaye's straight-talking nature gets to me, sometimes, and I rub my toe against the table leg irritably. "They want to prove it was a one-off, an accident, so that they don't get a bad rep. The Vibbington Weekly's going too, right?"

"That was only a rumour," Rosie counters, "but still, if they do turn up…"

"So what?" My heart is thumping wildly in my mouth, squeezing my tongue, restricting my breathing. I take another bite of brownie, just to give my mouth something to do. I can barely swallow.

"Well... that's why you're speaking, right?" Jaye and Rosie are glancing at me as though it's obvious, so I nod slowly, licking my teeth.

"You were there, Mace. Sharon was in the next field. Only you can prove it was an accident, that it was no one's fault."

"Yeah."

"So you'll have to talk about it." Jaye raises an eyebrow. "That's what everyone wants, Macey, even though it's messed up."

Rosie nods, though she's watching me anxiously. "She's right, you know. I know it'll be hard, Macey. We can't imagine what you're going through."

I nod.

What else is there to say?

# 13

Mum drops me off at 7:30, outside the chapel. She turns to me as I'm getting out of the car, frowning and trying for a smile.

"Tell Sharon I said hi," she says. "I won't stop. I'm ringing a client later, and I showed my face at the funeral, so I don't think anyone will notice if I'm not there…"

"Fine," I say, slamming the door behind me. She's probably right; no one will notice.

The sky's a soft blue, fading into yellow in the distance, and the lights are on in the chapel. My hands are shaking beneath my coat sleeves. I wander up the path with my fingers crossed and toes curled inside my Converse, heart inside my mouth and eyes watering.

I stop just outside, one hand against the door. Most people are early. It's not something they want to miss. I hear the buzz of chatter from beyond the walls, the breaking into packets of biscuits and gurgling laughter. No doubt there's cordial out, along with snacks and crisps, in pure church-style. Sharon raises her voice to get everyone's attention. I shudder as the room goes silent.

If walking in wasn't going to be awkward enough…

I push through the door, landing on the mat and rubbing my feet against it. Through the door, the people on the back row turn round to glare at me, frowning and shaking their heads as though I've disrupted something important. I slip off my coat and cross the threshold into the hall.

It's full, chairs lining the length of the room, an aisle in the middle to separate the crowds: guides on one side, parents on the other, Sharon in the middle. The lights are too bright, garish, causing my eyes to ache. She nods at me now, relieved, and tilts her head to the left as though inviting me to join her.

More heads have turned, peering at me in confusion. I hear a gasp from the far side and imagine it to be Lucy, or maybe even Kayleigh. I don't dare look at them. *One foot forward, two feet forward, don't step on the cracks…* I squeeze my hands into balls and breathe in deeply, smiling at Sharon and walking through the seats towards her.

"Macey!" she announces, smiling and holding out an arm to embrace me. "This is Macey Collins, everyone – the young lady in charge of the girls on the night that Lexie… Well, I think we all know who she is."

A few women to the front of the room and one bald man start to clap, so I nod back, careful to keep my expression light. I don't want it to seem like I'm faltering, like I'm nervous. I need to appear collected, as though I know exactly what's going on and am taking it all in my stride.

"Well…" Sharon continues, hugging me quickly and taking a step back. The hair on her upper lip is stiff with sweat and her eyes are twitchy and white, mascara stuck to her lids. "I think we'll start by playing the PowerPoint Lexie's friends have kindly put together for this evening. Chloe? Lucy? Would you like to come up to the computer, loves?"

I move to the side of the room, back colliding with the radiator.

As if in slow-motion, four girls rise from the audience. Chloe leads the pack, dark eyes glinting, Lucy just behind, a USB clutched between her fingers. Orla pushes her glasses up onto the bridge of her nose as they move through the seats, Kayleigh trailing behind with furious red cheeks and a hand clutched to her mouth.

Try as I might to focus, my eyes won't stop flitting back to Chloe. There's something about her expression – her smug, cold gaze, lips drawn into a thin line – which makes me feel uneasy. She steps out with confidence, gesturing for the others to follow her to the computer desk, then draws the USB from Lucy's hands and pushes it into the port with a satisfying *click*.

We wait, breaths held, as the folder opens up on the projector and Chloe clicks on the file. Lucy's bottom lip is trembling, green eyes filled with tears. I don't doubt that she made the PowerPoint. It's exactly the kind of thing she'd do.

We watch the tiny blue circle spinning round and round on the wall before us. It stops for a second, glitching and blurring, before whirring back to life.

The PowerPoint flashes up onto the wall, a mismatch of pinks and purples and blues, tacky, homemade. I don't let my vision focus; I don't want it to. I let the colours mix and merge, a kaleidoscope of twelve-year-old girly-girl splattered across the plaster.

Around the room, gasps echo and reminiscent gurglings ripple across the audience. I peak between my eyelashes, and my stomach drops.

There, on the wall, is Lexie.

She looks about eleven, toothy and beaming, wispy hair in braids around her head. She's stood in front of a forest, dressed in a strappy pink top and denim shorts, skin turned golden from the foreign sun. She's clearly been walking, and her cheeks are flushed pink from the hike.

She must've been on holiday in this one. I imagine Mrs

McCoy taking the photo, her husband's hand blocking the glare from the sun, Lexie's little brother parading beneath them and pulling funny faces. It looks like Cyprus, or maybe Spain, a typical British destination, a land chocka-block with tourists and ice cream vans and souvenir stalls.

The screen fades to the next slide. Lexie's stood by the fireplace in their beige living room, grinning, one arm slung over her brother's shoulders. The caption reads "Lexie and Daniel" – her brother, who isn't here, of course, along with her parents. The floor is scattered with wrapping paper, red and green and silver, streams of ripped paper and ribbon littered over the carpet, a Christmas tree cowering in the corner.

More photos dance across the screen, pictures of food parlours, pizzerias, Easter, various children and grandparents and fake Father Christmases. Lexie grows up before our eyes, transforming from a bold, red-faced pre-teen to a waddling three-year-old. She loses teeth, cuts hair, gains freckles and weight and endless summer tans. She lets go of friends and grandparents, and her baby cousin is born, falling into her arms like a tiny, bald kitten. The audience smiles – two or three even cry – as she develops into the person we all met upon her arrival at Vibbington all those years ago.

Lucy's done well, making it mismatched and chaotic, not lingering for a second. She's compiled the photos in a random order, flitting from baby snaps to selfies stolen from her Instagram, heavily filtered and edited to make the most of her face. I hate those. I hate the mask covering her mouth and nose, false eyelashes dangling from her sad grey eyes.

The ones I hate most, however, are the ones taken with her friends.

They're at the end, which is no doubt deliberate. Chloe is

always in the centre of each photo, holding the phone before them to get the perfect snap, dark eyes wide and lined with black. Kayleigh never stops pouting – it's like she can't help it – and Orla looks uncomfortable, squashed at the edge of the photo. Lucy beams, dimples in her cheeks as she leans closer into the frame.

And Lexie looks so *eager*.

Her expression is the kind Rosie pulls when she's trying to be sultry, lips pursed and eyes staring intently at the camera. Her hair's pushed to one side by the tilt of her head, spread across her shoulders. In the photos before Mr Sparkles disappeared, she's clutching him tight. After, her hands are empty.

There's one of her and Lucy together, outside a cinema somewhere. They have their arms around each other and are beaming at the camera, mid-laugh, streetlamps turning the ground around them tangerine orange.

Another shows Lucy, Lexie and Orla, on the school playground, mouths open wide as though they're screeching like the seagulls flying overhead. Lexie and Orla with that awful puppy-face filter, in someone's bedroom, smiling and leaning together. Lexie and Kayleigh in a science lesson, leering over Bunsen burners with tongs and vials and various bottles of chemicals around them.

Lexie and Chloe.

They're stood in front of a monument on some school trip or other. Chloe is clutching Lexie around the waist, so hard it looks like it could hurt, worried she'll take off at any moment.

The eyes are the worst part. Chloe's are black, the densest shade imaginable, lashes thick and long and menacing on her pale face. Lexie's are tired. They're ringed with purple, grey bags frowning down on us, peering from her badly made-up face as though they don't want to be there at all and are trying to escape.

Part of the screen disappears for a moment as a shadow crosses the projector. It's Chloe, standing up to face the audience and gazing round the room, mouth turned down at the edges.

"Thank you," she begins, "for being here. Lexie was one of our best friends, and we're so glad we were able to do this for her today."

Stepping back, she gestures for the others to step up and join her. With flushed cheeks, they scuttle up behind, Kayleigh clutching a piece of paper tight beneath her fingers. The whole room is watching.

"Erm... y-yes," Lucy stammers, blushing and biting down hard on her bottom lip. "Lexie was one of the kindest people we knew, and being her friend was the greatest honour of my life. I... I'm really going to miss her."

Orla takes a step closer to her, writhing and shuffling her feet. "We're grateful to Mr and Mrs McCoy for the photos they gave us. We're sorry they couldn't make it today, and we sympathise greatly with their loss and hope they feel better soon." She recites the lines quickly, as though they're rehearsed, then lifts her sleeve to her mouth and rubs it. "Our condolences to everyone affected."

Finally, Kayleigh steps up behind Orla. There are tears in her eyes and her cheeks are scarlet, and she stares at the paper with such intensity that I wouldn't be surprised if it combusted right before her.

"I..." She tries to speak, but she's trembling too much and her lips are shaking. "I'm so grateful for everything Lexie did for us, and will miss her very much."

The irony is too much, and it takes everything in me to not roll my eyes or stamp my foot. The audience are all shaking their heads and frowning sadly, whispering about the "poor girls" and their loss, sympathising, full of commiserations.

It's sick. It's so bloody *sick*.

"Thank you, girls." Sharon has joined them now, arms wrapped around them and expression full of remorse. "What happened to Lexie was a terrible tragedy, and no one has felt that more than her family and these four girls. As her best friends, they made Lexie's short life a joy, and we'll always be in debt to you."

Chloe drops her head, smiling at the floor. The others look like they're about to cry.

"And now it's time to speak to one of the people who knew and loved Lexie best." Sharon's eyes float around the room before landing on me, face breaking into a devastated smile.

"Macey?" she says, lifting forefinger to beckon me over. "Would you like to speak?"

# 14

Every inch of me is shaking as I make my way to the front once again, from where I'm settled against the radiator at the side of the room. My notes are in my pocket, tucked against my thigh. The piece has been folded and unfolded so many times that the seams are all ripped and it's almost completely broken, so I pull it out carefully and smooth it against my hand, words blurring before me in one grey blob.

Rosie's scribbled words stand out in blue biro:

*good luck, bestie xoxo*

I glance up then, remembering that they said they'd be here. My eyes scan the audience.

My friends are right on the back row, amongst the girl guides. Tyler sits by the aisle, dressed in a "going out" top and furiously tight jeans, tapping away at his phone on his lap. He's not even watching. The girls are beside him, Soraya next, smiling from beneath an emerald headscarf. Jaye presses up her thumbs reassuringly, and Rosie gives a huge, full-bodied wave.

Just seeing them makes me feel so much better, and I take in a deep breath.

*You can do this.*

I can do this.

Lucy, Chloe, Kayleigh and Orla have sat back down again, and the front of the room is empty. The projector's switched off, wall blank. I cross the floor, shoes squeaking, to the centre of the hall.

The audience stares back, a sea of people. The lights are always so bright in movies that the main character can't see the crowd properly, faces turned into blurry blobs. This isn't a movie. I can see every wrinkle, every freckle, every brown hair turned grey. The bald man on the front row catches my eye and I flush.

*Just speak.*

But my throat is dry and I can't breathe, the air in my throat trapped, constricted. I open my mouth to say something and yet no words come out.

I don't even know what I was planning to say.

"I…" I falter.

*Don't be so pathetic – you need to do this.*

"I'm Macey."

It's a weak start, and the audience are raising eyebrows and rolling eyes, confused, despairing. "What's wrong with that girl?" they'll ask, shaking their heads. "Can she not form words?"

I shudder, lifting the paper closer to my face. I *can* do this. I'm not stupid.

"I'm Macey Collins, and I was there the night Lexie died."

The room is silent. Faces stare back, impassive, unsure of how to react. It's not something we've said explicitly – not yet. It's something you avoid saying aloud, as if ignoring reality will somehow make it *not true*. I glance down at my speech, realising that it was the exact line I'd chosen not to say.

"Sadly, Lexie McCoy passed away three weeks ago, as the result of a terrible accident. Our thoughts are with her family and friends, and we hope to provide reassurance and support throughout tonight's session."

I sound robotic, forced, like Orla as she recited her lines. It's obvious I'm reading from the sheet. Catching my breath and clutching the paper tight, my eyes skim the next paragraph. "I knew Lexie well. She was a good friend of mine, and her death hit me hard, as it did everyone."

I can't read the next lines – not out loud, in front of all these people. I've written how she was "joyous", how she had a zest for life and loved everything about girl guiding, how she was happy and normal and *free*.

I can't tell that to a room full of people who know as well as I do that it's all lies.

"Lexie was an incredible young lady," is what comes out of my mouth instead. I'm not expecting it – not those words. Glancing back up, I meet eyes with the bald-headed man, who nods back coolly. It almost says, *you can do this*. "Lexie was one of the nicest, bravest girls I knew. She was adventurous, friendly, bold. She never stopped pushing through, and would do anything to better herself, to achieve her goals."

I stop, taking another deep breath.

"Lexie faced many challenges in her life, most of which went unnoticed." I look at the girls then. I can't help it. Chloe stares back, forehead creased, black eyes on mine. "She was stronger than most people realised, too. She got on with things, and didn't let anybody get her down, no matter how hard they tried."

Kayleigh's properly crying now, tears rolling down her cheeks, which are red and splotchy. Lucy and Orla are glancing at each other in bewilderment, clutching sleeves.

"She was a fighter, Lexie. Anyone who knew her would tell you that."

I turn to Sharon then, and she smiles and steps forward to join me.

It's over. I did it. Sinking back into myself, I clutch the paper between my fingers so hard that it growls. Relief takes over my body, but it's quenched as soon as Sharon clears her throat.

"Thank you, Macey, for that wonderful tribute to Lexie." With an awkward cough, she adds, "We understand that this is a highly sensitive topic, and so if you'd like to leave now, you may. However, we do think it's vital that we discuss this with as many of you as possible." She places a hand on my shoulder and squeezes, tight. Four people at the back stand to leave. "We'd now like to take the chance to talk about the night of the accident, and to answer any questions."

Silence settles around the room, as if a spell has been dropped. Nobody dares breathe.

"Macey, as we said, was there that night. I was in the next field in my tent. No one could have prevented what happened by the river. Lexie left the tent of her own accord, and the site was fully secured – no one could have left or entered through the perimeter fence, and it just so happened that part of the site wasn't as safe as we'd… assumed."

She squeezes my shoulder again then, taking a deep breath and glancing down at her feet.

"The river wasn't that rapid during the day – in fact, it was quite placid. I was with the girls the whole time we were out there, and, while I was watching, none of them could've come to any harm. Unfortunately, the river happened to pick up quite a pace that night, due to bad weather."

I don't want to be listening to this. I feel sick, heart beating fit to burst inside my ribs, pulse too quick. I want to run. Eyeing the door, I will my feet to move. They're stuck fast.

"We don't know why Lexie left her tent that night, or how she ended up by the river, or what compelled her to do what she did. All we know is that her death was the most tragic of accidents, something I'd step back in time to prevent in a heartbeat if I could." Choked up and eyes now glassy, she manages to continue. "I'll forever remember Lexie as a bright, cheerful young girl, one it was a pleasure to watch develop. I've always done my very best for the girls of our district, and Lexie was no different... If I could change what happened that night, I would, but I can't, and that's something I'll never truly get over.

"I can't thank Macey enough for her support and help, both on the camp and afterwards. The other girls, too, have been an absolute tribute to Vibbington Girl Guides, and it's been a privilege to get to know them over the last two years. I'll always do my duty, which is to protect the girls in my care the best I can. Lexie's accident was just that: a terrible accident." A tear slides down her face, into the crease of her mouth. "I'm so sorry for the loss Lexie's family have suffered, and I'd understand completely if you never wanted to send your girls here again. But I promise, from the bottom of my heart, to protect these girls in a way I couldn't protect Lexie."

She steps back then, shoulders shaking and eyes streaming. "Thank you for coming tonight. If you have any questions, we'll be here for the next hour to answer them."

As if by magic, the spell is lifted. Silence flitters away as people start to move, shuffling through the rows towards the aisle. They're heading straight for the biscuit table, of course.

Talk about death, then eat pink wafers. It's the obvious sequence of events.

My hands are shaking rapidly, so I push them between my knees. Rosie, Soraya, Jaye and Tyler are dodging the crowd, grinning and waving and smiling. I try to smile back yet falter, shrinking back against the radiator once again as they tumble my way.

"You did great!" Rosie announces, pouncing on me. I'm surrounded by beams and patting hands, clutching at my sleeves and nodding their heads. "God, Mace, we're so proud of you. Having to do that must've *sucked*."

"Yeah," Soraya agrees, smiling at me, brown eyes kind. "Want a Haribo, Macey?"

I take the gummy love heart, as usual.

"I'd have just wet myself with nerves, Mace," Jaye cuts in. "I'm awful at public speaking..."

Tyler doesn't say anything. He just stands there on his phone, shuffling his feet against the floorboards in some kind of dance.

"I think it went okay," I say, but my mind won't focus. It flits from Tyler to Sharon, face wet with tears, then back to Lexie and that awful, false image they played up in their minds. The image of Lexie as a fun-loving tween with heaps of friends who cared for her and respected her. The image of a girl with sun-tanned arms, a red face, stood in front of a row of trees on holiday with her family, having the time of her life.

Happy.

"It went better than okay, silly." Rosie bats my arm playfully, then turns to glance around the room. "Hey, Mace... we'll be over there if you need us, all right?" She gestures over to the other side of the room, and I turn just in time to spot two women wandering my way.

I recognise one of them as Lucy's mum, the other as Orla's. Shit. I wasn't ready for this – not the other mums. Holding my breath and crossing my fingers behind my back, I swallow and spin to face them, eyes bright and cheeks etched into a grin.

They're both dressed in beige, which is somehow worse than mourning black.

"Hi!" I say, holding out a hand to shake theirs. Lucy's mum takes it and shakes, eyes creased as she beams back. Orla's mother has the same worried expression as her daughter, eyes blinking anxiously behind her thick-rimmed glasses, and clutches the tips of my fingers as we shake hands.

"It's so nice to see you again, Macey," Lucy's mum says. "How've you been holding up?"

"Oh… you know." I switch back to a neutral expression then, just like that. It's easier than expected. "It's been tough. I really cared for Lexie – I cared for all of the girls." The obvious sentence lodges in my throat, lingering there.

*I'm so sorry for what happened that night – it must feel so scary, knowing it could've been one of your girls.*

But I still can't apologise, not when it still feels too much like admitting the truth.

"We know you did, Macey." Orla's mum pats my arm tensely. Her hand is still clammy from the shake, nails cut short and neat to the tips of her fingers. "We trusted our girls with you, and you didn't let us down. What happened was an accident, a terrible accident."

An accident. A chill runs down my spine. I nod and clutch the radiator, tight.

"Yes, we're very grateful for the everything you've done for Lucy and Orla… and the others." Lucy's mum's eyes fill with tears, pools of algae swimming in white. "We can't thank you enough, Macey."

Orla's mum nods in agreement while I stand there, unsure of what to say, knuckles tensed against the hot metal. It seeps through my hands and up my arms, twisting to my shoulders and stretching across my back, my neck.

"And... we're so sorry, Macey." Orla's mum is openly crying now, face red and splotchy beneath her glasses. I shift, moving my feet away. *They're* apologising to *me*. I back up even further, lump rising in my throat and heart pounding beneath my chest.

"If you ever want anything, we're here to help," Lucy's mum adds, lips trembling. "Anything, Macey, you hear that?"

I nod. I don't know what else to do.

"And thank you," Orla's mum says. "Thank you for looking after our girls that night. God knows what would've happened if they'd gone down to the river with Lexie too."

*They'd be dead!* I want to scream, heart racing and clenched fists shaking. *I'd have killed them too!*

But I don't say that, of course. The heat is seeping into my head, too hot, stark red, boiling... I just nod, smile, say my goodbyes.

# 15

The car park is cold. It's drizzling, just a bit, and the sky has long turned dark, pinpricks of light poking through the black. I stare at my phone screen, waiting for it to burst. It remains frozen in my hands.

The hedge rustles behind me, wind blustering past. Across the tarmac, families are climbing into cars, fathers and daughters holding hands, grateful to be alive after such a harrowing experience. They're probably thankful for Lexie's death, in some messed-up way. Thankful that it made them realise what really matters in life, ahead of their false priorities.

"Want a lift, Macey?" Jaye shouts from her car door. The others are stuffed in the back, illuminated by the LEDs in her roof, budging up to squeeze in tight. Tyler is in the middle. He lifts an emotionless hand as I stare back at him.

"Mum'll be here soon," I reply. I check the phone again; I already know she's ten minutes late and counting. "Thanks anyway, Jaye."

I'm sure she'll be here soon. She wouldn't have forgotten about me, would she?

I start walking half an hour later, toes numb with cold and fingers ready to drop off. My eyes are watering and even my face has goosebumps, though I'm not sure whether it's because of the cold. My heart's pounding beneath my chest and my eyes are moist with unshed tears, and I'm still reeling from the event, from the photos and memories, from what Lucy and Orla's mums said to me. Glancing up at the sky, I twist my hands into balls. I wish they'd never spoken to me. I wish I'd just left right after the speech... I shouldn't have stood there and listened whilst they preached, feeding me sympathy like I deserved it.

They apologised.

I killed Lexie, and they fucking *apologised*.

I hate it – I hate it *all*. There's so much utter detest inside me that I struggle to even breathe when thinking about it all, overwhelmed with a rage that climbs higher and higher through my body. It's not aimed at anyone else. It's targeted entirely at me, the disgust and dislike, the anger. As the streets empty and more and more stars burst into view, I clench and unclench my fists, unable to keep them under control.

*Just chill – that's the last time you'll have to lie.*

But knowing it's the last time we'll talk about Lexie is even worse. Not keeping her alive in our minds feels like letting go completely, leaving her ashes to rot in the air. That's one of the worst things about death. It's an ongoing battle afterwards, between moving on, accepting what happened, and trying to remember in great detail all that matters.

Maybe the struggle to lie is what I deserve. Do I really want the universe to go easy on me, after what I did?

The walk isn't long, but I'm freezing and shivering by the time I arrive home. The door isn't locked – that's the first thing I notice – and the house smells like cooking. I had a sandwich for tea, and Jenna joined me as I was making them. Peanut butter and cheese, an all-time guilty pleasure of ours, best on white bread with generous helpings of butter. Mum said she'd grab something later, but the spices floating down the corridor suggest she's done more than just knocked up a salad.

I take a deep breath, trying to slow my thumping heart.

*Calm down. Just a few minutes or so more...*

A few minutes or so more until I can punch my pillow, imbed my fist in the velvety duvet, scream into the eiderdown and hope it masks the sound.

The kitchen is full of unwashed plates, pots and pans, cutlery and equipment littering the sides, encrusted in rims of burnt chilli, kidney beans stuck to the bottom like tiny red droppings. There's half a lime on the side which has obviously been squeezed, and a carton of coconut milk sits with its lid off by the television.

The house is silent. I tip-toe across the hall with feet like ice, wishing Mum had put the underfloor heating on before she went to bed.

Making my way up the stairs, I'm careful to tread lightly. Is she in bed? Maybe it's like her to forget to pick me up, but to leave the kitchen in such a state and abandon a recently-used pan to fester... that's not something Lisa Collins would ever do. She's too neat, too tidy, too pragmatic. She doesn't do dirty, disorderly.

The door to her bedroom is closed, a do-not-disturb sign lodged on the handle. I stop for a second... and that's when I hear it.

A low, rhythmic thumping, coming from inside. The sound of something being hit repetitively, over and over, in the same fashion.

It's followed by gasp – then a breathless moan.

And then, "Oh Doyle!"

I freeze. Doyle?

Oh no –

"Oh Doyle, yes…"

I bolt from the door in disgust, cheeks flushed red and pulse thumping in my ears. The door looms before me like a huge, sick symbol for what's inside, leering so tall I think it's almost *laughing* at me.

Not tonight.

Any other night is bad enough, but tonight…

So that's why she couldn't go to Lexie's event.

The door at the other end of the corridor opens, and Jenna peeks out. She's wearing a headset and is frowning, but at least she hasn't been crying again. Her eyes are made-up and significantly less puffy, and she sniffs in disgust as she sees where I'm standing.

"Eavesdropping on Lisa's evening of pleasure, little sister?" she says, raising on eyebrow. "Where's Tyler? I didn't think listening to two grown adults doing it was really your thing."

I shudder glaring back and moving further away from the door. The thumping is still audible, but at least I can't hear what my mother's saying now.

"I… I just got back from Lexie's commemoration evening." I only say that to shut her up, but when her face falls and she juts out her bottom lip, I immediately feel guilty.

I read somewhere online that victims of trauma or grief sometimes turn to using the event as an excuse for attention or sympathy, which I thought would be the last thing I'd turn to doing. I was wrong, evidently.

"I'm fine, Jen, honestly. It was… nice. Nice to celebrate her again, you know?"

"Yeah… I can imagine." She pushes open her door, as if as an invitation. "You want to talk about it, little sister?"

"I'm fine – I just said." I back away again, towards my own door. It's ajar, pink covers welcoming. "Night, Jenna."

She looks back at me, and I know she sees right through me. "Night, Macey."

The door closes and I'm left in the corridor, alone.

# 16

Despite the avalanche of lies spilling out of the event last night, one thing I said was definitely true. Lexie McCoy was a fighter. How she managed to keep going to guides' sessions still baffles me, especially as spring rolled round and the bullying became worse. I don't know what it was like at school; I hardly ever saw her there. I know it can't have been *good*.

I remember seeing her once, outside the science block. She was carrying a sparkly rucksack and her eyes were pink, as if she'd been rubbing away at her makeup and the true colour of her skin had been exposed. Her nose was red, too, and she was frowning, bottom lip trembling.

"Lexie?" a voice called out, from somewhere behind her. "Lexie, are you okay?"

I stopped walking, hidden behind a wall. I was on my way to maths, but I didn't think anyone would mind if I were late... except perhaps Tyler. I watched, peeking out from the bricks, as a PE teacher jogged over to Lexie and placed a hand on her shoulder.

"Are you okay, Lexie?" she repeated, brows furrowed. "You're still in your PE kit."

That's when I noticed what she was wearing. Knee-length white socks; a polo shirt, the school emblem on her breast; a black pair of cycling shorts, showing her plump thighs and the line of her underwear.

She hung her head in embarrassment as the teacher waited for a response.

"I... I couldn't find my clothes, miss," she said. It was a pathetic excuse, and the teacher cocked her head like she didn't believe a word of it. "I think someone must have taken them by accident, or something."

A splotch of water released itself from her bag at that very moment, landing with a satisfying *plip* on the teacher's shoe. The pink of her rucksack was magenta on its underside, soaked wet, liquid seeping through the fabric.

"What's in your bag, Lexie?" the teacher asked, holding out a hand. "Let me see."

Flushing beneath her foundation, a subdued Lexie handed over the rucksack. The PE teacher took it and held it at arm's length, taking the zip with a hesitant finger and pulling it open.

"Oh – oh my!"

Dropping onto her knees, she pulled out a long, ink-black stretch of fabric. It didn't take me long to recognise them as a sopping pair of tights, bunched up and creased with water.

"Oh, Lexie!" the teacher cried, eyes wide in horror. "What on earth happened?"

"It was an accident," Lexie replied, though her voice trembled and her eyes filled with tears. "I was getting dressed in the toilets, and they just fell..."

Slowly, the teacher tugged out the wrinkled, yellowing blouse and skirt, finally emptying a pair of patent black shoes onto the tarmac. With a distressed moan and a saturated rip, two exercise books and a bedraggled history textbook were pulled onto the grey, along with a dripping Mr Sparkles.

I stared at them in dismay, ink and highlighter merged into a blob, cover hanging off the remaining staple with a tiny stretch of unaffected dry paper.

"Lexie... Lexie, dear, who did this to you?"

Why was that even a question?

Lexie just fell to her knees and began shoving the items back into her bag, tears streaming down her cheeks and nose blatantly running. The books were useless now. They were ruined, and the smell coming off her belongings was enough to make me gag.

"It was an accident," she repeated, through sobs. "I just dropped my stuff!"

With that, she turned and ran back into the building.

\*\*\*

Like I said, Lexie was a fighter. She wouldn't let it be known that she was weakened by their actions. She wouldn't cry in front of Chloe or the others, or skip a guides' session because she was too scared to face them. She was bold, right until the end, though her spirit was broken and Mr Sparkles had been long resigned to his fate without her.

She'd stopped smiling by March, had almost stopped speaking by April. She was a shell at this point, the skin of a snake, empty and pale and useless. She didn't laugh or play games or converse, but she was always just *there*, still with us, yet so far away.

When we first planned the camp, back in June, the girls were all for it. It was only to be a small affair. As year sevens, Lucy, Chloe, Kayleigh, Orla and Lexie were the only girls without exams or mocks that summer, so it was agreed that Sharon and I would take them away, organising a bigger event for the other girls later in the year.

"You can plan it yourselves," Sharon told them, passing

round sheets full of activity ideas and recipes. "It'll be your first proper camp, though we'll be on hand to supervise throughout. Right, Macey?"

I nodded. A weekend away from my friends during the precious summer holidays didn't sound ideal, but I could hardly say no. Sharon would need some help, and besides… maybe it would be fun?

"We have to do this," Chloe was saying, prodding at something on the list. "That looks *sick*."

Glancing over her shoulder, I noticed she'd found an image of a large, flat tyre, suspended with ropes and chains over a river.

Sharon was nodding, eyes filled with excitement.

"The tyre swing… I used to love it, back when I was a guide!" She smiled to herself, shaking her head in reminiscence. "Although we didn't have harnesses back then, dear God. The fun health and safety would've had with that!"

Lexie was staring at it. Catching her eye, I wandered over to the other side of the table and crouched down beside her.

"We don't *have* to go on the tyre swing, do we?" she asked, biting her lip. "It's just… I'm not good with heights, or water."

I grinned, patting her hand. "I wouldn't have done it when I was your age, Lex." Because I wouldn't. I never wanted to step outside of my comfort zone, even back then. "You don't have to do anything you don't want to."

"Wimp," I heard Chloe hiss, a few metres away. "It's a bloody *tyre swing*."

Kayleigh chuckled away at Chloe's mocking, whilst Lexie flushed.

"Don't worry, Lexie!" Chloe continued. "I'm sure there'll be time in our schedule for you to cuddle up with your teddy.

We weren't planning on inviting a baby to our camp, but we'll have to shift things around a bit if you're coming too."

"Chloe…" Sharon tried to cut in, but her weak authority stood out as usual. "There's no need for nastiness."

Chloe rolled her eyes, clearly above acting nice in front of Sharon. There was no point anymore.

Between them, Lucy placed two hands on the table with a huge smile. "I can't wait for this camp," she declared, nodding kindly at Lexie. "It's going to be the best weekend *ever*, I promise."

And for the second time in her short life, Lucy had no idea just how wrong she was.

# 17

It's Saturday night, and I'm alone with Rosie in my room. The lights are low and there's pizza discarded on the bed, a carton of garlic and herb dip tipped up on the greasy surface. Rosie has Shawn Mendes on the speakers and blasts out my favourite songs as we get ready, painting glossy smiles over our mouths and squeezing our eyelashes into the perfect, feminine *flick*.

I take a pin and push it into my hair. Rosie's braided it at one side, a long plait that snakes across my shoulder and glows faintly green in the harsh lights of my bedroom mirror. It's misshapen, hairs poking out of place above the bobble.

"You look fit," she says out of nowhere, snapping a piece of gum across her tongue. "Tyler's not expecting anything tonight, is he?"

I shudder, picking up the hairspray. With one final scoosh across my head, the plait is moulded into place, squashed into a lopsided, ash-blonde sausage. I don't usually do my hair like this for parties. Most of the time, Rosie and I smash out the curlers, perhaps touch up our roots over the bathroom sink, and pin back segments with a flower or pearls. But there was nothing else to do tonight. Rosie was fidgeting on my bed, restless, so I suggested she did my hair. I think we both felt ten years old again, squashed up on the carpet, her knees around my waist as she ran her fingers through my hair, twisting each segment into the plait.

"I don't know what he's expecting," I reply now, standing to inspect myself. There's a pizza crumb on my thigh, which I flick onto the floor. "But he's not getting *anything*."

I cock my head to one side and swivel, eyeing my reflection. Everything Rosie implied is exactly right. The skirt is just a tad too short, sticking to the tops of my thighs, and my top is low-cut enough to be deemed party-appropriate. It's the first time I've felt like my old self in weeks.

It's been three or four days since Lexie's commemorative event. I thought things would go back to normal somewhat, for better or for worse, but I can't seem to move on. The old Macey is stuck in the past, clutching her shot glass and pouting at the camera, glossy-haired and bright-eyed. I can separate them pretty easily in my mind... Macey before, and Macey after. They no longer seem like the same person.

I remember the days when I loved parties. The thrill of getting tipsy from Sourz shots in my bedroom, doing each other's hair and makeup before my mirror, trying on clothes and discarding the rejects in a corner. Turning up at someone's house to find the place in darkness, disco lights blasting colour onto the front lawn and music pulsing through the floorboards. The thrill of wondering who'd get with who, questioning why the door to the bedroom upstairs was locked, joking about the spiked punch in the kitchen. Darcie Carlton would be throwing herself about and eating all the pizza, stomach bulging over her belt, while we watched from the sidelines with cups of off-brand coke and enough vodka to have an effect.

I loved feeling nice, warm, wanted. Standing in the crowded living room as sweaty bodies writhed and shrieked to music, I was part of something. I was one of *them*.

"Are these jeans too much?" Rosie cuts in from the other

side of the room. She's wearing a pair of cow-print flared jeans, a little too short, exposing an inch of her ankle. She looks great, as usual.

"They're sick." The word feels outdated, not like something I'd say. "Anything looks good on you, though."

"I just feel so…" She frowns. "Frumpy?"

She's not wearing a top – not even a bra – but that's hardly unusual. Rosie doesn't have any kind of threshold when it comes to exposing herself, especially not around me. She's that kind of person. Every inch of her body is perfect, anyway, all smooth, slender limbs and freckles. There's no reason for her to be insecure.

"You don't look frumpy!"

"Are you sure?"

Rolling my eyes, I glance back at the mirror one more time. My eyes are pale and shadowed, skin a sickly shade, lipstick brushed hastily over the cracks. I look like someone who's trying too hard to be pretty, to be normal, to be liked.

I look like someone who doesn't deserve to be.

"I don't have a bloody clue what top to wear, Mace." Rosie wanders over to me with her bottom lip jutting out, still bare against the mirror's LEDs. "Do you think that dude will be there? The fit one, on exchange from France?"

"Everyone will be," I reply. "You know what Bob's like. He'll invite anyone…"

"But Francois, he's a sophisticated Frenchman, Macey." She performs some sort of mime, twisting her hands as though throwing a string of onions over one shoulder. "Frenchmen eat… eat… I don't know, coq au vin or cordon bleu. They don't scoff tortilla chips out of cocktail bowls at house parties!"

"Francois isn't a sophisticated Frenchman though. He's a

dick."

Rosie frowns. "Hardly."

I pick at my nails, pushing my index back into place. They're pale blue and tacky, and nail glue is spread across the cuticles. "Didn't he send nudes to Darcie's mate before the end of term?"

"She asked, he obliged." Rosie frowns, stepping over her straighteners and pulling a handful of clothes out of her bag. She drops them onto the floor behind her. "So which top, Mace? The white mesh, or the black crop?"

I roll my eyes again and bow my head, eyes flicking back to my phone. There's one notification, glaring yellow in the corner of my screen, presenting me with a text from Tyler. My heart stutters to a stop.

We've hardly spoken since the commemoration evening. My fault, really – I've been avoiding his messages. The party's one place I can't escape him.

**cant wait to see u tonite doll xx**

I feel nauseous. Phlegm rises in my throat and I swallow it down, switching off my phone and pushing it away.

"You ready, Mace?" Rosie's one step behind me, grinning and cocking her head. She went with the black crop; modest, yet somehow still sultry. "Jaye's got the car outside…"

I nod, risking a glance in the other direction, and the girl in the mirror nods back. I smile. She smiles.

"Soraya's already had too much wine," Rosie's saying, but I'm hardly listening.

I'm staring at my reflection, taking her in, trying to read her mind.

*Don't do anything stupid tonight.*

I know myself far too well.

***

The party's in full swing when we arrive, though you wouldn't know it from the street. Bob's house is semi-detached, one of those peach-coloured newbuilds on a quiet cul-de-sac, the kind with perfectly trimmed hedges and matching front doors. It's identical to its neighbours. A clone, the kind of neat, mum-loving home that only needs a Labrador to be complete.

There's music coming from inside, but only on the quiet, easily mistakable for a noisy television set. The blinds are all down and the porch is locked, but there's a gate at the side of the house beside a shoddily painted sign, reading, "Party this way, punks!"

"He thinks he's being original," Jaye says dryly, pulling open my door. "Classic Bob…"

We spill out onto the pavement, tottering in heels and boots, shivering in spite of the cool September evening. The sky is soft blue, the kind of warm shade you'd expect in a retro kitchen or splashed across a plant pot.

Soraya follows me out in a tangle of limbs, frowning and patting at the seat behind her.

"Mum made me bring *laddu*," she explains, finally grasping the paper bag with a triumphant grin. "If in doubt, bring sweets!"

I smile back as I take one.

We creep round the side of the house with our goods concealed under sleeves and elbows, Rosie's bottle of pink gin stashed beneath her jacket. There's a slow breeze echoing around the estate, tickling my knees and prising my skirt further up my thighs. I pull it down, shivering as we make our way to the back door.

Darcie Carlton's guarding the entrance, sipping something clear and still straight from the bottle. She's trying not to wrinkle her nose as she swills it down, neck flexing in disgust.

"You made it!" she cries, pushing her drink onto the kitchen side so that some splashes over the edges, and throws an arm around Rosie. "Thank *goodness* you're here, girlies. Mike and Steph, the geeky ones in our media class, showed up half an hour ago – I was hoping it wouldn't get any worse – and it's so frickin' *cold*, it's times like this you wish you'd worn something longer –"

"Bob!" Rosie cries out quickly, raising a hand and pushing past Darcie into the kitchen. "Bob! Awesome house, man! Where are your parents tonight? It was super they left the whole place to you…"

And so the party begins.

# 18

The living room is slick with sweat already. It permeates from every surface, clammy on the leather sofas and dotted across the mirror. My classmates gather in clusters, hanging from windowsills and leaning on the fireplace, splayed across the floor in a tangle of limbs and cans and bottles.

"Macey!" comes a voice from behind me. I turn. Tyler is stood in the doorway, swaying slightly, already drunk and clutching a red plastic cup. They're the kind the McCoys picked for Lexie's funeral. Seeing it clutched in his hand like that makes my stomach flip.

"Tyler." I have to force a smile. He leers into me with a smirk, taking a step away from the threshold, and pushes his face towards mine. His mouth tastes of cider as he kisses me, sour and metallic. There's far too much tongue.

"You look fu-ing lush," he murmurs, slurring his words. His hands go round my back and I try to turn away, but his fingers find the belt loops on my skirt and cling on, tight, locking me into place. "I've missed you…"

Someone changes the song at that very moment, and I shrink back as a beat envelops the room and Tyler lets go. No one moves at first, bopping as the song picks up and the lights flash dismally, purple and blue, red and yellow. That's when Darcie Carlton bursts into the room, green hair mussed up and cheeks pink, and stares around.

"You call this a party?" she scoffs, turning to Bob with

eyebrows raised. With a swift flick, her finger slides the dial up to the max on the speaker.

Music screams across the room, spluttering the curtains, shocking people onto their feet and burning through the ceiling. It's so loud it hurts my eardrums, and I have to clutch my hands over them to deafen the blow, squeezing my eyes shut against the glare of the lights. The beat seems to dance beneath our feet, carpet pulsing with life.

"That's more like it!" Darcie yells, letting out a high-pitched squeal of laughter and stepping back into the kitchen. "Who's for pizza?"

And just like that, she's woken up the entire room.

Mike and Steph, two geeky kids clutching sugary cokes and grinning like the Cheshire cat, begin to bop in their corner, gesturing for others to join them. There's jokey twerking and dad dancing, like the music has made everybody blind and they no longer care who's watching. I move back against the wall as Jaye darts forward, dragging Soraya by the hand, face alight with joy. Sweat and ecstasy mixed with the faint waft of pizza floating through the door hangs thick and claggy in the air. I close my mouth to avoid breathing in.

I don't remember parties ever being quite like this before. Last year, we were the younger kids at sixth form parties, the year twelves, anxious sixteen-year-olds, worried about what people would think, say. We'd watch the others dance, laughing and filming on our phones, part of the crowd yet still just spectating. We had fun, I think. Or maybe we just wanted to think we did.

Now *we're* in charge, as year thirteens. The "older kids" have left, sliding into university and leaving us to take shots and blast music as loud as possible to a street of families and pensioners. I feel the wall behind me, warm and sticky beneath my fingers, and slide down until my knees draw up to my chin and my trainers hit the back of my thighs.

Jaye and Soraya are dancing properly now, arms around each other, mouths open as they laugh. Jaye's shouting something at me which I can't quite hear, but I shake my head anyway and try to smile, spine aching against the plasterboard. They look like they're enjoying themselves, caught up with the blur of music and lights and alcohol.

I wish I could enjoy it. It's so hard to enjoy something so trivial when your mind can't focus, when you're stuck on the outside, looking in.

I wish I still had fun. I wish I were still happy.

I wish…

"Macey." The word, hot and slimy against my ear, drips down my cheek and stays there. I can feel breath against the side of my face but I don't want to move, to dislodge myself. "Macey…"

Tyler's tongue has found my earlobe and is lapping at my skin, wet and tender. I shiver, though the room's too hot and my skin prickles with heat. It edges further, slithering along my jaw and meeting my bottle lip with a delicate nudge, colliding against my own with a fizz, one which tastes like those awful sour sweets you get at pound shops. My heart's racing as I turn my head to meet him, bringing my lips to a close and pushing back against him.

"Oh, Macey…"

The mumble is enough, and I raise my hand to his cheek. It's smooth and cool beneath my thumb, devoid of spots and stubble, a perfect expanse of bare, freckled skin, golden from the Italian sun.

"Mace…"

It's coming back in waves, the desire and panic I once felt every time he leant to kiss me, nibbling the inside of my lip with those perfect teeth. I don't know if it's the alcohol on his breath or the dark, clammy room, but something draws me back, drags the old Macey from her shell and pushes her into full colour… and I love it.

I kiss Tyler back like the last few weeks didn't happen, like we're sixteen again and falling in love, clutching hands at house parties and searching places I didn't think my fingertips belonged. The room's a blur of dancing and laughing and pulsing music, sweat heavy around us and hanging in a thick mist to protect our bubble from anyone else. I remember Tyler once laughing at my distaste for PDA, clutching me tight and telling me he didn't mind showing me off, that I was worth the attention. I feel like that now. A prize turkey, Tyler's girl, someone innocent and perfect and free from scandal.

*Are you the girl who killed Lexie McCoy?*

Here, I'm just Macey Collins, girlfriend and teen, nothing more.

His hands are at the rim of my skirt now, fingers searching just beneath, circling my skin. I go to push him away with a breathy gasp and instead cock my head, pulling back and gesturing towards the door. *Garden*, I mouth, hoping he takes the hint. A slow smile spreads over his face as he nods and lifts me to my feet.

We cross through the tangle of bodies with fingers interlinked and hearts racing, wandering through the crush in no hurry, all the time in the world to get what we want.

In the kitchen, it's just as crowded. There are four pizzas on the table, sprinkled with toppings. Tandoori chicken and chorizo, sweetcorn and mushroom, ham and pineapple, sausage and bacon. Tyler lets go of my hand to reach for a slice and I watch as he lifts it to his lips, biting down, hard. It's like an addiction. His jaw flexes as he chews, a globule of cheese stuck to his lip, crust held between his finger and thumb.

"Want some?" he asks, holding the slice out to me. I shake my head. It's not what you do; it's unladylike. He wasn't really asking, anyway.

We go to leave, moving to the back door with his arm snaked around my waist and eyes trained on the space before us. Just as his hand reaches for the handle and goes to push down, there's a hand on my shoulder, and I spin around to come face to face with Darcie Carlton.

"Macey!" she exclaims, though her words slur and she elongates the "e" sound. "Are you leaving already?"

Turning to Tyler helplessly, I shrug and try for a smile. "Needed some fresh air, that's all!"

Darcie narrows her eyes at me, before they widen in realisation and she claps a hand over her mouth. "Oh! You're going to have sex." A gurgle of laughter bursts through her fingers and she creases over, shaking her head. "I'm so *dumb*. Well, enjoy it while it lasts, Macey. He's really good."

I flush, taking a step backwards. Every part of me wants to shrivel up and collapse onto the floor, and as Tyler's arm tightens against me, all instinct causes me to lean into him.

"Thank you?"

"Don't want to hold you up," Darcie continues, raising an eyebrow and flicking us away with her hand. "Stay safe, kids!"

Then she turns away and we push our way outside, away from the party.

It's cold outside, darkness enveloping us whole. A splinter of light shines from under the kitchen blinds, but aside from that it's pitch black, the sky dotted with murky clouds. We can still hear the music but it's quieter here, drifting far, far away, the soundtrack of a time before instead of the present.

"Come with me..." Tyler whispers. I hear the grin in his voice as he pulls me down the path.

Bob's garden is the ordinary, suburban kind, rectangular and neat, the odd dying bush sat beneath the fence before a clean-cut lawn. I remember it from when we arrived and clutch Tyler's hand in the dark for reassurance, a nod to safety. I don't like the way the wind hits my bare legs, the way it brushes my face and hair with its long, cold fingers. I don't like what it reminds me of.

Creeping around in the dark on a summer night, the river rushing before us, Lexie running on ahead, desperate to reach the water's edge. Crashing, pounding, lapping at the silvery banks, hungry, waiting for its first victim...

*Shut. Up.*

We reach a door – a shed door – and Tyler grapples with the latch before pushing it open and spilling inside. There's a lamp hanging from the ceiling which he somehow already knows about, and turns on with a quick flick of the switch.

The shed's warm and dry, laced with cobwebs. It must be Bob's dad's sanctuary, and tools litter the surface of the workbench, screws, nuts and bolts scattered across the wood.

"Can you..." Tyler gestures to the bench, cheeks flushed pink, and with his fist pushes aside the clutter, creating a naked expanse of surface. I pull myself up, heart racing, swinging round so that my legs hang over the edge. The light flickers softly as wind whistles through the cracks in the windows, and Tyler squeezes between my legs, gazing up at me with those liquid brown eyes and long, elegant lashes. "Oh, Macey..."

Then he kisses me again, lips colliding with mine in a mess of pizza breath and lipstick, tongues everywhere, saliva thick with cider and heat. His hands are on my back, beneath my top, roaming my shoulder blades, fingers edging beneath my bra strap...

My mind's fizzing with ecstasy, an overload of joy and happiness, tingling at my fingertips. It's not Tyler I'm thinking about, not really. It's not *anyone*.

It's just a relief to finally be free.

# 19

I once thought I loved Tyler. Daft, isn't it, the way we think we feel when we're young and don't have a clue? It's not as if I ever really loved Tyler the *person*. I fell for his social status, his clear skin and big brown eyes, the broad chest and shoulders, the mirror selfies he'd post to Instagram. People said I was lucky to have Tyler Campbell interested in me.

Maybe I was.

Our first date was like something out of a romcom. A movie screen; reclining seats at the very back corner; a cardboard box of nachos and cheese, served with salsa, sour cream and minced beef. He bought me a large diet lemonade, my favourite, and a packet of chocolate buttons to share, and held my hand the entire time, stroking my palm and lifting it to his mouth to kiss.

The movie was something Marvel, but I wasn't really concentrating. I couldn't believe it was all really happening to me. Me, Macey Collins, master of blending in, of being invisible, dating *Tyler Campbell*, the most popular boy in our year.

Those recurring thoughts seemed to underline everything.

Tyler was my first, though I knew he wouldn't be my only. Boys like him got bored easily, no matter what he said about love and fate and being "soulmates". I wasn't stupid. He liked me well enough now, but how long would that last?

"Just enjoy it!" Jaye would say, eying me jealousy. "You

don't want turn to turn up to uni with your v-card still intact – you'd be a laughingstock!'"

"Take it slow," Soraya would contradict, frowning. "You don't want to do anything unless you're one hundred percent comfortable, Macey. Promise us that."

Rosie didn't like him. She could tolerate him, sure – they could have a laugh, and she agreed that he was ridiculously fit – but she never really trusted him.

"It shouldn't be a big deal," she'd say, lounging against my pillow with her feet in the air. "It's just sex, you know? But I don't want your first time to be rushed, Macey. You have to be ready. This means something to you, remember – Tyler's a boy, and an experienced one at that. It won't matter to him. Not as much, anyway."

So I did try to take it slow. We officially started dating that December, and up until then, we'd just kissed a bit, held hands. He was respectful of the fact I'd never had a boyfriend before, and promised we'd never do anything I wasn't completely comfortable with. It was one thing saying that, however, and completely another in practice.

He met Mum the week after the Christmas holidays. She invited him round for dinner, a chickpea curry concoction she spent the entire afternoon making, with posh salad (quinoa and all). It wasn't an unusual meal for us, but I could see Tyler struggling as he ate, too used to chicken nuggets and burgers and fries.

"Don't you like it?" Jenna asked from the other side of the table, always the first to step up and embarrass Mum. "It's just chickpeas and spices – super simple, nothing complex at all. Can't you finish it?"

Tyler flushed, shovelling an extra big forkful into his mouth. Between chews, he grinned with curry-stained teeth.

"It tastes amazing! You're a wonderful cook, Mrs Collins. Have you practiced this recipe a lot?"

He knew exactly how to schmooze her, too.

Afterwards, he came upstairs to my room. It was the first time we'd been properly alone together, somewhere other than the park or bus stop, and I was suddenly nervous, jittery, on edge. Mum wasn't fussy – she was that kind of parent – and didn't even tell me to keep the door open, instead pushing a condom into my hand and throwing me an artful wink.

That somehow made it worse.

On my pink bed in my pink room, in my sanctuary, my safe place, Tyler crossed the threshold. He was confident, calm, in control, and wandered round the edges with a disinterested expression, picking up my possessions and frowning at them, one by one.

"What's this?" he asked, fingering a tiny stuffed bear I'd had since I was a child. It was falling apart, arm hanging on by a singular thread, but he tossed it from hand to hand like it was a ping-pong ball.

I perched on my bed, pushing the condom under my pillow. *We won't be needing it*, I instructed myself with a shudder. *We've only been dating a month...*

The floor creaked as he made his way over to me, a smile tugging on his lips. Brown eyes clear and shining, he dropped onto the sheets beside me, lying with one knee in the air and his arm behind his head.

"Hi," he said, face breaking into a grin.

Shuffling closer, I swallowed my nerves and tried to beam back. "Hello."

"Your mum's curry was nice..."

"She likes all this healthy food, see." I didn't want to mock her with him. It felt too much like betrayal, especially since she was clearly such a fan. She'd told me as much when I first mentioned him, gushing with excitement and adoration at how well I'd done. "She's learning to cook"

"I can see that." His eyebrows were raised, dark brown and heavy against his skin. "*Trying* to learn, that is…"

Then his arm went around me, pulling my down against the pillow. With a soft tug, he leant to pull the bobble from my hair, brushing his fingers through it and splaying it all across my shoulder.

"You're so pretty when you hair's down…" he whispered – and then he kissed me.

It was a different kind of kiss to the previous we'd shared. He was softer, gentler, kissing with less urgency, less pressure. His lips met the corner of my mouth and lingered, and I closed my eyes against him as he dipped down my chin and neck, planting soft, wet flowers against my skin, hugging my body closer until I was cocooned against him in a soft, warm bubble, wrapped in his Ty-ness like a blanket, arms heavy around me.

It was a kiss with intention, not a "just because" kiss, the kind that would follow after a date or to fill an awkward silence. It was a kiss that was leading somewhere, that I was sure of. I hardly knew how to react, lying against him and feeling the heat radiating from his body.

"Are you okay?" he whispered, stroking my face. "Tell me if I go too fast for you…"

As if I'd ever tell *him* that.

He was allowed to stay over for the first time later that year, in June or July. I don't think his mum was too pleased about it. She still wanted to keep him young, like all mothers do, despite the fact he'd slept with at least three other girls before me. The fact I didn't know for sure should have been a red flag.

"Just be safe," was all Mum said to me. "I don't need to have the talk with you, do I? I always knew you'd figure it out by yourself…"

I told Rosie and the girls, of course – and even Lucy, Chloe, Kayleigh, Orla and Lexie seemed aware of what was happening. I don't think I had a clue what sex *was* when I was twelve, but they seemed pretty clued up, giggling and prodding me throughout that night's guides' session, collapsing into peals of laughter at whatever Chloe was whispering to them.

"Surely that's not how it works!" Lucy exclaimed. She didn't realise I was listening, and blushed when I tapped her on the shoulder with both eyebrows raised. "Oh, hi, Macey. We were just talking about…"

"Maths," Orla prompted, and Lucy nodded vigorously.

"Yes, maths!" She smiled, though her cheeks were red and her mouth trembled. "Just maths…"

Rosie leapt into action the minute I mentioned it, dragging me into town the minute our biology lesson ended. She was fizzing with excitement, overjoyed that I was finally "ready".

"Hats off to him for taking it slow," she said, walking backwards along the pavement, so we could talk properly. "Just don't get too attached, okay? You never know how long guys like him will last, not once they've got what they want…"

But by this point, I wasn't bothered. I loved him. We were together, and that was just what couples did.

Wasn't it?

She dragged me into Primark first, proceeding to thumb

through the underwear section while I hung back, flushing furiously. I refused to go up to the till with her, and instead waited by the door for her to pass me the paper bag.

"Perfect!" she announced, pushing it at me with a grin. "He won't be able to resist you, Mace."

I wasn't too sure about that.

\*\*\*

In the end, it wasn't even that good. Maybe I wasn't ready. Maybe I just didn't care about him enough. It was hot and sweaty and heavy-handed, hurting far more than I was prepared for, and the build-up was so little that I was almost convinced he didn't care about *me* at all, only interested in getting to the action.

Once it was over, I just lay there. Tyler was asleep, snoring on his back in a tangle of sheets, mouth open. I was lying on his arm and it was digging into my back, but I was too scared of moving and waking him up, so I stayed there, silent, scarcely breathing.

Would Rosie want to know all about it? What would I tell her? Was it so bad that Tyler wouldn't want to touch me again? Would we break up after tonight? The thoughts ran round and round in my mind, tripping over themselves in haste.

But the main one, standing out above all else, rang loud and clear.

*I don't love him. Do I? No, of course not… but do I?*

Maybe that should've been obvious.

# 20

I wake up on a hard floor, something digging into the base of my back. I roll over and instinctively claw beneath me, fishing out a tiny metal bolt, the size of a peanut. Confused, I open my eyes and twist left, colliding with something warm and solid: an expanse of golden-brown skin.

Shit.

Scrambling backwards, I push myself onto my feet and stare with eyes wide at Tyler, laid out across the floor, trousers around his knees and boxers tangled up with them.

Shit, shit, *shit* –

My hands scrabble on the floor as I feel for my clothes, fumbling in the half-light. The lamp above has long blown out, and a scattering of gold flits through the window on the far wall. The benches are in darkness, their undersides black, webs looming like silvery yarn.

I dress silently, back turned. Tyler hasn't moved, breathing against the wooden slats, mouth slightly open. His hair is all mussed up, the back sticking up from where he's been laid on the floor, and the base of his back is imprinted with a smattering of tiny screws.

I watch him for a second, heart racing, then drag myself up to cling to the workbench. *Don't do anything stupid*, I told myself all those hours ago. But the drink, mixed with the flashing lights of the party and a pair of warm lips which tasted of pizza and comfort, had other ideas.

How could I have let myself get so carried away?

Tyler grunts, rolling fully onto his back. I don't want to see this. Did I ever? His body, stretched out before me, clothes in a jumble against his calves, feet still with their Nikes intact. His abdomen, laced with hairs, leading to a nether-region I can't bear to look at.

Why did I ever think I *loved* this man?

And, just like that, I begin to cry.

The tears are silent at first, flowing down my face as I try to gulp them away, shaking my head in horror. I sink to my feet and bury my mouth in my knees to mask the sound as the world collapses around me and the only thing constant is my pale hands, clutching the leg of the workbench, clinging on for dear life, nails digging into the wood, pulse thumping through my fingers –

I hate myself, I hate myself, I *hate* myself. I hate that this is my life, that I'm so dumb, so irrational, so unfeeling. I don't love Tyler. I didn't want to sleep with him. I loved Lexie. I didn't want to kill her. But I killed her. I killed her, and now she's dead, and *I killed her*.

My knees are wet and my throat is hoarse, but I sob and sob and sob until my heart feels heavy and my stomach aches, tough and clenched beneath the waistband of my skirt. I killed Lexie. I killed Lexie. I killed Lexie, I don't love my boyfriend, I killed Lexie –

I killed her, and now she's *dead* –

There's a movement from Tyler's sleeping body, a jerk which ricochets through his taunt, golden-brown torso. I freeze. Eyes slick and puffy with tears, I watch as he rolls over onto his side, facing me, and opens his mouth to murmur, "Macey…"

I jump to my feet at once, careful not to rattle the

floorboards. Placing one foot after the other, I tiptoe from the room, heart thumping in my eardrums. This is it. He's going to wake up, I'm sure of it...

I press down on the latch quietly and push the door open, just a crack. It lets out a creak, one which sounds like a desolate cat mewling, and I hold it to as I watch him anxiously for a response. There's nothing. Tyler remains silent, sleeping away on his side as I cross the threshold and close the door with a *clack*.

The garden's cold and dew-strewn in its early morning state. The stretch of grass we crossed last night is green and saturated, the few dead bushes sagging desperately against the fence. The house, just a sallow new-build in daylight, sits on its foundations with a frown. I can see pizza boxes stacked up against the kitchen window. Four flavours, overpriced and greasy, oil dripping through the cracks.

I wonder who's left. Those who don't return home from teenage parties are usually the ones who have sex, the ones who get so drunk they can barely stand, or the speccy types who stay to clean up the mess. I fall into the former category, so it would seem. Did Rosie not wonder why I didn't go back with them?

I creep around the side of the house and let myself out of the gate. The street is silent, suburban, ordinary. My trainers squeak on the pavement. Across the road, a man is power-washing his car, a smart number he wants to show off. It's too early for this, but he's cleaning in the forgotten hours of Sunday morning, hoping to finish before the kids come out to play and the pensioners go off to church. He glares at me as I walk past, angry that I've caught him by surprise.

I check my phone. Rosie *did* try to ring me, it seems, and I never answered, no doubt lying on the cold floor of the shed in Tyler's sweaty arms. I don't want to think about him making love to me. There was no love involved, simply pleasure, perhaps desire, with a healthy dose of alcohol. I don't think Tyler's ever *made love* to me.

I try to imagine describing last night to my friends, but shudder. Am I completely delusional?

I turn right at the end of the street. Bob's cul-de-sac is right at the edge of Vibbington, completely hidden away, one of the new estates built to expand the town. Left would take me back into the centre, where I could go home, get something to eat, and fall asleep under the covers.

But my feet propel me in the opposite direction, out of the estate, past neat gardens with privet hedges and perfect turf, past watering cans and flowerpots, hand-crafted door signs and plaques reading "beware the dog". I pass a woman walking her own mutt and she lifts a hand to wave at me, the cheerful wave of an early September morning, still hungover from summer and hanging onto the last dregs of cheer.

I think of smoothies and bikinis and joy, staring at the grey tarmac before me. Summer is gone, leaving a cascade of autumn in its wake, once again splitting my existence into two parts, once again. Before and after, clear as night and day.

At the edge of Vibbington, the forest looms. It's just a copse of trees, really, littered with energy drink cans from tacky teens attempting to be "edgy", kicking back on chunky trainers and trampling seedlings beneath obese thighs. The track has been flattened by bikes and scooters, crisp packets stuck to the branches like brand deals.

I'm running now, faster, darting through the trees as my hair streams out behind me and my heart races. Twigs crackle beneath me and breath catches in my throat, and I raise my hands above my head to catch a moment of ecstasy between my fingers, a sliver of excitement, before wood greets me and the world wobbles to a stop.

The planks are wet and slimy beneath my feet, moss-ridden and cold, lime green in the golden light. I clutch the edges of the bridge with my hands, heart still thumping wildly in my ears, wind cool on my face.

The sound of running water, the tinkle of breeze through viridescent leaves. I watch the blue splash over pebbles, so keen and cold, icicle clear.

It's shallow, much shallower than the river Lexie died in. Would it cause me more pain? If I tumbled right now, falling towards the stream and landing against the bottom, would I die on impact? Is the rush enough to push me downstream, for my fingers to clutch the bank, the way Lexie's did, or would I break my neck and just *lie* there, silent, despondent?

The rush of water, filling Lexie's lungs, lapping over her tongue and filling her throat…

I close my eyes and clutch the wood tight, feeling the air against my bare legs, arms, belly, chest. *Just jump*. One hurtle over the rotting rail, one swift move, two feet forwards, eyes clenched shut. I could do it. I could do it so, so easily.

I lift my feet, one by one, to rest on the first rail. It's easy, too easy. Foot by foot, I clamber so that my body is on the outside and the backside of my skirt is green from sitting on the slimy edge. One slip and I'd fall. It's what I deserve. I killed Lexie. I didn't stop the bullying when she was alive, and now that she's dead, I'm *enjoying myself*, like it never happened. I'm selfish, so selfish, so disgustingly vile and selfish –

My feet are loose on the wet surface. Beneath me, the stream trickles on by. I can see each pebble, each strand of green, each deadened leaf, saturated with spring water. It's not that deep. It would hurt.

But would it kill me?

No.

The answer's no.

It wouldn't kill me, not like it killed Lexie. Lexie deserved to be alive. That's what made her death so tragic.

Me? I don't deserve it at all.

# 21

I don't tell anyone about what happened on the bridge. I'm not stupid. I know what they'd say.

When I was in year eight, a girl in our year tried to kill herself. She took an overdose, swallowing a large amount of ibuprofen to numb the pain of her father's death. They found her on the outskirts of Vibbington, in that very forest, unconscious and freezing cold. After she recovered from hypothermia, she was placed on something they called "suicide watch". She had to check in with the school staff every half hour, to make sure she was still breathing.

I don't want to be watched.

I want to disappear.

So I keep my mouth shut.

Tyler messages me, of course, the minute I get home. It's a vulgar, grainy snap, from where he's woken up on the shed floor, and I feel sick as I quickly skip past it. Did it even cross his mind that I maybe didn't want to see that, or that I wasn't in a position to? But of course it didn't. It's Tyler, and Tyler doesn't *think*.

I need to tell him, I know I do. I can't spend another night like that, not now I know how I really feel. I couldn't stop Lexie's fate, but I have the power to control what happens to Tyler. I don't want to put that to waste.

I ring him from the edge of my bed, gnawing on my hangnail, fingers trembling. Despite my nerves, I'm sure about this. An edge of doubt creeps into my mind but I swallow it whole, holding the phone up to my ear to listen and crossing my legs.

"Tyler?" I whisper, heart racing. There's a pause at the end of the line, then the sound of someone coughing.

"Macey." Tyler's voice eventually sounds, rough and croaky from bad sleep. "Where'd you go this morning? I woke up and you'd gone!"

"Sorry." I hesitate, the silence awkward between us. "I didn't want to disturb you –"

"Right…" I can hear the frown on his face. "Did you want something, Mace? I'm in the middle of a game."

Which means he's on his Xbox, of course.

"I was just wondering…" I take a deep breath, crossing my fingers on my lap. "I was just wondering if you wanted to meet this afternoon, somewhere in town? We could grab something to eat."

I realise too late that it sounds like I'm asking him on a date, but he's already agreeing, suggesting the new café on the corner of the main street, pushing forward times and a place to meet.

*At least I can get it over with*, I tell myself, though I feel sick to my stomach at the very thought. *You have to do this, Macey. If not for Tyler… do it for Lexie.*

\*\*\*

Tyler is stood outside when I get to the café, on his phone. He's dressed in a slouchy pair of tracksuit bottoms and a fitted top, hair still messy and eyes unfocused as I approach.

"Hey."

He looks up at the sound of my voice, breaking into a

grin. "Macey!" he says, holding out his arms and pulling me into a hug. My face disappears inside his monstrous chest, and I smell aftershave and last night's pizza on his skin. "Last night was… well, incredible, Macey."

I flush, unsure of what to say. Everything suddenly seems very, very real.

"Shall we…" I gesture towards the door, and he nods in response.

The café's small and warm, sunlight flitting through the windows and onto the table. We grab a booth at the back, one with sky-blue padded seats and a glassy table, and sit opposite one another, feet just touching. I try to move my toes away but Tyler follows, tapping me under the surface and smiling.

"They're supposed to make the best quesadillas here…"

He orders them for both of us, his chicken, mine plain cheese. We sit in silence as we wait. Tyler is on his phone, turning it landscape every few moments to carry on playing his game. It's not an uncommon scene. It's just how we are. Tyler likes his phone, and I like to people-watch, to observe.

There's a grandfather and a small boy on the table to our right, sharing a stack of blueberry pancakes. They must've been for an early autumnal walk, because the boy's wearing striped wellies and an anorak, mud splattered up his chinos. They're playing snakes and ladders on a napkin, drawn by the grandfather with a purple biro. I smile – I can't help it – and take a sip of my J2O.

A middle-aged couple sit in the corner, with milkshakes and sandwiches, clutching hands across the table. Rosie and I always try to predict people's life stories, figuring out how they came to be here, together, like this. I've mastered the art by now. They've just met, I assume, from the way they're looking at each other. Both divorced, a few kids between them, two houses, both newbuilds. The woman would be in exactly the same position as Mum, if Mum preferred cotton t-shirts and dark blue jeggings to sharp suits and yellow bikinis.

"Selfie?" Tyler says suddenly, holding out his phone to capture us both. I smile at my reflection. A plastic smile, a white smile.

"You're not posting that, are you?" I ask, and he shakes his head.

"Nah, not right now. Maybe another day."

Thank goodness.

Our quesadillas arrive moments later, steaming away, oozing cheese and grease onto the plate. Tyler licks his lips and goes to pick it up. I watch as he lifts it to his mouth, eyes like saucers.

"Oh my God," he mumbles, shaking his head. "Soraya was right – these quesadillas are *bomb*."

I pause, fork in the air, first mouthful hovering beside me.

"Soraya said that?" I gulp. "How did she know we were coming here today?"

Tyler looks sheepish then, chewing before swallowing. "I... I think it was just in a group chat. I can't remember where it came up."

"What group chat?" I'm forceful now, pushing the fork down onto the plate and watching him. There's something in his flushed cheeks and shifty eyes that I don't trust, and my stomach writhes with unease as I stare.

"The group chat for Bob's party." He takes another bite, lifting the quesadilla up this time so that grease drips down his fingers. I watch it slip down his wrist, over his forearm. Onto the table with a gentle *plop*. "Yeah, that's right. The group chat for Bob's party."

"I'm in that group chat," I say, but my voice is wavering now.

Shit.

Am I going to lose it before I've even said what I came here to say?

"Oh." Silence laps at the edges of the booth, threatening to spill over into awkwardness. My hands are frozen at my sides. "Well... it must've been another group chat then."

"It must've been." I nod in agreement, then glance back down.

"Look, Macey," he starts, just as I say, "Tyler..."

We're forced to stop again, staring at each other across the table with such intensity that I can feel his eyes burning into mine, brown and dark and smothering.

"Tyler..." I begin again, only this time I don't stop. "Tyler... I think we should break up."

I can see regurgitated chicken and cheese on his tongue as his jaw drops open. "B-b-break up?"

I might have imagined the stammer.

With my fork, I spear another piece of quesadilla. To our right, the grandfather and little boy are leaving, picking up their flimsy snakes and ladders board, receipt, a toy car, pushing the items into a rucksack and laughing amiably. The grandfather takes his hand and they smile, wandering towards the exit, meandering through tables. I watch, unmoving.

In our booth, time has stood still.

"You want to..." Tyler shakes his head on disbelief, finally swallowing his mouthful and staring at me with wide eyes. "You want to break up, Macey? After last night?"

My J2O tastes sour as I go for another sip.

"I just think we've changed," I say, by way of explanation. "A lot has happened, Tyler, you know it has. I'm... I'm not the same person. The whole thing with Lexie has changed a lot for me, made me realise some things."

"Things?" he repeats, still watching me in abject surprise. "Like what, Mace? That you don't love me anymore, is that it?"

There's a lump in my throat and I don't know why. I bite down the fork and cheese oozes over my tongue, sharp and salty, like sick.

"I need some time," I say, though I'm just making things up now, unable to say what I really want to. How could I word it, in a way that wouldn't sound so nasty? *I'm sorry, Tyler, but I just don't love you anymore – I don't think I ever did.*

"Time for what?" Tyler protests. He slams both fists down on the table and I jump, oil splashing over the edges of my plate and landing on the table.

"Tyler…" I start.

He shakes his head again and lets out what almost sounds like a growl, low and throaty, full of anger and despair.

"Time for *what*, Macey? Time to get over that girl who died? It was an accident – you couldn't have prevented it – and it's been *weeks*, Macey. *Weeks*." He stops for breath, fists still flat against the glass surface, face red with objection. "And what, some girl dies and you let it ruin your relationship? You let it ruin us?"

"No," I say, beginning to stand. My hands are trembling and I can feel myself falling, falling, back into a place of defensiveness, a place of distrust and uncertainty. I can't let that happen. I can't let my mind take control.

*Just get out of here.*

"It… it just made me realise what's important to me." I grab my bag, shifting it over my shoulder and shuffling out of the booth of wobbly knees. "I'm sorry –"

"You're sorry?" Tyler snarls this, staring at me with those huge brown eyes, the whites off-colour and fuzzy. I can't move, locked by his gaze, trapped in the aisle before him. "You're *sorry*, Macey?"

I don't know what to say to that, shivering all over, legs unstable –

"You will be, Macey. You will be."

# 22

I knock on Jenna's door.

"Come in!" she calls through the crack. "Just don't step on the painting, okay?"

There's a canvas sat among sheets of newspaper as I push through and over the threshold. I'm careful not to step on it, but my foot meets wet paint anyway, and I step back in alarm as it seeps through my sock.

"Sorry about the splatters." Jenna frowns from across the room. "Got a bit overexcited. The carpet's ruined anyway – I don't think it makes much difference."

She's painted Megan, of course, her pierced face leering from a blood-red abyss. It's dark, almost black at the point of which her neck meets colour, flashes of white like bone taking on the form of her ribs. Two twin breasts peer from the crimson, nipples brown, like chocolate eyeballs.

She must've gone crazy with the splatters of paint, as they decorate Mum's cream carpet like the remnants of a murder scene. I blink, noting flecks on the skirting board and wall, as high as the pinboard covered in tattoo designs and pictures of punk bands. Blood scrapes the ceiling, forming puddles leaking from the attic above.

"Like I said, the carpet's ruined anyway." She pulls a face at me, then adds, "Don't tell Lisa, okay?"

I shake my head as I sit at the edge of her bed, a few feet away from her. She's wearing her dressing gown and earmuffs, and is frowning intently at her laptop screen. "Bloody college."

"How's it going?"

"Shit."

Jenna started a hair and makeup course two weeks ago at a local college, just for something to do, after failing her A-levels back in August. She doesn't want to do it as a *job*, but Mum said she had to at least try and do something with her life. If she refused to go to uni, this was the next best option. She mostly works from home, completing the bare minimum and complaining about the brain-dead bimbos on her course, repeating each teatime, "You'd get on well with them, Macey."

I pick at the duvet now, unsure of what to say. When I look back up, Jenna's staring at me with narrowed eyes.

"What do you want, then?" she asks. "I'm assuming this isn't just a social call."

"Well..." I glance back down at my hands and shudder. "I broke up with Tyler."

It's hardly an exaggeration to say that Jenna looks surprised. Her eyes pop and her jaw drops open, revealing a blue tongue, and she shakes her head in abject disbelief.

"You did what?"

"I broke up with Tyler –"

"Why?"

We stare at each other for a moment, silence hanging heavily over the bed.

"I slept with him last night. At the party."

Jenna's mouth drops further open, agape with what could be shock, but might as well be horror. "You did *what*? Where? At Bob's?" She pauses for a minute, then gasps and adds, "Of course, I knew there was a reason you didn't come home last night! My, Macey, you are the dark horse. House parties are *well* grotty!"

"I know," I say, and phlegm rises in my throat at the very thought of the sweaty, pizza-infused living room, pulsing with horny teenage bodies and adrenaline. "We did it in Bob's dad's shed."

"In his shed? As in, middle-aged man cave, screws and all?"

I nod, unable to stop the smile from spreading over my face. It helps, somehow, bringing light to what happened. Making it seem humorous.

"God, Macey." She shakes her head again, still in shock, yet somehow in awe of me. "And then... you broke up? Why? I thought you were mad about him?"

"I don't think I ever really was." It's a surprise to hear that come out of my mouth. It's not something I expected to say out loud. "I just thought I was, because he was popular and desirable, and everyone kept saying I was lucky that someone like him liked me." My cheeks flush pink as I notice her raised eyebrows. "You think I'm pathetic, don't you?"

A smile spreads over her face. "No, Macey. I don't think you're pathetic." Turning to the side, she glances down at the painting again. "I'm actually pretty proud of you. You've figured it out already. I'm still a *mess*."

Subtly, I try to take her attention from the carnage, tapping on the windowsill. "You're coping with it well, then?"

"Oh, wonderfully." She scowls and flits her eyes back to me. "Megan was a bitch. I don't know why I always go for girls like her. It only ever ends in trouble."

"You weren't to know," I lie, but that just makes her snort.

"It's like with Tyler," she says, "we knew he was a player, a dick, a big penis – whatever you want to call him – but girls love him anyway, because he's sporty and fit and all that, whatever straight girls like. And with Megan... She was exciting. I don't know, all the tattoos, the piercings, the clothes... I knew she wasn't really into me, but I wasn't bothered, I liked her anyway."

"How do you know she wasn't into you?" I ask.

That just makes her burst with another sharp laugh.

"Lesbians are kind of thin on the ground around here. It's always just... I don't even know, nothing meaningful, if you get my drift. I don't think I've ever met another girl who's wanted more than that – it's weird to want an *actual* relationship." She pulls herself together for a moment, sitting up straight and staring back at me. "Anyway, enough about her. She's been given way too much attention already. That painting's going to completely blow up my Instagram."

"Won't she find it a bit weird?" I ask, though I try to say it softly, so she won't get annoyed. Jenna's short fuse is the reason we've never really got on, and I don't want to blow it now – not while we're on a roll. "I mean, isn't it basically like leaking nudes?"

"Nah." Jenna grins. "She's not shy about who she flashes her tits to anyway."

I know better than to argue.

"So..." Jenna wrinkles her nose again, then says, "What made you realise you weren't into him? It kind of came out of the blue, not gonna lie."

I shrug.

Where did it come from? Was it just last night? Or did I know well before that?

I think back to the last few weeks after Lexie's death. His reaction, the way he didn't know how to help me, to comfort me, what to say as I grieved in those early days. We barely spoke, really – he didn't even try to communicate, not properly.

And I just ignored it.

"I don't know," I answer truthfully. Because I don't know. I don't know why things with Tyler went downhill, or why I stopped feeling... things.

I don't know what I ever really felt, though. Was it always just desire, like I felt at the party? A desperation to feel... wanted?

"I never really connected with him," I find myself saying. "Not on a deeper level, not like I should. He was just hot. That's all."

Jenna bursts out laughing again, closing her laptop and leaning on it as her body heaves up and down. "Oh, Macey," she gasps, between wheezes, "That's the most sense I think I've ever heard you speak!"

"Shut up," I retort, shoving her lightly, but I can't help but smile. "I think... I think maybe Lexie dying put everything into perspective for me. Does that make sense?"

Jenna glances up and frowns, still trying to stop laughing. "Yeah. Yeah, Macey, it really does."

"I just..." I close my eyes and breathe in deeply, leaning back. "I just think about things so much more now. I can't stop. And I suppose I've been thinking more about Tyler, too, and noticing more, things I would've ignored. I never wanted to make a fuss or to ruin things, but now... that's just not important."

"What do you mean by ignore?" Jenna asks, frowning. "What did you ignore?"

"Just..." I think back to the bullying, to everything I ignored before Lexie died, to the way she changed, right up until that night by the river. I think about my feelings, the way I didn't want to rock the boat, how I breezed through everything in order to just stay under the radar.

Mind whirring, I swallow quickly and finish with, "Stuff."

"Stuff?"

"Yeah. Just... I don't know, Jenna, I can't explain it."

She cocks her head. "You're too closed off, Macey. You don't say what you really think. You just get on with things – you have done since Lisa and Dad got divorced. You think I wouldn't have noticed that, but –"

I shake my head, squeezing my eyes shut.

That's *not* true – I'm not closed off, and I do say what I think, sometimes. It has nothing to do with the divorce.

"You stopped dancing, you stopped trying mega hard at school... I've said that heaps, Macey, but you don't believe me."

"Because you're *wrong*," I say. "Please, Jen, just shut up about the bloody divorce!"

She raises her eyebrows at me then, as though she knows best. "Right."

We stare back at one another in silence, my fingers still tapping on the windowsill, faster and faster, picking up pace, cuticles roaring with pain. I'm cold, socks still soggy with paint against her duvet.

"I'm sorry," I say. "Sore spot."

"I know," she replies, smiling weakly. "I'm gonna get on with this work, if that's okay, Macey. It's due tomorrow."

"Okay." I stand up to leave, pushing my legs over the edge of the bed. "Thanks for talking. I think... I think I needed that."

"No problem." She opens her laptop up again, but before I have chance to leave, she glances back at me and says, "Hey, Macey? How do you feel about going out next weekend? I want to take some photos for a new project, so I was thinking of going up to Whitby…"

"Whitby?" I say, frowning. "But we haven't been since Dad left…"

"Exactly." She smiles. "I think it's about time we went back, don't you? And besides – it's lush up there."

I'm unsure still, fiddling with the zip on my hoody. "I don't know, Jenna. Why don't you take one of your other friends?"

"Because you deserve a day out," she says simply. "I'm not taking no for an answer."

I shiver, pulling my sleeves down over my hands.

"Fine." I nod. "Deal."

## 23

"You broke up with Tyler?" Rosie explodes, the moment I step through the gates. She's stood with her hands on hips, staring at me incredulously, as though she doesn't know who I am or where on earth the real Macey has gone. "Why the fuck didn't you *tell* us, Mace?"

I carry on walking, unresponsive to her cries and yells, the tapping of fingers against my arms.

"Macey Collins, get back here!" Rosie jogs alongside me, eyebrows knitted and mouth cemented into a firm line. "What's going on? One moment you're sleeping with him, then the next, Soraya tells us you've broken up!"

I stop then, swivelling round to face her. "How does Soraya know that, Rosie? How does she know so much about Tyler recently?"

Rosie stares back at me, realisation dawning on her face. "You mean, you think..." She shakes her head in disbelief. "No, Macey – Soraya wouldn't do that. You know how her parents are with relationships –"

"You don't know that," I counter, though there's an edge in my voice now, a hard line. "And Ty..."

"Don't you trust him?" Rosie watches my face carefully.

I think we both know the answer to that.

"But why now?" she presses. "You must've known you felt this all along..." She frowns, realising what she's said, and adds, "It was Lexie, wasn't it? Who made you realise? The accident... it changed you, Macey."

I freeze, hands still by my sides. "What do you mean?" I ask. "How has it changed me?"

"You're more... I don't know, *aware*. You think about things. You're cautious. You notice things you'd have ignored, once upon a time."

"Do I?" I don't believe her. I've always been like that... haven't I?

"Yeah, Macey, you do." Her expression is sad then, as she takes another step forward towards me. Around us, the playground is alive with kids running and playing, smiling and kicking at the leaves on the ground, chasing each other through the Monday morning playground. "It's not a bad thing. I just miss my best friend."

"She hasn't gone anywhere," I murmur, pulling my hands further up my sleeves. "She's still here. I'm still the same person."

"But you're not, Macey." She smiles again, albeit flatly, and reaches forward to take my hands. "You've changed. I still love you, but... you've changed. Maybe it's time we all grew up a little, I don't know, but you seem to have done so way before us."

"Lexie *died*," I whisper, though my voice falters and tears spring to my eyes. "That's not something you recover from lightly, Ros. If I've grown up, it's only because I watched my friend die."

I regret the words the minute they spring from my mouth.

"You watched Lexie die?" Rosie repeats, face forming a frown. "I thought you were in your tent, and Lexie died alone?"

Shit.

Shit, shit, *shit* –

"That's what I meant."

We stare at each other, an awkward silence lodging between us as the school whirs on the outside.

"Well…" Rosie hesitates, then glances down at her phone. "I said I'd meet Jaye in the common room. You coming? We were gonna get bacon sarnies to take to photography…"

"I think I'll go straight to maths."

"Okay." She smiles as she turns to leave, giving me a small wave. "See you."

As she walks away, I know for sure that I'm losing her, too.

\*\*\*

The maths room is empty; not even the teacher has arrived yet. I wander in on tiptoes, eyes flitting to where my usual seat is. It's right behind Tyler's, which has gum stuck along the rim in a long, raggedy line.

"Macey!" a voice from behind me exclaims. I turn, coming face to face with Miss Marian.

She's one of those young teachers, the kind everyone hopes will go off pregnant ASAP and who only teaches year seven and eight. She wears ankle boots and flower-print tunics, tucking her pin-straight hair behind tiny ears, always clutching a faux leather handbag under her armpit. She's squeezing it now, watching me as I dawdle in the doorway.

"I was hoping to catch up with you," she says. "I haven't talked to you in forever, it seems! And now you're doing A-level maths… I always knew you had a talent for it, Macey."

I don't say anything. We haven't talked in "forever" because she hasn't taught me since I was thirteen. No doubt she only knows me from the disastrous assembly, when Mr

Roberts brought my existence to the attention of the entire building and beyond.

"I taught Lexie," she continues, and my heart shudders to a stop.

Just one day without having to talk about it is all I want. One day away from the memories, the guilt, the pain. Is that too much to ask, or do I want the impossible all over again?

"She was a wonderful student," Miss Marian continues, shaking her head and smiling. "So positive, always willing to give everything a chance! A credit to the school, too – and a credit to you. I understand you were one of the leaders at her girl guide group?"

I nod, slowly. "Yeah. She was a wonderful person."

How many more times will I have to say that sentence, or words to that effect? Too many.

"You must be struggling, Macey," she says, pulling a face and holding out a hand to place on my shoulder. It's awkward and clammy, sticking to my coat. "It must be really tough, going through all of that, losing such a close friend. I bet she was almost like a sister to you."

"She was a wonderful person," I repeat, before catching myself and flushing. I don't want to seem completely out of it. "I really do miss her."

Miss Marian nods, the hint of a frown on her pale face, and lifts her hand from my shoulder. Jerking her head backwards, high heel ready to snap as she pushes down on its point, she moves to disappear down the corridor.

"I think you should think about getting help, Macey."

I freeze.

"My friend overdosed when I was your age, and having a professional to talk it all through with was really beneficial..."

A professional? She means a psychiatrist, someone to tell you everything that's wrong with you, how to cope with things that are none of their business. Jaye saw one for a short while, after her grandma died. She'd ask invasive questions and try to get to the "root" of Jaye's problems, asking for personal information about her grandmother's life and their relationship, completely disrespecting her privacy. It didn't help, not even a little. Opening old wounds made everything *worse*.

Mum tried to get Jenna to see a specialist therapist when she was in sixth form, to get to the bottom of why she'd veered so far off the rails. It didn't work. Jenna stopped going after a month, instead using the money Mum had given her to buy ice cream and chocolate.

"I'm doing okay, but thanks for the... suggestion." I try to smile at Miss Marian. It's like there's cling film stretched over my face, impossible to move my jaw.

"You're a very brave girl," she says, before twisting and backing away down the corridor. "It was nice speaking to you!"

I'm frozen, hands shaking beneath me. I watch her back retreat and disappear down the stairs, feet tip-tapping against the tiles, and shrivel up into myself with tear-filled eyes and a sticky, horrified feeling lurching within me.

*You should think about getting help, Macey.* Like I'm some sort of psychopath, needing someone else to try and control my feelings for me.

Is that what everyone thinks of me?

I tiptoe back into the room, whole body trembling beneath me. My cheeks are bright red. I feel hot, too hot. I don't head for the seat I usually inhabit, instead aiming for the other side of the classroom, where nobody really sits. A quiet girl named Nima sits there, alone, lesson after lesson. She's not very good at maths, and spends most of the time doodling hearts and cartoon dogs along the edge of her lined paper.

I push my coat over the back of the seat, dropping my bag onto the desk. There's a kitten sticker on the edge of the table, which someone has illustrated over with a crude penis drawing.

The lesson isn't due to start for another ten minutes, and most of my classmates are still in the common room. It's tradition to get bacon sarnies and paper cups of tea before a period one lesson, something I've partaken in for most of my sixth form experience so far.

I'm over it now.

I cross over to the window, which looks out over the whole playground. Kids are still trickling in through the gates, dragging their too-long trousers and with rucksacks strapped around their chest. The smokers continue puffing away just outside on the edge of the road, skin cakey with fake tan and foundation, false eyelashes sticking up in all directions. A group of nerdy kids play Dungeons and Dragons on a picnic bench, squealing with laughter as they battle elves and gnarly warlocks, heads no doubt filled with dreams of Princess Leia and Katniss Everdeen.

And there, just by the main entrance, are Lucy, Chloe, Kayleigh and Orla.

They look subdued, stood together in a circle and yet silent, unspeaking. Chloe is glued to her phone, Kayleigh watching over her shoulder, and Orla is reading from a hefty hardback. Even during the camp, Orla read whenever she got a spare minute. She's still reading the same series.

Lucy is still, eyes flitting round the playground at the

other kids. She's unsmiling.

It's unusual to see her looking so dour.

It feels wrong – almost invasive – watching them like this. The classroom window is high up on the top floor, and the glare from the sun would prevent them from noticing me, even if they were to glance upwards. I raise a hand to wave, just pretending, for a second, that someone will wave back.

They don't, of course.

I go back to my seat, staring down at the kitten with the biro illustration covering its mouth and eyes.

It's funny how pretty things spoil so easily.

# 24

The girls hyped up the summer camp right from the beginning. Despite Lexie's reservations about going away with her bullies, even *she* was excited. The activities, the food, a whole weekend away from parents and pressures and technology... I was buzzing, too, as it drew closer and closer.

The camp was always meant to last two nights. We'd arrive on the Friday, set up shop, then pack away again on Sunday morning. We'd have the whole campsite to ourselves. The field we were staying in had a toilet block, showers and a kitchen, as well as a small fridge and chest freezer, a distance away beside the car park. We weren't going to use the kitchen, Sharon decided. There was an outside cooking area near where we'd place the tents, with a big brick round, perfect for a fire.

Sharon and I planned all of this to the nth degree, going over meal plans, shopping lists and equipment on various spreadsheets. She told me we'd need lentils and doughnuts and celery, and I bought each item a week in advance, storing it all in Mum's fridge until the big day.

I hadn't realised the fruit and veg would go off so fast – I wasn't brought up with an awareness of basic housekeeping skills – and so we chucked the fresh food on Thursday, rushing round Lidl to pick up more. Adulting wasn't my strong point, clearly.

"Are you sure this camp has been planned well?" Mum

asked as I returned to the car. "It all seems very last minute…"

Yet somehow, everything still seemed ridiculously well put together.

The week before we were due to go, we had a meeting in the chapel, just for Sharon, the girls and me, parents on standby. They brought makeshift examples of their bags, packed full of clean underwear, snacks, and spare socks, torches and sleeping bags hooked on top and tied with string to stop them from exploding everywhere. Chloe carted a pink holdall in through the fire exit, which was the only door wide enough to fit it, while the others stuck to sensible camping rucksacks.

My own baggage was pathetic. A suitcase filled with clothes and shoes, and my school rucksack, which I'd crushed a sleeping bag and pillow into. Mum said she wouldn't let me get any of our other bags dirty, and it'd be a waste of money to splash out on something new, not for one weekend of sleeping outdoors. I could use extra carrier bags, if I really needed to.

"Well, Macey!" Sharon said, raising her eyebrows. "That's certainly an… *interesting* way of packing."

We crossed into the main room and stood in a circle with the bags, Sharon in the centre. She had a list of things she needed to go through, with forms for the parents to sign, and instructed me with the task of handing them out. Lucy and Orla's mums took them nervously, still uncomfortable about letting their daughters leave them for the weekend, however safe they may be.

"Lucy gets very bad homesickness," her mum muttered to me, pinching her t-shirt between her nails. "She won't be taking her phone with her, so if she gets upset, just ring me, okay?"

I nodded, smiling. There was nothing else I could do, other than act natural and nod and agree. Kids like Lucy were the product of overprotective parents; there was no way of getting around that.

Mrs McCoy stood at the very edge of the room, by the door. She was holding Lexie's coat and rucksack and smiled as I approached, taking the form from me.

"Macey!" she exclaimed. "It's lovely to see you again. Are you excited for the camp?"

I nodded back, putting on a falsely enthusiastic voice in order to say, "It's lovely to see you, too! I can't wait for the camp – is Lexie looking forward to it?"

That's when Mrs McCoy's face dropped, and she shrugged as she said, "Oh, I suppose so. She doesn't give much away, not anymore. Growing up too fast, I think!"

I smiled, as if I believed her. As if I didn't know the real reason behind her indifference.

"It should be really great," I replied, turning to leave. "Feel free to ask any questions, we're here until nine!"

Back in the main circle, Sharon was running through her activity cards. She'd planned climbing, kayaking, the tyre swing and campfires, and was trying to make it all sound as interesting as possible, holding up laminated images and gushing about fresh air and "good vibes". I took a seat between Kayleigh and Orla, watching Sharon produce recipe cards and attempt to hype up red lentils, shaking the packet about like the tiny pellets didn't look at all like cardboard.

I could tell Chloe was itching to ask something. Her face was tense and her hand was poised to raise in typical Chloe Alize style. Spotting a break in Sharon's speech, it shot straight up and interrupted her precious recipe cards. We all turned to watch her, waiting to see what she'd say next.

"Excuse me." Her smile sickly sweet, eyes wide and imploring. "I was wondering about sleeping arrangements. You haven't mentioned that yet."

Flushing, Sharon glanced around at everyone. She pretended to consult her planning sheets, finger skimming the page and landing on the bottom left corner. "We're borrowing tents from Vibbington 2nd Brownies; two tents which will fit two people each, and three one-man tents. Macey and I have to have our own tents for safety reasons, of course, or we would've sorted out different arrangements. Unfortunately, one of you five girls will have to sleep in a tent by yourself."

The look on Chloe's face was positively evil. Beaming, she turned to Kayleigh and said, "You'll share with me, right, Kayls?"

Lucy and Orla immediately clutched hands too, though Lucy frowned and added, "This is unfair on Lexie, though…"

Lexie's face was like stone. She'd been silent for most of the night, stormy eyes surprisingly tranquil, arms crossed over her stomach.

"It's fine," she said, expression flat. She'd attempted to draw on her eyebrows and they perched like slugs across her forehead, far too close together. "I don't mind."

"Are you sure?" Sharon checked. "Because I'm sure the other girls wouldn't mind swapping if it makes you uncomfortable…"

Although some of them clearly felt sorry for Lexie, none of them wanted to miss out on the chance to go camping in a tent with their friends. I wouldn't have, either, if I were them.

I glanced over at Mrs McCoy, who was staring at Lexie with an expression full of hurt, eyes shining with tears. Is this how she'd felt all these years, watching Lexie get left out of things time and time again? Phlegm rose in my throat and I glanced back down on my hands, interlocked on my lap.

Should I say something? Was it my place to?

"Does anybody have any more questions?" Sharon asked, smiling round at the circle. She thought things had been smoothed over, completely oblivious to the elephant in the room. "I've brought some bourbons, so help yourselves... I'll hang round here until nine, checking over the way you've packed your bag, any equipment you need to borrow still, things like that!"

The group started moving around again, shifting places and wandering up to parents to view forms and ask permission to eat some of Sharon's biscuits. Chloe, however, didn't head for her mother, who was stood with Kayleigh's by the radiator. She headed straight for Lexie.

"Hey, Lex!" she announced, voice dripping with poison. "Are you excited for the camp?"

"Yes, thank you," Lexie replied. She went to stand, but Chloe put out a hand to stop her.

"Look, I'm sorry about the sleeping arrangements... I guess you understand that we're just a lot closer to each other than we are to you, so we'd feel quite uncomfortable in a tent alone with you."

Lexie flushed bright red beneath her makeup, getting to her feet properly and stepping away from Chloe.

"It's fine," she replied. "I'd feel uncomfortable in a tent alone with you, too."

Nima doesn't acknowledge me as she enters the room. She plonks down her cat notebook and smooths her skirt, perching demurely on her seat as she lines up her gel pens and highlighters, a rainbow of bright coloured ink. I take the next seat and push my bag to the floor, trying to act like I sit here every day that it isn't completely weird and unusual.

The other students start trickling in, going straight to their desks with the remnants of their breakfast butties, sipping their tea. I don't glance up. No part of me wants to see Tyler, not even a little bit.

When our teacher arrives, stiff-necked and exhausted from her morning at the maths department's meeting, she sets us up with a task then disappears into the staffroom to warm up some porridge. The room lapses into conversation, the boys at the other side of the class tripping over themselves in order to speak to Tyler. I know they're whispering about me. I can feel it, ears burning as they turn their heads backwards and forwards in my direction.

Nima is drawing the title in her book, using those fancy brush pens and six different colours of gel pen. There are at least three rolls of washi tape scattered around her.

I gulp. One of Tyler's friends, a loud-mouth named Rhys – the one Jaye claimed stuck his hand up her dress – is staring right at me now, spotty face set into a snarl.

"Macey!" he shouts, right across the room. I freeze. "Hey,

Macey!"

Nima glances sidewards at me, blue eyeliner squashed as she narrows her eyes, as if to say, *I've sat here in peace for the last year. Why are you bringing attention to us?*

I know my face is burning.

"Macey!" Rhys calls again. There's a dangerous spark in his eye, one I don't like the look of. "How do you feel about Tyler dumping you?"

It's as if the world has spun to a stop.

"What?" I whisper, hesitating on the word.

Rhys bursts out laughing as his mates smack him on the back, egging him on.

"He dumped you because you had shit sex at the party, didn't he?"

Horrified, my mouth drops open and my hands begin to shake. I don't know why I'm angry. It's not as if it *matters* what these goons have to say.

"I broke up with him," I say, in the coolest voice I can manage. "I don't know what lies he's been telling you, but…"

Tyler finally speaks up at this point, guffawing and shaking his head, pen behind his ear. "*You* broke up with *me*?" he repeats, tone veering on incredulous. "Did everyone hear that? She's shit in bed *and* a manipulative cow!"

My cheeks are deep red now, practically on fire. I grab my bag and rise to my feet, pushing the straps over my shoulder and reaching to grab my books. They're laughing at me, all of them, even some of the bland, fake-tanned freaks like Darcie Carlton, the ones I've spent the last six years befriending. They point and giggle and take photos for Snapchat as I make my way to the door.

"This'll teach her to not tell lies…" comes a bitter voice from just below me, before a foot sticks out from beneath the desk and I go flying, exercise books and sheets scattered everywhere, landing on my hands and knees in the middle of the floor.

I try to grasp my work in an attempt to salvage some of it, but the boys are everywhere, grabbing sheets of paper and tearing them in half, grinning gleefully. The test I got an A* on – the one I desperately needed for revision – gone. The flashcards I made on trigonometry, dipped into Tyler's mucky sports bottle, ink running in every direction. I watch, a lump in my throat, as Rhys rips my revision timetable into two, four, eight tiny pieces.

A hand comes into my peripheral vision, slender and gentle, as it starts to help pick up the sheets and slide them into a pile. I glance up to meet Nima's eyes, and she pulls a disgusted face back at me.

"Guys are dicks," she whispers, pushing the papers to me. "Come on, let's go before Miss comes back!"

We hurry from the room, still under fire of insults as we disappear through the door and down the stairs, shoes loud against the silent corridor. We make sure not to stop until we're out of the building and away from the staffroom, walking faster as the main door comes into sight.

"We'll just tell her you didn't feel well, and I went with you to the nurse," Nima says, stopping to catch her breath. She doubles over, wheezing, then grasps the pocket of her baby-blue bag to fish for her inhaler. "Shit, remind me not to partake in getaways while my asthma still sucks."

I try to smile, but my heart's still racing.

I can't *believe* Tyler would turn on me like that, not after everything we've been through. Why? What did he gain from doing that?

But more than that, I can't believe everyone would take

his word for it over mine. Not my friends, acquaintances, the people I once thought liked me. The only person to stand up for me was a weird nobody who barely ever speaks, announcing the severe demotion of my social status. Nima seems friendly, but she's a freak, a total nerd, and her friendship group renowned for being icky.

So much for being invisible.

"What do we do now?" Nima asks, raising an eyebrow. "If you're okay, I'll go back up there and smooth things with Miss..."

"I'm fine."

We stare at each other for a second, before she nods and turns back towards the building.

"Jeez, Nima, thanks for helping me – I couldn't have gotten out of that alone!" She rolls her eyes and tugs on the straps of her rucksack, cocking her head at me. "Why are you friends with those douchebags, anyway?"

I don't have an answer.

"That's what I thought." Her smile is sad as she backs up so that she's perched against the fence, skirt splayed out against it. "You broke up with Tyler, didn't you?"

I nod. Despite everything else, it means a lot that she believes me. She doesn't have a reason to, not like everybody else.

"He used to bully me, back when we were kids. He thought I was weird for having a Disney party when I was twelve. He lives near me, so my mum invited him; the next day, he told everyone I was a psycho with princess dolls all over my room, and I lost at least seven friends. I can *totally* see what attracted you to him."

I can't help but laugh at that. Nima smiles again, bemused, and glances at her feet. "You were there when that girl died, weren't you? At the camp."

"Yeah," I say, though my voice wavers. "Lexie."

"I think I knew her," Nima continues. "My cousin went to dance class with her, so we'd pick them up together sometimes. Mind you, that was ages ago, before she quit."

I'm silent again, wrapped in my thoughts, the lump returned to my throat. I'm trying to imagine Lexie at a dance class, but I can't picture it at all. I did dance, when I was a kid. I guess we had that in common.

"You can sit with me in maths from now on," she adds, meeting my gaze once again. "I don't really care, but if you need somewhere to go, that seat's always free."

I don't know what to say to that. I just stare, holding back tears, as she wobbles back and forth on that fence.

"Anyway, I'm gonna get back to class. It was nice speaking to you, Macey."

I watch as she disappears back inside the building, skirt swishing around her slender thighs, rucksack bobbing up and down beneath her pigtails. I hardly notice the tear sliding down my face until it touches the corner of my mouth, stinging. I hate that she was so kind to me, so helpful, for no reason whatsoever. I don't really deserve that, do I?

I pull my phone from my pocket and click onto my contacts, scrolling until I find the right one. I click 'call' and hold it up to my ear, hearing the familiar beep and holding my breath until someone picks up.

"Hello?" Jenna's voice fills my head, sleepy and disorientated. "What do you want, Mace?"

"Are you free today?" I ask, sucking in a breath hopefully.

I wait a second as she hesitates, before replying, "Why?"

"I was wondering if we could take that trip to Whitby early. I need something to take my mind off… everything."

Jenna is silent for a moment longer.

"Macey Collins is *skiving school*?" I can hear the smile in her voice, the amusement, and my heart pounds as I wait for her answer. "I'm sure I could manage a trip to Whitby, if that's the case. Pick you up in fifteen?"

By the time I hang up, my breathing has returned to normal and I almost feel… okay. I don't have to worry about Tyler for the rest of the day. That's one saving grace, at least.

\*\*\*

When Jenna pulls into the car park in the clapped-out car Mum bought her for her seventeenth (which she subsequently trashed), relief floods through my body. I drop my bag onto the backseat and climb in, as she pushes into gear and starts to pull away from the curb.

"My sister, the rebel," she says, rolling her eyes. "Come on then, what happened? Someone stole your mascara? Got less than a B on a test?"

I flick my middle finger up at her, which I know surprises her. I'm not the type to swear out loud unless I'm really angry, especially not in front of her and Mum.

"Tyler's telling everyone *he* dumped *me*," I say, pulling a face. Making light of it seems to dull the pain. "He told everyone I was rubbish in bed, the hypocrite."

Jenna turns to me with her mouth open wide, almost ramming into the car in front as it slows to a stop. "He said *what*?" She toots the horn furiously, before overtaking the car in a manoeuvre that most likely could've killed us. "Did you tell him your sister had a black belt in karate, Mace?"

"No," I reply sourly, "because that'd be a lie."

"Minor details, Mace."

"What exactly did you need to do in Whitby?" I ask, aiming to change the subject.

Jenna grins.

"I don't like that face," I say. "It's not more photography, is it?"

Ever since Jenna started doing art properly, she's been using me for photoshoots. She'd parade me all over the county when I was eleven or twelve, roping Rosie along for the ride and dressing us both in all colours of the rainbow, positioning us beside railway tracks, busy main roads and dodgy-looking back alleys. I haven't agreed to help in years, too busy to traipse around modelling for my older sister.

"Just a few snaps, down by the harbour. It's different this time. My mate's starting a jewellery business, making stuff out of natural materials, you know, shells and all that crap. He's paying me a hundred quid for shooting the pics for his launch. You'll be famous, Mace, plastered all over his Instagram!"

"Jenna…" I start, but she puts up a hand to stop me.

"I'll give you a twenty percent cut," she says. "Not bad, eh?"

"My photos going all over some stranger's Instagram, for *twenty pounds*?"

Jenna grins again. "You want to show Tyler what he's missing, right?"

I smile weakly, but that's where she's wrong.

After everything that's happened, I just want to disappear.

# 26

We used to go to Whitby all the time when we were kids. Dad would take us on his days off, driving the forty-five minutes across the North Yorkshire moors to pull into the overcrowded car park by the harbour, breathing in salty sea air and lifting us out of our car seats to catch the first glimpse of the water. Jenna was never that fussed about fish and souvenirs and the wide blue ocean, but I *loved* it.

We'd race up the one hundred and ninety nine steps first, tiny feet pointing on the old stone slabs in order to reach the top fastest. Jenna was only a year older than me, but she was still much quicker, and I'd yell at her to wait as she pounded on ahead.

Right at the top, Dad would reward us with our fish and chips. He kept a big bottle of ketchup in his bag and we'd douse it generously over the chips as we sat on the bench, all squished together. Jenna always got mushy peas with hers, which would've made Mum happy, and Dad would buy a soggy battered sausage to replace his fish. The portions were always too big for me, so they'd finish off quite happily.

Dad would force us to try crab, shrimp, jellied eels from the harbour, too, cutting the salty fish into tiny pieces for us to manage without retching. He loved the taste of seafood, eating cockles and lobster with those weird salad cream sachets. We'd clamour for ice cream and candyfloss, and he'd bargain for cheap offcuts from the stalls to take home for our tea.

The beach would come next.

Jenna and I would tear off our sandals and rush towards the water's edge, toes cold against the lapping tide. Sea spray would wet our cheeks and dance salt along our tongue, and we'd screech with laughter as the waves rushed in and out, splashing up our legs and exploding in fireworks of white foam.

Sometimes, we bought those rainbow turbines, the kind of cheap plastic that blows round and round when it catches the wind. We'd hold them up against the blue sky and watch as they spun, six thousand miles per hour, faster and faster and faster, a kaleidoscope of colour whirling out of control.

The arcades, however, were always a highlight of the trip.

I can still smell it now, the cheap, metallic scent of 2p coins on our skin, clutched in sweaty palms, pressed through the gaps in the plastic to slide down and land among the rest. We each have boxes under our beds where we'd keep our prizes, like buried treasure. Sparkly teddies, bracelets, plastic flip-phones filled with lip gloss. Jenna would aim for the artfully placed five pound notes, but I preferred the tacky toys and teddies.

We always wanted to go on the big kid machines, the motorbikes and air hockey table, but Dad said we were too young. He'd find another poor father to race against instead, and we'd watch them battle with wide eyes and trembling lips. After a few hours, Dad would get frustrated by the tiny, hot room, irritated by the clashing music from each machine and the sound of coins clinking against one another, American accents screaming their congratulations as little boys hit their targets. He'd refuse to hand over more cash for us to convert into grimy coins, and we'd promptly burst into tears, demanding that we weren't leaving unless he paid for more rounds.

It never worked.

We were always silent on the way home. If it wasn't the arcades that we'd argued over, it'd be something else. Dad would get bored of being the doting father, the cracks in our family finally showing.

At home, Jenna and I would run upstairs to her bedroom to listen to the fallout. We only ever felt safe under her covers, as six or seven-year-old kids, listening to their parents scream at each other.

It always went something like this.

Mum would start out criticising Dad for taking us away to a strange town, claiming he wasn't responsible enough to keep an eye on us both. He hated that, hated being told he wasn't good enough by Mum, who could be quite demeaning. He took it as an insult to "all men".

She'd start on our diets next, asking what he'd fed us, whether we'd had anything healthy besides fried food and spun sugar. Even before the divorce, she was always big on healthy eating, force-feeding us lettuce and sticking salad in our lunch boxes. We were never allowed the hot school meals in the primary school canteen, instead carrying containers of cucumber, carrots, couscous and cereal bars in our bags.

She despised that Dad wouldn't feed us the right things. She didn't care what he ate – he worked out often enough – but filling her daughters with rubbish just *wasn't* acceptable.

They'd yell and throw things until well into the night, like Mum still does with Jenna now. We'd curl up in bed to listen, eyes squeezed shut and arms wrapped tight around one another as they shouted. Every now and then we'd hear our names mentioned and flinch, convinced that we were the cause of their arguments, that it would've been better if we were never born.

"Do you think they'll get divorced?" Jenna whispered one time, bottom lip trembling. I couldn't answer that. It wasn't something either of us wanted to consider.

The day finally came when I was eight. Mum and Dad sat us down around the kitchen table and reached to clutch our hands so that we were united in a ring, both of them pink-cheeked and guilty.

"Girls. Your daddy and I won't be living together anymore."

That was how she put it. Like things would still be normal, they just wouldn't be living in the same house. I think we both imagined him moving in next door, or something silly like that.

Then again, we were pretty stupid.

Mum fought all the way for full custody over us. She tried to prove that he wasn't a responsible father, that he was lazy and inattentive, a danger to himself and others. She was an estate agent, owner of her own company, the respectable Lisa Collins. He was just a manual labourer from Hull, sloppy and with a strong Northern accent that turned the court officials against him in a heartbeat.

In the end, he stopped fighting.

We weren't worth it.

Jenna and I are silent for most of the drive, hands tip-tapping to the sound of her radio. She listens to alternative stations, crazy screaming and head-banging rockstars with long hair and skull tattoos. She mutters along to the words as I stare out the window, watching the moors roll by in a blur of green, purple, blue.

The roads are bare this high up on the hills, a car passing us every now and then at a crazy speed, windows open and breeze rushing through the metal box. We hurtle round winding corners and over hills, whirling past those little black and white signs and stones sticking up from beneath the heather. Jenna is forced to stop three times as sheep wander into road, baa-baaing and staring at us with beady eyes, not budging until we beep the horn right in its face.

"Bloody sheep," Jenna murmurs, frowning and pushing us back into first gear. "I swear half of them are suicidal…"

We stop off to buy sandwiches at a tiny village garage; ham for her, tuna mayonnaise for me. We eat them in the boot, feet hanging over the edge, a 7up between us in a two litre bottle.

"You can pay for the chippy," she tells me. "They're always overpriced in tourist spots…"

Then we're on the road again, driving past tiny stone villages and old-school pubs, village greens and lakes, bus shelters and primary schools. The air is significantly saltier now, the sky blue and clear, despite a brisk wind whipping through the windows. My hands are still lodged under my sleeves, an act of protection. My head thumps and my neck aches, and I can't stop thinking about everything, thoughts tumbling through my head at a rate of knots. It's not just Tyler and the boys. It's Rosie. My friends. The "old Macey". I don't know when I got so... serious.

*The accident... it changed you, Macey.*

Maybe Rosie was right, and the accident did change me. I'm skiving school, driving to Whitby with Jenna, overthinking, overreaching, scarcely breathing –

Is that such a bad thing? It wouldn't be fair for me to continue learning, having fun with friends, participating in sixth form life, when I stole each of those opportunities from Lexie.

"You okay, Mace?" Jenna asks, eying me sidewards. "You look a bit... white."

I shake my head, trying for a smile. "I'm fine."

I'm always fine.

We pull into the car park fifteen minutes later, finding a spot surprisingly quick for September. Jenna wanders off to find a parking meter while I wait in the passenger seat, clutching the edges of my bag and huddling inside my coat. The wind seems to have died down now that we've left the hilltops, but it still looks nippier than back home, tiny droplets of sea spittle hitting the windscreen. As she returns, slapping the ticket onto the dashboard, she pulls back to watch me with her hands on her hips.

"It's okay if you're not ready for this, Macey," she says. "I know it'll be a bit weird, not coming here with Dad..."

That's not really the issue. It's been too long for me to still care about my father.

Sucking in a breath, I nod. "I'm fine, Jen. Let's go!"

\*\*\*

The harbour is packed, despite the reasonable car park, and the air is alive with laughter and chatter. Music dances from stalls and shop windows, and a brass band plays on at the end of the road. The pavement is gritty beneath my Converse. The air smells strongly of salt and vinegar, wafting nostalgia my way, but it's easier than I expected to cut out the memories, and Jenna and I are soon laughing along with everyone else, pointing and roaring and doubling over with fits of giggles.

Swept away by the tide of joy, we're soon immersed in the Whitby life we once loved. Jenna buys us chewy, over-cooked lobster from a bald man, which we eat sat on the sea wall with two sachets of ketchup she just happened to have in her bag. She snaps away at everything that catches her eye, seeing light and colour and texture in everything, from my blue trainers to my ketchup-stained fingers and blonde hair, the rough brick wall and adjoining metal railings, a seagull soaring overhead.

"I just want to do this forever," she says, sighing. "Take photos, paint, draw, create. Real life sucks, Mace."

We get ice cream next, a staple part of the trip. Jenna goes for raspberry ripple and I surprise her with pistachio, which immediately sends her into a spiral of snapping green photographs against the weathered background. She insists on ducking into jewellery stores to "stake out the competition" before we embark on our photoshoot, and fingers each necklace with an air of contempt, making the owners uncomfortable.

We decide to start taking photos down on the beach. It's

full of holiday makers, who sit behind windbreakers in bikinis and tiny trunks, bellies bulging over nylon and sand clinging to leg and belly hairs. A British summer is one of sticking out the cold air just for a day on the beach, lying on towels with goosebumps all over your body in an attempt to catch a fragment of sun.

Jenna insists I take my coat off, then lies me against the sand with my head sunk into the grains, hair splayed out around me. She takes one of her friend's handmade necklaces and laces it around my neck, so that it lies across my t-shirt and stands out against the white. She instructs my poses, telling me to reach towards the lens, cover my eyes from the sun, look moody, glance away.

Not once does she tell me to smile.

We take photos sitting upright next, the busy beach with its brightly coloured costumes blurred together in the background. She tugs the t-shirt down my shoulder and I don't complain, thinking all the while that maybe Jenna was right, that it won't do any harm to show Tyler what he's missing.

Flicking through the photos on her camera, a lump forms in my throat. I look kind of… nice. Normal. Almost pretty. I'm makeup-free and freckled, sand dusting my cheeks and a natural smile tugging at my lips, one that's in no way forced.

"Don's gonna love these," Jenna says, eyes bright with excitement. "They're amazing, Macey!"

We wander along the sand to the water's edge then, socks and shoes tugged off. The sea foams against the sand as it's dragged in and out, in and out. We drop to the ground and watch as it laps our toes, freezing cold and smooth, like cream.

"Anklet time!" Jenna says, pulling one out of her bag.

"Give me your foot, Mace."

"I haven't shaved!" I say, gazing up in horror. "There's no way you're taking photos of my hairy ankles!"

"Mace, you're my model. I'm sure I can edit out the longest ones –"

"Let's use your feet."

Jenna glances up at me then, eyes wide. "No way, Mace! I have manky feet."

"It's your feet or no feet…"

I end up taking the photos in the end, snapping at Jenna's chipped nail polish and white ankles, covered in golden freckles. It's weird how similar we are, beneath her choppy dyed hair and heavy eye makeup, the dark clothes and angry expression. We share sharp blue eyes, blonde hair, the same milky white skin, so pale I look ghost-like if I don't fake tan. We might wear different shells, but we're just the same as each other, really.

"Why are my toes so long?" she asks, flicking through the images with a scowl. "We're telling everyone these are your feet, okay?"

The last thing to shoot is bracelets, which Jenna hasn't planned for. She flicks through Google to find examples holding them towards me to get my input, eventually taking screenshots of several she likes for inspiration. We traipse back up the beach towards the harbour and drag our shoes and socks on over the sand, then I wait as Jenna goes for props.

"Here you are," she says, handing me a bright orange ice lolly. "Don't eat it before we shoot the pics, even if it starts to melt…"

We continue taking photographs until well into the afternoon, as the sun starts to dissolve and the sky turns a faded candyfloss blue. I'm hot and sunburnt, despite the breeze, and my coat is beginning to annoy me as it hangs over my arm. We traipse back up the front in search of food as Jenna flicks through the photos, a smile playing on her face, and I check the price on every other chalkboard to find something reasonable.

We eventually come to a dinky fish and chip shop which doesn't seem too bad. It's greasy, the windows covered in a thick layer of sludge and the tablecloths sticky. We take a table in the very corner of the room, one with a "sea view", and examine the menu as a waitress fusses around us. A breeze drifts through the open window.

She places salt and vinegar before us, along with a huge pot of chip spice and all sorts of off-brand sauce sachets, before taking orders for our drinks and bustling off to get them.

"Fish, chips and mushy peas?" I suggest, smiling faintly at my sister. "I think I'll be able to finish a full portion this time…"

"I prefer battered sausage now." Jenna flushes as she says this. "I think it's time that stops being Dad's thing."

The food arrives in slimy polystyrene containers, along with our J2Os. The waitress makes us pay there and then, apparently to stop kids from nicking chips after school. We tuck in with our little wooden forks as the sun begins to set outside, ducking below the clouds as the tide draws nearer and nearer to the sea wall, the first drops of seaspray tumbling onto the pavement.

It takes a minute for me to realise that Jenna is watching me, eyes narrowed as I swallow.

"What?" I ask, reaching for another chip. The room is slowly emptying, families moving back to the car park and couples finishing their Twix desserts before wandering home, hand in hand, breathing in the sea air. Jenna frowns at me and takes a bite of the sausage, crunching with her mouth open.

"You don't think I brought you all the way here just for a photoshoot, do you?"

I freeze. "Why else would I be here?"

Swallowing her mouthful, Jenna sighs. Another minute seems to pass as she taps against the table, and I hold my breath, knee jiggling up and down, as she finally says, "We need to talk about Lexie."

It's like the whole world has stopped. For the third time today, my heart is in my mouth and hands are trembling, just at the very mention of Lexie's name.

"What about her?" I ask, once again attempting to sound nonchalant. "You never even knew Lexie, Jenna. What do you want to talk –"

"I want to talk about the night she died." Jenna's face is set, eyes fixed on my face. "Because I know you're hiding something, Macey. I can tell."

"I don't know what you mean," I say, though my cheeks are burning. "I don't know anything more than you do –"

"Don't give me that bullshit, Macey."

"It's true!" I argue, but there are tears in my eyes and my voice comes out all wobbly. Why doesn't she believe me? What happened to sisters standing by each other, no matter what? "I'm not hiding anything!"

"Fine," Jenna says. "If you're being honest, then tell me about the camp. All of it." There's a pause. "Tell me everything you know, Macey."

I stop, heart pounding. Does she really mean that? Does she really want to listen to the whole story, from start to finish, here in the fish and chip shop over our J2Os and platefuls of chips? Does she really care that much?

"I mean it, Mace."

We stare at each other levelly, and I know she's being serious.

"Tell me the story."

# PART TWO

Dear diary,

The truth is a funny thing.

Telling lies is, too. Are you really lying if you merely withhold information? If someone asks if I know how Lexie died, I say no, not really. Because I don't. I'm not the coroner. I don't know the ins and outs of what happened to her body that night, of how and when her heart stopped working. I'm not lying when I say I'm oblivious, that I can't help the investigation. If anything, I'm telling the truth.

Saying that makes me feel artful, like Chloe. She does the same when people ask about Lexie's life, her friendships, how she felt in school. Did you ever witness Lexie being bullied, Chloe? No, no, of course not. Did you ever see anyone being mean to her?

Because how could she? She never witnessed the bullying, never saw anyone pulling Lexie's hair or making fun of her cheap trainers, her clothes. She didn't have any out-of-body experiences that year, as far as I know.

Bullies get away with being nasty because they know how to bend the rules, to manipulate the people doling out punishments. I know that. I witnessed it first hand when... when I watched girls lie their way out of admission, gloating at me from across the bridge in Vibbington forest.

I used to detest bullies. I thought there was nothing worse in the world you could become. I wanted to pay them back, to make them realise how much damage they'd caused me - and Lottie.

What happened? Why couldn't I stand up for myself, stand up to them?

When did I become one of their own?

# 28

The camp came round sooner than any of us expected. I was lounging on my bed with Rosie and Tyler, feet in the air, when the clock struck two and I sat up immediately.

"I've got to pack my bags!" I announced, climbing off the bed and wandering over to my wardrobe. "Sharon's picking me up at half past. I wish I could stay home and go to the movies tonight with you all..."

The group – my friends and Tyler's – had planned the night out well in advance, and I assumed I'd be free without actually checking the date. They were going to see the new Marvel movie in town, since Tyler and Jaye were so obsessed, but had fallen on the same evening of the camp, which was just typical.

"We'll be tucked up on those reclining seats while you're singing camp songs and wiping kids' noses," Rosie said, throwing one of my teddies up into the air and catching it deftly. She sat at the other end of the bed from Tyler, a huge gap between them. "Rather you than me..."

"I don't know why you bother with all this girl guide stuff anyway," Tyler added. He was on his phone, no doubt playing Flappy Bird and trying not to hit the ground. "You waste so much time there, playing babysitter. Who wants to hang out with a bunch of little kids anyway?"

Tyler's own younger sister was too "cool" to be a girl guide; she did dance that night instead, prancing around in a leotard with a spiky ponytail and too much foundation. I rolled my eyes as I pulled my suitcase from above the wardrobe, and he stuck his tongue out in return.

"It'll look good on my uni application," I said. "Volunteering, community involvement, social skills. It'll be useful if I do decide to go into speech therapy."

That'd been my plan for at least a year now. They did the appropriate course at the local uni, which Jaye and Soraya were also applying to, and the grade requirements were pretty low. It wasn't an outstanding goal, but it was something. At least we'd all be together.

"Why do you even want to be a speech therapist?" Rosie asked, catapulting the teddy higher into the air so that it hit the roof. "What's your reason?"

I shrugged. Opening my draws and proceeding to tug out clothes and underwear, I consulted the list, ticking off items here and there. "It sounds like a good career – I can help people, you know? It'll be nice to do something useful."

Rosie frowned, kicking herself back upwards to sit on crossed legs. "Mmmm. I guess."

"It's well-paid, too. Steady."

Rosie nodded.

"What about you?" I threw my waterproof into the case, along with my trainers and torch. "What do you want to do next year?"

But Rosie shrugged, leaning back again to rest against the backboard. "Live? Do a random job to get paid, spend more time doing things I want to do? I'd love to travel, visit my grandparents in South Africa. Education's kinda burnt me out."

I didn't know if I recognised my best friend, in that moment. She was so blasé, so *Jenna*. We'd always been a fairly smart, studious group, the prettier version of Mike and Steph's clique, the Dungeons and Dragons playing nerds. While the other kids drifted off to the nearby college to study animals and sport, we stayed for A-levels, the "academic" option. That was just who we were.

Now, hearing her speak about education as if it were a waste of her time, something she'd grown out of, made me feel like a child. This was *Rosie*, my best friend and partner in crime, study buddy and metaphorical twin.

"Won't you regret not going to uni?" I asked, trying to keep my voice light, despite my shaking hands. "It's supposed to be a good experience…"

"I don't need twenty-seven thousand pounds of debt to have good experiences, Mace."

The room fell silent, aside from the sound of Tyler tip-tapping away at his phone, blunt nails on the screen. He began hitting it faster and faster as his bird soared into the sky, letting out a disgruntled sigh as it crashed into a pillar.

"Dumb fucking bird," he murmured to himself. Rosie and I exchanged amused smirks. He glanced up and caught me watching him, adding, "Need any help packing, Macey?"

We finished filling my suitcase ten minutes later, squashing spare pairs of socks down the sides to bulk it out, blankets and pillows and a string of LED fairy lights sat on top, three portable chargers thrown into my rucksack. Rosie had brought me a bag of snacks, filled with Minstrels and Pringles and cans of coke, and I hid it deep in my suitcase where neither Sharon nor Mum would ever find it.

"You'll have a great time," she said, grinning and slapping me on the back as Tyler snorted his disagreement. "It'll be an adventure. We're just watching a crummy movie – don't sweat it."

So I smiled, trying to nod determinedly. "I know. And you better text me at all times, okay? Let me know how things are going, keep me updated on any drama!"

Rosie rolled her eyes. "As if there won't already be enough drama at your camp!" There was a hint of sarcasm on her tongue, so I forced a laugh.

If only she knew Lexie and the girls.

Tyler carried my suitcase downstairs for me, to where Mum was sitting with Jenna at the breakfast bar. They were going over the arrangements for Jenna's new college course, snacking on a bowl of drained chickpeas as a hunk of pork roasted away in the oven. Jenna was seemingly disinterested, sneaking chocolate from her pocket with her other eye wandering.

"Mace!" she exclaimed, watching our procession move through to the hall. "Looking forward to your freak camp? What time will that woman be here, again? You know, the one with awful roots and saggy boobs…"

I scowled at her as the sound of tyres sounded on the drive outside, a door opening and closing in the back of my ear.

"That must be her!" Jenna said. "See you on Sunday, little sister."

The sky was light blue and clear as we stepped outside, the sun beating down on us, too hot even for August. Sharon was making space in her boot for my bags, leaning over so her khaki shorts strained around her posterior, and turned around with a huge smile as we progressed down the drive. The front of our house was protected from the main road by a clump of trees and bushes, but the sun was positioned right above us in the midday heat. It shone from her car like a lamp.

"Macey!" she called, waving me over. "Isn't this exciting?"

I tried to smile, but the dread was getting to me more and more as time went on. Aside from the weekend outside, half an hour making small talk with Sharon in the car was putting me off camping altogether – and an evening at the cinema with my friends had never looked so appealing.

"She can't wait!" came Tyler's voice from behind me. I felt a cool hand slide onto my waist, fingers dancing just below my waistband. "She's been going on about the trip for weeks…"

"She has?" Sharon smiled, shocked, and I grinned back guiltily. Every part of me wanted to elbow Tyler in the ribs, but his fingers were sliding further and further into my jeans, hand hidden from them behind my back. "I'm so glad you're looking forward to it, Macey. I've tried my best to make it exciting for you and the girls!"

"I'm sorry Sharon, but do you mind if I nip to the loo?" I tried to wriggle free from Tyler's grasp, suppressing a snort, as I began to move back towards the house. "I thought it'd be better to go before we set off…"

"I left my phone inside," Tyler added, as his feet joined mine on the tarmac. "I'll come with you, Mace."

We hurried back up the stairs together, heart in my mouth, collapsing in a pile on the landing. Lying there, head against the rug and elbows flush on the floorboards, he readjusted himself so that he was lying on top, arms to my sides in some sort of cage. It was uncomfortable, but Tyler was too strong for me to object.

"Do you have to go on this trip tonight?" he murmured, right in my ear. I could feel his breath against my neck, hot and metallic. "Everyone's coming round to mine afterwards for pizza, and staying the night… Jed's bagsied Rosie and Rhys wants Jaye, so I'll probably be lumped with Soraya."

I couldn't help but smile at that, twiddling the hair by his ear and scraping his face with my fingers. Of all my friends, Soraya was the one I most trusted to sleep beside my boyfriend. Aside from her strict parents, she wasn't that interested in "casual dating". She had strict views on waiting until marriage, and would much prefer to settle with a Muslim man, as her religion was so important to her.

"Don't be tempted by her..." I whispered back, while he planted a floret of kisses along my neck. "Soraya has some good moves!"

He jerked back up then, eyes wide. "She does?"

I rolled my eyes and poked him gently on the cheek, though inside I felt funny. "Don't be so gullible!"

He grinned, dejected, and sunk back in with a sigh. His lips moved along my skin to my collarbone, hands diving under my shirt and pulling it up, up, up, until it was resting on my chest. It was only a month since I'd slept at his for the first time, and he'd stayed at mine several times since. My heart was in my mouth as I let him paw me, listening to his heavy breathing as his fingers travelled below me to the clasp on my bra.

"I need to go soon," I reminded him. "Sharon's waiting!"

But Tyler just grunted, moving against the strap and pulling it off, tossing it and watching as it landed on the edge of the staircase, about to fall. "I'm not gonna see you for three days, Mace – cut me some slack!"

Tyler had never been the gentlest of boy, but I sucked in a breath sharply as he tugged at the zip on my shorts so hard that the waistband dug into my back and most likely left a mark. He lifted himself up for me to undo his jeans, and I knew what he wanted me to do. I was well practiced in the language of Tyler Campbell.

"Ty," I said, trying to wriggle away, but he frowned, confused. "Tyler."

"Come on, Macey…" But he pulled back with a roll of his eyes, and I moved away, relieved.

"It's only a few days," I reminded him, as he pulled away and began to do his jeans back up, fastening his belt and tugging his t-shirt over his flat stomach. "You can come round on Sunday, if you want?"

Tyler smiled, only briefly pecking me on the lips before reaching for my bra. It was weird, letting him see me like this, and the seriousness of what almost happened was only just kicking in.

If Jenna had wandered upstairs at any time, or Rosie had decided to see where we'd got to…

It was stupid.

It was so, so stupid.

"I'll come round on Sunday, yeah." Tyler nodded. "At least I'll have this to remember you by…"

I tried to catch his eye and smile back, but he wasn't looking at my face, not even a little.

His eyes were trained on my chest.

"You've got heaps to remember me by," I argued. It was true – Tyler had enough photos and videos to keep him going for a week. "And like I said, it's *three days*, Ty!"

I reached for my bra – it was dangling from his hand, just out of my reach – but he moved his arm higher away from me, a smirk playing on his lips.

"I really do have to go," I repeated. "Please, Tyler!"

Sighing, he flung it back to me. I caught it deftly, pulling it back on and doing up the clasp.

"Fine," he said, rolling his eyes. "You win."

"I'll be back on Sunday," I reiterated, for what felt like the hundredth time. "Then things will go back to normal!"

*\*\**

Sharon and Rosie were still talking when we finally made it back outside, into the sunshine. Sharon was telling Rosie all about her travelling days, visiting Indonesia and China and Morocco, living in yurts and feasting on cow testicles and cauliflower couscous.

Rosie glanced up in relief as we approached, raising a hand to wave us over.

"Thank you so much for the advice, Sharon!" she said, nodding enthusiastically. "I'm a lot more excited to travel now!"

I climbed into the passenger seat beside Sharon and watched her turn the dial on her radio, flipping the channel to some hippy, acoustic trash, the kind they play in shops that can't afford a licence for proper music. Rosie and Tyler waved as we travelled down the drive and onto the street, Sharon focusing hard on the road and trying not to crash into anything.

"I'll expect you to be my eyes and ears whilst we're in this car, Macey," she said, dead serious. It was as though we were about to drive on a busy motorway, not the country lanes of rural East Yorkshire. "There are snacks in the glove compartment, if you just pull on that lever... yes, that's right! They're cheese and onion flavour, made with organic pea shoots!"

And so the journey began.

## 29

We arrived at the campsite just as my phone announced it 3:30 in the afternoon, later than we'd scheduled. We drove through the gates under the cover of trees and towering weeds, making our way through an English jungle in order to arrive in the car park beside the large field. The other girls and their parents had already arrived and were carrying bags and wellies and food contributions, making a pile of belongings on a large tarp someone had placed by the garage.

Lucy and Orla huddled with their mums, Lucy snuffling and Orla trying to tug a book from her mother's grasp.

"You're not bringing a book with you, Orla!" her mother protested, as I pushed open the door and took a cautious step outside. "You'll just spend all your time reading, and you need to learn to *socialise*!"

"I can socialise *and* read!" Orla objected, pulling the book back into her hands. It was a hefty hardback, the one I'd still see her reading three weeks later, unable to get past a certain chapter. "I need something to entertain me, Mum!"

Chloe and Kayleigh were comparing mascara wands, brushing them against their palms to check the "clump factor".

"Yours is crap, Kayls," Chloe said, flicking a ball of black from her skin. "You don't want tiny balls on your eyelashes, like that. It's the sign of a cheap mascara!" She frowned and glanced over at where Lexie was standing, a little way off, with her parents and younger brother. "Hey, Lexie! What brand of mascara do you use?"

"It's from Lidl!" Mrs McCoy called, delighted that her daughter should be asked such a question. "I bought it for her birthday!"

"Thanks," Chloe replied, throwing back a horrible, tacky beam. Turning back to Kayleigh, she muttered under her breath, "You definitely don't want to buy *that* mascara, then. It's even more lumpy than her foundation!"

Sharon helped me to pull my suitcase from the boot while I unloaded the tents. There was a hint of tension as Mrs McCoy stepped forward to grab Lexie's one-man bag of fabric and poles, but Chloe quickly broke it by rushing in for a pink tent, snatching it up and marching up the field, Kayleigh hot on her heels.

I watched as Lucy's mum gave her daughter one last hug, wiping her wet cheeks, before climbing into the family's sensible black car and backing off down the road. The sun was still beating down, just dipping below the treeline in the summer evening, sky pale blue and warm. Orla clutched her novel in triumph as her own mum pulled away, and the other three cars began to leave. Lexie's, however, lingered by the gates.

"We'll pick you up on Sunday," Mrs McCoy was saying, not blind to the tears in her daughter's eyes or her trembling lips. It was an expression begging her not to leave, though the McCoys were oblivious as to *why*. "Have a good weekend, love."

"We can pick you up at any time," her dad added, trying for a smile. "Just make sure it's before tea, or I'll have had a beer!"

Lexie let out a snort of laughter, ducking her head.

"Thanks, Dad."

"I'm not kidding, Lex." He held out a fist for her to bump, and she greeted it weakly. "Keep your phone switched off to conserve the battery, so you can text us if you need anything. We're only half an hour away."

"We can make pancakes when you get home!" her brother Daniel piped up from the back, all toothy grin and wide grey eyes.

"With banana ice cream and extra syrup?"

"Obviously!"

Breathing in deeply, Lexie nodded. I watched as she took a step back from the car and waved at the retreating vehicle rolling out of the gates. She turned around, just a small girl looking incredibly forlorn against the forest's backdrop, hands laced before her in a ball.

"Have your mummy and daddy left you?" Chloe called, letting out a squeal of laughter. Her and Kayleigh had been watching the exchange with eager eyes, listening to the McCoys and overflowing with giggles at the way they seemed to "baby" their daughter. "Too bad, you'll have to manage without them. We'll look after you, Lexie!"

From the look on her face, being "looked after" was the last thing Lexie wanted.

We carted the tents and tarp up to the corner of the field, where the brick surround and sooty grass made way for an open fire and two grills. There was enough space for us all to pitch our tents in a row, so we got to work, digging pegs and metal hooks into the ground Sharon had marked out for us. It was a shady spot, set under the cover of trees which made up the back forest, which in turn led to the river through a stone path that wound through the copse. Cold, dark trunks loomed out of the darkness.

"Do you need help with that?" I asked Lexie, resting the hammer beneath my thighs. I'd been on enough camping expeditions as a girl guide to know how to put up tents. It was so far ingrained I could do it with my eyes closed. My own tent had been simple, taking brief minutes to assemble and secure against the grass. It was pale blue and compact, but I felt a buzz of excitement as I turned my back to it.

"I'm fine," Lexie replied, though she was huffing and puffing as she struggled with the ground ropes. "I just need someone to hold the other side…"

"I'll do it!" came a voice out of nowhere. It was Kayleigh, face bright red and hair scraped back into a ponytail, out of breath from figuring out her own piece of canvas. "You just hold that side, Lexie, and I'll grab this to make sure it doesn't collapse on you."

It was like a scene from a movie. Somewhere deep inside me, I knew what was about to happen – it was obvious. And yet I watched, too anxious to do anything about it, as Kayleigh pulled on the other side of the tent so that less weight was focused on Lexie and the whole thing was suspended in mid-air.

"Have you got it?" she called, face still pink and voice nervous. As Lexie began to respond, she let go of the tent with both hands and watched it swing straight towards Lexie, hitting her with full force and knocking her to the ground, submerging her in blue.

The clearing was silent for a moment, sun beating down through the trees, the field absorbing the lightest of breaths.

"Oh my goodness, are you okay?" Kayleigh seemed sincere enough, but as she rushed over to where Lexie lay beneath the tent's shell, a tiny smile pulled on her lips. "I'm so sorry, I didn't mean for that to happen –"

"Lexie!" came another cry, as the other three girls came tumbling across the field. Lucy and Orla immediately attempted to pull the blue from Lexie's body, throwing it to one side, poles and all. "What happened?"

I wasn't stupid enough to not notice the high five Chloe gave Kayleigh.

Once the tents were fully up and functional, bags and sleeping things rolled out into our compartments, I reached into my bag to pull out my fairy lights. It was cute, almost romantic, to hang the tiny LEDs around the opening and roof. It looked like something out of a cheesy movie, Peter Kavinsky about to emerge from the flaps with a tray of entrées. It would've been nice to have Tyler there with me, but, as I finished stringing the last few bulbs around the ground ropes, I couldn't help but think that this weekend wouldn't be quite so awful after all.

# 30

Sharon insisted on cooking us sausages for tea, on the open fire. Despite the masses of organisation around the kids stepping in and helping to cook the meals, seeing the flickering flame and red-hot pan seemed to have caused a change of heart, and she ushered us all away from the surround with flapping hands.

"Don't get too close, girls!" she said, eyes wide. "There'll be oil spitting everywhere!"

We were instead restricted to salad chopping duties, on the rickety camp table a little way off. The sun was fully setting now, belching orange and yellow and vibrant pink across the sky as it sunk lower beneath the trees. Lexie had the biggest knife, chopping onions into tiny slivers to fry off, whilst the other girls attempted to shred lettuce, tomato, pepper and cucumber, frowning as they put their year seven food tech skills to the test.

"That's not how you chop a tomato," Chloe pointed out, rolling her eyes at Lucy. "You're gonna get seeds everywhere, dimwit!"

Yet somehow they managed to prepare an entire bowl of salad, dressed generously in oil and raw cumin seeds, which Sharon had for some reason brought with her in the Tupperware full of equipment. She had a pan of sausages sizzling lazily over the grill, seven identical buns sat beside it, buttered and ready to apply ketchup and mustard. We gathered round to take one each then sat on our camp chairs around the fire to munch on them, fingers warm and greasy. They tasted of summer barbeques and happiness, of secrets and burnt flesh.

This was the part I remembered most from camping as a kid, with the other girl guides my age. Sitting around a flickering flame, eating good food, and feeling *part* of something, though our group couldn't have been more disjointed.

Chloe and Kayleigh were giggling and flicking through something on one of their phones, whispering behind hands and taking delicate bites from their hot dogs. Sharon sat with the other three and attempted to engage them in a game of 'I went to the shop and I bought', despite Lucy acting severely disinterested and confused. I sat in the middle, goosebumps rising on my naked legs, as the sun set fire to the world around me.

Something felt off, right from the beginning. There was this uncomfortable sense of foreboding, unease, ripping around the clearing and draping us in jilted silence.

Or maybe that's just hindsight. It's easy to remember things the way you want to, to subdue the guilt.

Digging into my pocket, I pulled out my phone. Tyler had messaged me, just a grainy snap of him and the others in the cinema, Jaye leaning too close to Rhys and Rosie hogging Jed's entire lap. Soraya perched demurely on the edge beside Tyler, out of focus. She was wearing an orange headscarf – her favourite – and snacking on popcorn straight from the bag.

**Looks like you're having fun xx**

Tyler replied instantly, his little icon popping up in the

corner with a bold grin and quiff waggling.

**eh films shit and popcorns soggy lol**

**wish you was here xx**

I couldn't help but smile at that. Tyler was *very* particular when it came to food and experience; we'd only ever been to the high-end cinema in the nearest city, which could still be dodgy from time to time.

Leaning back and giving a subtle pout so Sharon and the others wouldn't notice, I sent back a grainy selfie, half-smiling, half-sultry. The fire lit up my face just a tad, and smoke blew against my bare legs. I waited, heart pounding, for him to send one back.

In the end, it was taken in the mirror in the cinema's toilets. He stood with his hand just resting on his belt, hair all messy, eyes bleary.

I switched my phone off abruptly, shoving it back into my pocket.

I could reply later.

"Right!" Sharon cut through my thoughts, standing from her camp chair and sending hot dog crumbs tumbling onto the floor. "Since it's our first night and it's still light, we're going to play hide and seek! Everyone needs a partner."

Lucy and Orla's eyes lit up at the suggestion, nodding their heads with enthusiasm. I glanced at Lexie, who was smiling weakly and clutching the rim of her shirt.

"Can I go and get a hoody?" she asked, her voice wavering.

She looked as though she was about to cry.

We were washed up and ready to go in the next fifteen minutes, after all the dishes and pans had been scrubbed under the nearby tap, and the food equipment had been carted back to the fridge in the garage area. Sharon had several torches in her hand – one for each team – and was holding a stopwatch round her wrist. Lexie had only just appeared, traipsing across the field in a baggy hoody with her hair pulled up into a bun. She'd clearly been crying, as her eyes were all red and mascara had been smudged right down her cheeks. Lucy smiled at her but she was unresponsive, and glanced back down at the ground with a trembling lower lip.

"You'll have ten minutes to hide," Sharon said, glancing down at the stopwatch. "Are we all in pairs? Chloe and Kayleigh, Lucy and Orla, Macey and Lexie. I'll come to find you in ten minutes – but try to move around a bit, that just makes it more fun!"

Lexie seemed relieved at the prospect of not being partnerless, and sidled over with a shy smile.

Then Sharon blew the whistle.

Chloe and Kayleigh were off straight away, legging it across the field in the direction of the back copse. Lucy and Orla hesitated for a moment before exploding in the other direction, towards the toilet block, hands linked.

"Lexie?" Sharon pushed. "Macey? Are you going? You only have ten minutes!"

I felt a bit ridiculous, in all honesty, rushing round playing hide and seek at the great age of seventeen. But Lexie was gazing at me with those imploring grey eyes, bottom lip trembling. I couldn't say no.

"Come on," I said, reaching to grab her hand. "We've still got time!"

With Sharon still stood in the centre of the field, gazing around, I began to tug Lexie in the direction of the back forest. It was the obvious option. There were so many places to hide, to move under the cover of big, dark trees. Lucy and

Orla had no scope to move from behind the garage and toilets without being seen, but the forest was the perfect place to disappear.

"But Chloe and Kayleigh are already in here!" Lexie whispered as we reached the edge of the trees. The sky was cobalt blue now, the forest pitch black. Shivering, I flicked on the torch and directed it forwards through thick trunks and undergrowth.

"There are heaps of places we can hide," I hissed back, beckoning to her. "Come on! Just grab hold of my top and don't let go!"

Nettles swiped at my shins and bracken scratched my ankles as we tore through the forest, far chillier now that we were encased in foliage, rustling leaves echoing all around. It was the hiding spot we needed most, somewhere we could turn off our torch and hide from Sharon properly.

And yet I didn't really *want* us to win. It felt like Chloe would use anything as a reason to hate Lexie, and that wasn't what I needed at all, not in the slightest.

"We'll hit the river soon!" Lexie whispered, tugging on the back of my shirt. "Then there'll be nowhere to hide!"

She was right. The torchlight had hit something some way off through the trees, glistening like running water, gently trickling downstream. We were slower as we approached it, feet hitting hard decking as the floor opened out into the straight, fast-flowing river.

"What are you doing here?"

Lexie and I turned to find Chloe and Kayleigh, huddled up inside what looked like a tractor's tyre. It was attached to a harness, which in turn was unclipped and lay against the wet decking. If the tyre began to roll there'd be nothing to connect it to the embankment.

"We're looking for a hiding spot," Lexie said. She slipped her hand into mine again. "Come on Macey, these are all taken –"

But the sound of footsteps could be heard through the trees, torchlight flickering around us. Sharon was already on her way.

"Budge up!" I hissed at Chloe, pushing Lexie forward. "We can all fit in there if we try!"

Shivering and covered in spray from the river, we clambered inside the tyre, Chloe and Kayleigh squishing right up to let me in. Lexie hung back, cheeks flushed pink, as we tried to make enough room for her.

"Chloe!" I repeated, more urgently now. "Chloe, come on, be a team player!"

It was only a game, but I was so caught up in it all that the whole thing suddenly felt like a military operation. I felt like a twelve-year-old again, huddled in that tyre. I certainly didn't feel like their *leader*, even as I insisted, "Move, we need to get Lexie in!"

Begrudgingly, Chloe shuffled into the side of the tyre and watched as Lexie hopped in, half on top of me, knees scrunched up to her chest. We all moved deeper inside the tyre, hearts racing, trying to pull our feet in as far as possible so that Sharon wouldn't spot us. We could hear her crunching over the undergrowth towards us, calling our names, the light from her torch bouncing off slimy pebbles and branches.

"Lexie?" she shouted, walking right up to the edge of the water and peering down. Spray splashed over her feet, voice carried away with the sound of the fast-flowing river. "Chloe?"

I pulled Lexie against me even more, feeling her

quivering, hearing her heart beating fast through her hoody. Even Chloe had fallen silent, nestled next to Kayleigh, brown eyes like pockets in her moonlit skin.

We waited like that for a moment longer, until Sharon could be heard moving off through the trees, still calling our names. She'd find Lucy and Orla now, unless they'd taken a chance and ran whilst Sharon was safe within the back forest. I prodded Lexie gently to force her to move, and we crawled out of the tyre swing onto the slippery decking.

"I've never been so scared!" Kayleigh whispered, shaking her head. I noticed Lexie was smiling at her through the darkness. Even Chloe was shaken, stood some way off and staring down into the water.

"This is where we're going tomorrow, right?" She was watching at me expectantly, eyes flicking down to the crashing current every few moments. "We're going to use the tyre swing, after lunch."

I nodded, crossing the deck to join her. The water was the darkest shade of dense black, ripples lit up every few seconds by the moon shining through the trees. It looked like a swirling black hole, right in the centre of the forest.

"Yeah," I said. "You'll be using the tyre swing."

Kayleigh and Lexie had joined us by now, stood on either side, staring into the abyss. Kayleigh was swaying slightly, legs buckling, face faintly green in the half-light. "Isn't it a bit dangerous?" she asked, glancing at me for reassurance. "The current's way too fast…"

"It'll be calmer during the day," I told her, though I wasn't too sure myself. "Trust me."

"I had a cousin who drowned once." That was Chloe, of course – always putting a dampener on things. She said it with a grin, like the story was *funny*. "They were surfing in

Cornwall, and a big wave caught them. They fell under the water and couldn't reach the surface again, because the waves were too random, too tall, and kept crashing over them. When they eventually washed up on shore, they were all blue and covered in seaweed, lips swollen and bulbous. Apparently their lungs were so full of water that they'd doubled in size."

We were silent, staring at her. There was a tiny smile playing on her lips, which only grew as she noticed our shocked expressions.

"There'll be rocks and all sorts in this water. If you fell off the swing, you'd probably die on impact."

"There's a harness," I added quickly, but Lexie and Kayleigh were still wide-eyed and queasy. "It's completely safe, honestly. If it wasn't, we wouldn't be allowed to let you use it!"

"That's what they say at theme parks," Chloe added. "Until a ride goes wrong, and you get your legs sliced off and your fingers trampled under the wheels, all mangled and bloody."

"Have you ever thought of writing a horror book?" I asked drolly. "Because I think you'd be perfect for it, Chlo."

"I saw it on YouTube!" she insisted, spinning round and moving towards the trees. "Come on, she will have found Lucy and Orla by now. They're probably making s'mores!"

Kayleigh hurried after her through the forest, the light from their torch flickering as they moved away from us. I turned to Lexie, who was still staring down into the dark, swelling river, licking desperately at the slick mud banks and overflowing onto the decking. It lapped against her trainers before backing down into itself, all dark eyes and thick, oily tongue.

"Could you really drown in this water?" she asked,

glancing up at me. "Would you hit the rocks and die on impact, like Chloe said?"

It was strangely eery, standing here in the dark with Lexie, shivering in my thin t-shirt and shorts. The bun on her head was messy and wispy, hairs flying about her pale face.

"Would you, Macey?" she repeated.

"I don't know," I said. "But it's perfectly safe, Lex. Like I said, you'll be attached to a harness, it'd be impossible to get hurt."

Nodding, she looked back down into the river and gulped. "Okay."

"Okay?" I repeated. "Don't worry, Lex. Shall we go back and get those s'mores, yeah?"

She nodded again, eyes flickering back towards the water for one last time, before taking my hand and letting me lead her through the forest and away from the monster within.

# 31

The tents were all quiet later that night, trees rustling around us and owls hooting. I was used to living on a quiet suburban street, the only sound coming from the occasional mewling cat or wind whistling through hedgerows, and camping always put me on edge. This was the first time I'd had a tent all to myself.

Phone clutched in my hand, I gazed down at the moving dots, watching as Tyler typed. His little Snapchat icon grinned back.

**u on ur own xxx**

I replied quickly, fingers skipping over the keys. His answer was immediate.

**send pics, miss u so much xxx**

I wanted to – I *so* wanted to – but something was stopping me. The fact that I knew he was with Rosie, Soraya, Jaye and the guys right now even though I knew they all did it too. Underwear photos seemed like a common fixture of sixth form life, despite all those talks about how it was illegal and they stayed on the system forever, logged by the social media companies, easy to track down. I was almost eighteen, but it still made me uneasy, especially since I was at a *camp*. At home, I'd prance in front of my mirror with no worries, but this didn't feel right.

### I can't atm xxx

I watched as Tyler disappeared off screen without replying. He wouldn't just ignore me because I wouldn't send stuff, right? Something had probably come up. It was only half nine. Maybe they were watching a movie, or playing a game.

I got my answer ten minutes of scrolling later, when Rosie sent me a hazy snap of them all playing Cards Against Humanity in a big circle. She was practically straddling Jed, Jaye snuggled up against Rhys, Soraya perched demurely beside Tyler.

That was good, at least. I trusted Soraya. Everything was okay.

Lying back against my pillow, I breathed in deeply and twisted onto my side. It was chilly in the tent, dots of water lacing the outer layer, sleeping bag like ice against my leggings. Outside, leaves brushed together and branches crackled, and the smell of smoke drifted through the wind away from the remaining smouldering coal.

That was when I heard footsteps on the grass just outside. I crawled across the sleeping mat in my fluffy socks, heart racing, and stuck my head out the tent's entrance.

It was Lexie, traipsing across the grass to the toilet block. She was clutching her washbag and had big wellies on her feet, bright pink with luminous googly eyes.

"Lex!" I called, into the night. She turned around, glancing about her in fright, eyes finally landing on me as relief flooded her expression. "Lexie, where are you going?"

"I'm going to clean my teeth," she yelled back, over the

sound of the forest. "I forgot to go earlier."

Nodding, I pulled myself back inside the tent and tugged the door closed, zipping it all the way up. Perhaps I should get some sleep now. After all, there was a busy day ahead, however early it may currently seem.

But as I crawled back into sleeping bag, socks sliding against the slippery material, there came another noise. I jerked upwards again, ears pricked, as the sound of tiny feet against wet grass sounded from just outside my tent.

"Shh!" a voice hissed. "Macey's tent is right there, dummy, she'll hear you!"

It was Chloe.

Heart thudding, I moved closer to the zip. They were clearly planning something, but I knew that if I interrupted them, I'd never find out what it was. They were heading towards Lexie's tent, all four of them, wellies crunching against the ground. I froze, so as to hear as much of their conversation as I could.

"What if Lexie comes back while we're in there?" That was Lucy, unmistakably, forever anxious. "She'll only tell Sharon we were in her tent…"

"She won't come back yet," replied Chloe, and I could hear the smirk in her voice. "I pushed a camp chair in front of the toilet door to jam it shut. She'll be stuck in there until we let her out."

I couldn't help but inhale sharply, heart thudding. Although she was just twelve-years-old, there was no doubt in my mind that Chloe was the biggest bitch I'd ever met.

Yet I still didn't want to leave my tent. I needed to know what they were doing first. I needed to know everything was *okay*.

I heard the zip on Lexie's tent go up, the flaps peeling

back and attaching to their Velcro holders. There were giggles here and there, the odd playful shove, suppressed squeals ricocheting through the night. No doubt Sharon was tucked away with an audio book plugged in, blissfully unaware of what was going on.

"What the..." I heard Chloe exclaim. "Guess what I found!"

I imagined them all clustered around her, staring in awe at whatever object she'd managed to produce, just like that first night two years ago when we all first met Lexie. My heart was in my throat, pulsing against my tongue like a baby bird, slippery and painful and flapping to escape.

"Chloe, you can't take that!" Lucy hissed. "You mustn't!"

But Chloe never listened to anyone.

"Why?" she said. "It's falling to pieces anyway!"

"She loves it," Orla piped up, voice wavering. "You'll only upset her, Chloe."

"And?" Chloe's voice was hard, cold, as she held up whatever it was she was holding and the girls all gasped. "We don't want to be nice to her, do we? She's an annoying little busybody, Orla. Imagine how much fun we'd have if she weren't here with us!"

The others couldn't disagree.

"Let's take it, we can have some fun with it tomorrow..."

Giggling, I heard her pass it to Kayleigh, who murmured something about getting germs.

"I have a plan," Chloe continued. "It's gonna be hilarious, just you wait and see..."

I heard the tent flap zip itself back up, wellies slick against the grass. I stuck my head out of my own door quickly, into the dark night.

"Chloe?" I called. She spun around, quickly stuffing

something behind her back before grinning and giving me a wave. "What are you all doing out of bed?"

"We were going to check Lexie was okay," Lucy said, though her cheeks burned with the lie. "But we think she must be in the toilet block still."

The others nodded while I frowned.

"What's that behind your back, Chloe?"

If I could pull my wellies on fast enough, I'd rush right up to them and check, grab whatever Chloe had and place it back in Lexie's tent. But they were in their carrier bag, tucked away beneath piles of clothes and toiletries.

"Nothing," Chloe replied, acting innocent. Her face was blank, eyes wide. "Why would you think anything was behind my back, Macey?"

"I just saw you come from Lexie's tent." My tone was light, but Chloe glared back anyway, eyebrows knitted.

"We were just going to check on her now," she said, moving towards the toilet block with her back still turned. "Come on, guys, let's go find Lexie…"

But I shook my head, moving closer to the entrance as though I was about to go after them. They didn't know I had no shoes on; I just wanted to get to Lexie first.

"I'll go. You lot get back into bed." I watched as they made no attempt to move, booted feet stuck still in the grass. "If I hear another peep from any of you, I'll be waking Sharon."

Slowly, they traipsed across the field away from me. I waited until they were all safely back in their tents with the flaps closed and torches off, before digging into my suitcase for the wellies Mum bought me three years ago, pulling them on over my fluffy socks and stepping out onto the damp ground.

It was freezing now, the sky black and covered in stars. A

breeze blew across the site and into the trees, rustling my hair and the surrounding trees. In the distance, the sound of the river crashing down the banks and over jagged rocks sounded faintly, like a whisper in the back of my ear.

The toilet block's door was lit up by a solar-powered lamp, suspended on the peeling wall. The door hung open, a row of grassy sinks laid out behind it, caked in mud and dried spittle. There were laminated signs beside each one, reading something about remembering to use soap.

"Lexie?" I called down the aisle. There was one door closed, right at the end. It was cold, a breeze blowing through the door behind me. "Are you in here?"

A snuffling noise came from that cubicle. My wellies were loud against the tiles, clomping towards her with little to no dignity, huddled in my hoody against the icy evening air.

"Are you okay?" I whispered. "Come on, Lexie, it's cold in here. Let's go back to bed."

She pushed open the door, emerging in pink Superwoman pyjamas and her mum's beige fleece. She'd clearly been crying, face puffy and red in the harsh toilet lighting.

"I want to go home," she murmured, clutching her washbag in tightly wound fists. "Everyone hates me, Macey."

"I don't hate you!" I said.

Her eyes filled with tears again and she sagged back against the door. "I'm going to ring my parents tomorrow, ask them to pick me up."

"Lexie…"

"I don't want to be here, Macey! I never wanted to come in the first place!"

"Then why did you?" I stared at her, this poor, crying twelve-year-old, stood before me in her kiddie pyjamas and too-small pink wellies. In that moment, it just *hurt*. The fact that Chloe could make her feel like this, for no fault of her own.

"I don't want my parents to know anything," she whispered, voice trembling. "They think I'm good friends with the other girls. When Chloe didn't invite me to her party, her mum said there was an accident with the invitations and a few got covered in juice, and they had to rewrite some, but must've forgotten mine. I've never properly stayed away from home before, just on sleepovers. I wanted them to be proud of me."

"They are proud of you!" I insisted, though she just stared back in disbelief, like she didn't believe me. "They love you, Lexie. You need to tell them what's going on, so they can help. Or tell the school – they have a really good anti-bullying policy! You can move classes, or…"

She started to sob again at that, shaking her head hard. "I can't, Macey! Then my parents will know no one likes me and that I have no friends!"

"You have Lucy and Orla!" I said, though we both knew they'd choose Chloe every time. "It'll be okay, Lexie. But don't go home tomorrow. We have so many fun activities planned, you'll have a great time!"

It was clear she didn't believe me, but Lexie shrugged anyway and took a deep breath. "We'll see."

"I promise." I held out a hand to high-five her, and she met it cautiously. "Let's go back to the tents, shall we?"

We made our way back to the tents, where I hugged her goodbye and watched as she disappeared into her own. I pulled off my wellies and crawled back into my sleeping bag, using my phone as a torch, shivering.

It was only a minute or two until I heard a scrabbling from the next tent. Lexie was looking for something, searching fervently through her possessions to find whatever it was that Chloe had taken.

I should've got it back from Chloe there and then, knocking on their flap and poking my head in, catching them in the act.

But I didn't. I was too tired, too weak, too unbothered by it all.

That was my first mistake.

# 32

The next morning, Sharon awoke us by banging two saucepans together, the metal clanging in my ears. I rolled over, nestling further into my pillow. It was still freezing in the tent, and dew stuck to the material above me. I groped on the canvas beside me for my phone, finding it still stuck to its charger, icy-cold.

There was a snap from Rosie, and I opened it without a second thought.

It was a selfie of the six of them, squashed up on Tyler's double bed beneath his dark blue covers. It was the bed we'd slept together in for the second time, feeling dangerous for sneaking up there in the middle of the day while his mum was at work. Now, however, Rosie and Jed were cuddled up together beside Jaye and Rhys, an empty pizza box between them. Soraya was leaning against Tyler, a lazy smile on her face, eyeliner smudged.

But it wasn't that that made me feel so uncomfortable. It was his hand, resting on her ribs, just below her armpit. Too close, in a position it really, really shouldn't be. I clicked away quickly, shaking my head to try and rid it of the image.

"Macey!" came a voice from outside. "Sharon wants you to come and help cook the breakfast. We're making eggy bread, and she says you need to show us how!"

Still trying to remove the photo from my mind, I shouted back that I'd be out in a second, that I just needed to brush my hair. I shoved it into a bun instead, throwing my feet into my still-muddy wellies and hurrying outside.

It was chilly, the air still draped in pale golden sunlight, and Sharon had already lit the fire. The girls clustered around the table with a big pack of eggs and a loaf of bread, trying to find a bowl to mix up the egg and milk mixture in, debating whether the oil needed to join the liquid or just the pan.

Chloe seemed sour, mouth closed to avoid anyone realising she had morning breath. I smiled at her, only to be greeted by a stern, dark-brown glare.

"Someone got out the wrong side of the bed!" I said, only partly joking.

"It's a *tent*," she replied. "There is no bed."

Breakfast was a shabby affair, served on our plastic camping plates, each slice either undercooked or black around the edges. The girls ate quickly and clamoured for pancakes right after, just those packet ones you heat in the microwave, and Sharon even produced a jar of Nutella for them to spread over liberally. Chloe was the only one to complain, moving the bread round and round on her plate and frowning at the chocolatey pancakes, muttering about calories and sugar and waistlines.

Sharon had a whole host of activities lined up for today, and more for Sunday morning. She wanted us to go climbing last, as it was the thing that needed the least special equipment and preparation. We'd go kayaking and on the tyre swing today, then have a paddle in the water, perhaps have a go on the rafts in the garage. We all needed a swimming costume on under our clothes, and old clothes we wouldn't mind getting wet and muddy. There were showers in the toilet block, she told us. We could use them before bed.

Back in my tent, I changed into a yellow bikini, pulling a

pair of shorts over the bottom half. It was the one I'd worn to the beach only a week previous, when we'd all gone on the train. Tyler had loved it, claiming it set off the blue in my eyes. We snogged a bit in an unoccupied beach hut, his lips hot and salty against my skin, and the thing was still tainted with the memory now, too bright to be distinguished.

I still couldn't push the image of him and Soraya from my mind.

Sharon dragged the six of us through the forest to the river, where golden light spilt through the trees and cast a glow atop the running water. It wasn't quite so choppy in the daylight, meandering through the forest floor beside carpets of green moss and twigs. It was so still that it almost looked... inviting.

"Can we not just go swimming now?" Chloe whined, but Sharon shook her head, disappearing to the side to start unlocking the four large, padlocked kayaks from their chains. They were "tandem kayaks" made for two people each, but Sharon had one all to herself – she was the only one experienced enough to handle it.

I helped her hold them steady to the side of the decking as Lucy and Orla climbed in first, wobbling about on the tiny seats and terrified of falling in the water.

"What if they drown?" Chloe asked, trying to frighten them. "What if it turns over in the water, and they both get trapped underneath?"

"That's why they're wearing lifejackets," Sharon retorted, giving the buckle on Orla's a tug. "They're perfectly safe, very stable. But if it *did* turn over, the girls inside would float back up to the top!"

Kayleigh and Lexie were instructed to share, being the same height and weight to balance each other out. I think everyone was expecting Chloe to moan about this, but she shrugged and started to tug ours towards the water, sandals slip-sliding against the decking. Truth be told, I think she thought Kayleigh would be dead weight in a kayak.

I'd kayaked heaps of times as a kid, but I never remembered it being quite so *fun*. Despite her age, Chloe was good at using the oars to move us through the water and we rowed ahead of the others in no time, gliding along like a knife through butter. Sharon held back to help Lexie, Lucy, Kayleigh and Orla as they hit the riverbanks time and time again, but Chloe and I were in a whole other league.

We broke free of the forest eventually, paddling down the river between fields of cows, which gazed at us dismally as we glided past. Ducks and geese honked and flew up the banks upon noticing us, and reeds drooped our way, watery weeds like long, green nails. As we gained momentum, I stopped rowing for a second to just reach out and touch the water, fingers cold against the icy depths of the river.

The sky was blue above us, filled with fluffy clouds. I could hear the others approaching, giggling as they learnt to row in the right direction, oars slipping through the water. Sharon held up the rear end, beaming, delighted that we were enjoying ourselves, as we turned around and headed for home.

Lunch was simply sandwiches on the riverbank, about half a mile from the campsite. We ate with our legs dangling over the edge, feet submerged. We'd brought our own from home, kept in the fridge overnight, and tucked in greedily. A farmhouse watched from a distance, smoke steaming from its chimney. I'd never felt quite so peaceful.

We rowed back in silence, enjoying the tranquillity of the river and surrounding Yorkshire countryside, paying much more attention to each bird and flower than we usually would. The decking soon appeared in the distance. Sharon helped us out, throwing our bags and lunchboxes into a pile beside a tree.

"Right!" she exclaimed, a huge smile lighting up her face. "Who's ready for a swim?"

The girls were all wearing swimming costumes under their clothes, and undressed beneath the canopy. Chloe was the only one to be wearing a bikini, like me, despite being flat-chested and on the skinny side, but Lexie and the others gazed at her in envy.

"My dad would *never* let me wear that!" Kayleigh murmured, shaking her head in awe. "He always says I'm growing up too fast…"

Chloe just smiled smugly, shrugging her perfect shoulders. "When we're older, we can go shopping together and buy you one!" Kayleigh's eyes lit up at the sound of that, and she nodded. "You just need to lose a bit of that chub, Kayls. Then you'll look *fab*."

The water wasn't as cold as we'd anticipated, so I went first, leading by example. The others watched as I ducked my shoulders and arms under, gasping at the feel of it.

We swam around for half an hour or so, mainly wallowing where the water was most still, up to our necks in weeds and bits of leaf. There were rocks on either side, as Chloe had predicted, but they were fairly deep-set and not too jagged, so we didn't have to be careful. We stuck to the middle of the water anyway, where it wasn't *too* shallow and we could float on our backs, gazing up at the criss-crossing branches above and watching the clouds drift by.

Lexie's costume was babyish, pink and studded in sequins in the shape of the American flag, but for once, no one said anything about it. There were no snide comments, no laughing and pointing, no whispering about how she looked like a five-year-old. She hadn't done any makeup and her hair was in a loose ponytail, and for the first time in weeks, even *she* looked happy, smiling and laughing along with everyone else.

Until Sharon went and ruined it.

"Who wants a go on the tyre swing?" she asked, gazing round at everyone. She herself was in a sporty swimsuit, which rode up her sagging bottom and clung to her breasts in all the wrong places. There was a smattering of stubble under her armpits, and the hairs on her legs were dark with water. "Come on, don't all shout at once!"

Chloe was the first to raise a hand, stepping out of the river and clambering across the rocks. She pulled the harness on over her bikini, shivering, and grinned at Sharon.

"I'll give it a go!"

Sharon was careful to clip Chloe into place, tugging on each strand of rope and checking each clasp had been done up properly. Finally, she clipped the tyre onto the large piece of wood that stuck out above it, then grabbed hold of the rope to hoist Chloe into the air.

Her legs were white and dangling as she rose away from the decking, high above us. It was all perfectly safe, approved by health and safety, yet I couldn't help but feel worried as she was tugged up into the clouds.

Once she was high enough, Sharon breathed in and glanced back down at us, before counting down from three and letting go. The speed of which Chloe dropped from the sky was alarming. The tyre became a black blur, scream high-pitched and dragging in the wind, as the swing whipped through the air and back up again, just like that, bouncing on the end of its rope. We watched as she swung back and forth, slower each time, the expression on her face losing its terror and becoming a steady grin. Then she was laughing. It was a nervous giggle at first, switching to the screeching cackles of a witch as she swung through the air above us.

"That was sick!" she called, waving. "You've got to give it a go!"

Kayleigh went next, screaming so loud that I swear you could've heard her back in Vibbington. Her face was pink with fear and her podgy legs kicked desperately, almost crying as she was pulled back onto the decking.

Lucy and Orla reacted in a similar way, petrified but eager to have a go. They seemed to enjoy it, entering the water again with big smiles.

"That was awesome!" Lucy said, eyes wide. "You'll love it, Lexie!"

But Lexie was staring at the swing in horror.

"I don't want to," she said, shaking her head. "I... um... I don't like heights."

Chloe was gazing at her with a gleeful glint in her eye, mind ticking at a rate of knots.

"You're scared," she said, voice barely a whisper. "You're scared of the tyre swing!"

Lexie shook her head in objection, sinking lower under the water, so that her chin just touched the surface. All the girls were staring at her now, judging, Sharon still clutching the swing so it wouldn't go flying.

"You don't have to try," she told her. "Not if you don't want to."

"It's only a tyre swing," I added, patting her on the back. "No big deal!"

"Yeah," Chloe echoed, as the other girls giggled and

Kayleigh added, "No big deal."

Lexie slid further into the water, out of reach.

# 33

Sharon roped us into cooking her lentil dahl that night. The girls all thought it an awful idea, complaining bitterly as she sent us to gather ingredients from the fridge, though Lexie was silent all the way there and back.

"You okay, Lex?" I asked, nudging her shoulder. "You're being very quiet…"

She shrugged.

The garage was a cold, airy building, filled with bits of equipment and outdoor games, the concrete beneath our feet covered in mud and grass clippings. We weren't wearing shoes and it was icy against our toes, but we made our way over to the squat fridge-freezer without complaining, late summer sunshine pouring in through the door.

"Here we are," Orla said, pulling out the veggies I'd bought two days before. "Cucumber, carrots, pepper, celery!"

Sharon instructed us to get chopping back at the camp, even trusting the girls with big knives, though she kept glancing over at them to check. I was in charge of stirring the big pot of dahl, making sure the bottom didn't burn, stood in front of the fire as smoke billowed in my face and made my eyes water.

The meal was surprisingly good. We ate yellow-red lentil dahl, full of spices and onions and veggies, with a yoghurt raita and deflated flatbreads. There were doughnuts for afters, bought by Sharon at Lidl and covered in sickly-sweet icing and sprinkles, and we made hot chocolates in our flasks, stirring in the mixture and dotting marshmallows on top. We even had golden sprinkles, courtesy of Lucy.

I think it might have been the over-the-top hot chocolates that did it, though it could have been the doughnuts. We were sat around the campfire, all seven of us, when Sharon suddenly lurched forward, retching violently as she vomited over the fire.

"Oh, shit!" she moaned, leaning back and wiping her mouth with the back of her hand. She flushed and glanced up with a shifty expression. "Excuse my language, girls." And then she bent over the fire again, missing the flame completely and hitting the metal grill we'd just cooked our food over.

The others were unimpressed, trying not to wrinkle their noses. Lucy patted her on the back and attempted a smile, but there was an awkward edge now, and the bricks were beginning to smell.

"Are you okay, Sharon?" Chloe asked, pulling her very best straight face. "Do we need to call someone?"

"No, no." Sharon shook her head, though she was suppressing further belches and was bright red now, either from effort or embarrassment. "I've just eaten way too much sugar. I knew it was a bad idea to bring all that sweet stuff, I just thought it'd make a change for you all…"

"Maybe you should have a lie down?" Chloe continued. She stood up and crossed round the fire to Sharon, clutching her shoulder and helping her stand. "We'll be all right here, and we'll put the fire out before we go to sleep. You probably just need some rest!"

Sharon smiled gratefully and stood to leave with Chloe, but we all knew what she was really doing. She wanted

Sharon out of the way so that they could have free reign over the camp.

The four of them waited a few minutes for Sharon to disappear, Chloe helping her make her way from the fire. Sharon zipped herself into her tent and jammed plugs in her ears so she could sleep properly, while the rest of us settled into our camp chairs and helped ourselves to more hot chocolate. I had to pour for everyone, careful with the scalding water, then placed the kettle off the fire to let it cool down. It wasn't that late and the sky was a shade of velvety blue, keeping us from darkness.

Lucy and Kayleigh huddled together, muttering about their summer history project, Orla with her book tilted forward so she could read by firelight. Chloe, however, was staring down at her hands with a concentrated expression, deep in thought.

"Let's play a game," she said suddenly.

They were twelve-year-old girls, still hung up on kiddie sleepovers and a craving for Haribo, and I knew exactly what was coming next.

"Truth or dare!" Kayleigh suggested, eyes alight and sparkling, and the others nodded their agreement.

Typical.

Chloe went first, just to show off. She picked dare, of course, grinning as the others gathered round in a tight bubble to decide on her punishment. Lucy eventually broke free after minutes of frantic whispering.

There was a nervous smile on her face as she said, "Go up the climbing wall in the dark." Kayleigh and Orla nodded eagerly. "Although we can think of a forfeit, if you think that's too dangerous…"

"No," Chloe replied, a smile spreading over her face. "That

sounds perfect."

Of course it did – to her.

The climbing wall was a pathetic wooden structure pushed against the garage. Chloe was wearing trainers and had bare palms, but she gripped the little holders and swung herself up with ease. At the very top, she pushed her leg over the gutter and sat, one foot on the roof, another on the wall, staring down at us with those almost-black eyes.

"Easy," she said, rolling her eyes. "Who's next?"

Kayleigh volunteered, probably just to copy Chloe, and picked truth. The inevitable preteen question came flying out of Orla's mouth before she could stop herself.

"Who's your crush?"

Kayleigh flushed as Chloe came tumbling down the wall towards us, practically flying over the tiny holders to reach our huddle. I observed from a distance, careful not to get involved.

"Go on, Kayls," Chloe urged. "Tell us!"

Apprehensive, Kayleigh sucked in a long, deep breath. "I… I think I have a crush on Martin."

I had no idea who Martin was, but the others immediately burst into peals of excitable squeals and cries, shaking their heads and jumping up and down. Even Lexie joined in, hitting Kayleigh on the back as the poor girl flushed, sheepish, and ducked her dark head.

"He walks me home from the bus sometimes," she admitted, which drove more giggles and whoops. "I gave him my number before the holidays started, but he hasn't messaged me yet."

"He's probably just shy!" Lucy exclaimed, eyes bright. "What if he asks you out when we're back at school, Kayls? What will you say?"

Chloe was the only one not laughing now. Her face was set, brows knitted, as Kayleigh gushed about her romantic success.

"Anyway," she cut in, throwing her best friend a tacky smile. "It's Macey's turn."

I went to shake my head at once, adamant that I wouldn't be playing. I was just supervising, making sure they didn't get up to too much trouble, while Sharon had her rest.

"We insist!" Chloe continued, putting one foot against the climbing wall and hauling herself back up, so that we were stood eye to eye. "Truth or dare?"

I picked truth. There was no way they were getting me to run around the campsite like an idiot, completing their daft quests.

"How does it feel to have sex?"

We all blinked at Chloe's question. She was hanging from the wall with a straight face, gazing straight at me, eyes dark.

"Come on, Macey, we all know you've slept with Tyler Campbell. It's a simple question. How does it feel to have sex?"

I tried to stare back with equal intensity, but I could feel myself flushing, and had to lean back to steady myself. I tried to look Chloe in the eye as I replied, but the atmosphere was awkward now, the younger girls watching as though they too were curious.

She was twelve.

Chloe was *twelve*.

"It feels nice," I said. "That's why people do it."

Nodding, Chloe leapt from the wall. She landed just before me. "See? That's all you had to say."

"Why did you need to know that?" The voice came from behind us, judgemental. "It's not really any of our business, is it?"

Lexie. I looked at her, trying to understand. To figure out why she'd say that, *do* that, knowing the consequences.

"It's only because Chloe's seeing Ben Margate, the year ten!" Kayleigh grinned triumphantly, as Lucy and Orla exchanged glances. "He's way older, and her mum's dead furious about it!"

"Shut your mouth!" Chloe exclaimed. She stared at them all in disgust, surprise wavering on her face. She clearly wasn't expecting to be ganged up on – not by Lexie and Kayleigh, anyhow. "You're just jealous because I snogged Ben, and stupid Martin's too pathetic to even message you. He's probably not interested in you anyway."

There was a pause, everyone looking at Chloe, waiting to see what she'd say next.

"I mean... Who *would* be?"

Silence enveloped us as Kayleigh leaned back, stung. "It's Lexie's turn," she said, flushing as she diverted the attention away from herself. "Truth or dare?"

Chloe was still glowering as they all turned to Lexie, who shifted from foot to foot and wrung her hands. Careful not to meet anyone's eyes, she muttered, "Truth."

Lucy and Orla tried to recreate the huddle to discuss the matter, but Chloe had already stepped forward.

"Why didn't you want to use the tyre swing?"

We all fell silent again, watching Lexie for a reaction.

"You can have a forfeit if you don't want to answer," Lucy cut in, and Lexie nodded gratefully. "But it has to be a dare."

"Well, well, well." Chloe grinned. "I can think of the *perfect* dare."

I think we all knew what she was planning, but waited for her to say it out loud anyway.

"Go on the tyre swing," Chloe said, eyes gleaming as she caught Lexie's horrified expression. "It'll be perfectly safe, and Macey can set it all up and operate the rope. It'll just be dark. And the river will be choppier. Blacker. Full of God-knows what."

"No –" I tried to object, realising how stupid they were being. Chloe raised a hand to stop me.

"You picked forfeit, Lexie." She smiled, mouth curved up in a malicious shape. "Are you scared?"

"No," Lexie whispered, but her bottom lip was trembling. "It's just too dangerous, it'd be stupid to go at night –"

"Lexie's scared!"

"I'm not scared, I'm –"

But the others were already giggling at her.

"You're so pathetic, Lexie," Chloe said. "You won't even use a harmless tyre swing because you're too frightened of it. It's health and safety approved, it's just a bit of fun!"

"I just don't want to," Lexie said feebly, but Chloe and the girls were gloating too much, filled with joy at the fact that poor Lexie was too frightened to use the swing and they weren't.

"You're such a baby," Chloe added. "Such a weird little wimp." Then her expression began to gleam, a smile spreading over her face like poison. "If you don't go on the tyre swing, we'll throw Mr Sparkles in the river."

Mr Sparkles. Lexie's old unicorn teddy, with its missing one eye and half-unpicked mouth. The one she claimed to have thrown away after the girls made fun of it.

My stomach dropped.

"It was you who took him from my tent," Lexie whispered, realisation dawning. "Last night, while I was brushing my teeth."

"You got it," Chloe replied. "It's been sleeping in my tent, happy as Larry."

Lexie's eyes had filled with tears and she was shaking her head desperately, gasping for air.

"Chloe, you give that back to Lexie right before bed tonight, or Sharon will be finding out about this." I didn't want to intervene, but I couldn't *not*, even though it'd turn the others against me for sure. Things had already gone too far. "Chloe? Have you got that?"

"Whatever," Chloe muttered. "You wait, Lexie. You don't go on that tyre swing, and Mr Sparkles might just have an accident…"

Lexie didn't reply. Instead, she flushed and glanced down at her feet, and wouldn't say another word for the rest of the night.

After that, truth or dare got boring. The girls couldn't think of anything challenging enough for them to do, and none of them wanted to pick truth, for fear of revealing something they genuinely didn't want the others to know. It was like if they refused one of the quests, they'd turn into Lexie, ridiculed and weak.

I decided to call it a night half an hour later, insisting they crawled into bed. They were reluctant, bribing me with more doughnuts and hot chocolate, but I stood firm. Chloe returned Mr Sparkles begrudgingly, though the look on her face said she wasn't giving in.

I cleaned my teeth in the bathroom, staring into the mirror at my pale, makeup-less face and thin eyelashes, my white nose and tangled hair.

I peeled on my pyjamas, sinking into my freezing cold sleeping bag.

I checked my phone one last time, replying to Tyler and

Rosie and Jaye, turning it off and slipping it into my bag at the bottom of the tent.

And then

I went

to

sleep.

# 34

"So that's it," I say, smiling at Jenna through my eyelashes. The fish and chip restaurant has fallen completely silent, sunset orange light leaking through the sludge on the windows. I've finished my meal – I kept breaking off at points to take mouthfuls – but Jenna's plate is still half-full of food, and she's watching me with a dumbstruck expression.

"That's it?" she echoes. "You went to sleep, and when you woke up she was gone?"

"Yep," I reply, though my cheeks are pink and my chest feels all tight. "Sharon went round with her saucepan to wake us up, and asked me to go check on Lexie. She wasn't answering, so I went into her tent, and there was no one there."

"So Sharon called the police?"

"Not straight away. We went for a walk around the site to try and find her, and called her parents to check she hadn't been picked up. Then the police came out."

"And you found the body later that afternoon?"

I swallow. Nod.

"And the tyre swing?" Jenna frowns. "They think she wasn't clipped on right, and she fell into the river? I don't get it. You must know more, Macey. It makes no sense that she'd even *try*."

I shake my head, willing her to stop speaking. It doesn't matter, not now, not ever. We don't need to dig up the past, not when it won't bring Lexie back, not when it'll only stir things up for her family again.

"You must know. You were there!"

"I *don't*, Jen!"

Jenna stares at me, shocked by my outburst. I lean back, face bright red, fingers scrabbling at the sticky tablecloth in an attempt to distract myself. The waitress comes to take our plates, breaking the awkward silence. We listen as her footsteps squeak on the tiles away from us.

"Sorry," Jenna says, pulling a face. "I shouldn't have pushed you."

"It's fine." I bite my lip, taking a final swig from my J2O and placing it back on the table. "Shall we just go? It'll be dark soon, and we've got to drive home."

Jenna sighs as she agrees.

We don't talk on the way back to the car park. My sister crunches her knuckles and stares straight ahead, and my throat is still thick and hot and slimy, painful to swallow. Elderly couples stroll past us, smiling and nodding, as families skip down the harbour with linked hands. The stalls are packing away, and we get a free bag of cockles from a man who claims they never sell once they're a day old. Jenna's car squats lazily beneath the dark blue sky, and we sink into it, exhausted and ready for home.

The drive back is quicker than it was this morning, the roads empty and the moors stretching out like a great black canvas. It's later than we both thought, and the only light comes from our headlights, spilling over the road beyond and not much further.

It's past eleven when we eventually pull into our drive. Jenna curses violently under her breath. The street has long gone to sleep, but Mum stands on the doorstep in her silky robe and sliders, hair piled above her head and expression like ice.

"Inside," she says, folding her arms and glaring. "Come on, now!"

She hasn't had the heating on, and the house is freezing. We perch on the edge of the sofa as she closes the door behind us, shaking her head in anger.

"What were you thinking? I got a call from your maths teacher, Macey, asking if you were feeling better, and then the head of your sixth form – that tubby man, Mr Roberts – gave me a ring to ask why you hadn't been to your UCAS session. And then neither of you came home, and your car was gone, and I was so, *so* worried –"

And just like that, she starts to cry.

"You can't just do that girls, you just can't. Since that young girl died, I can't – I can't –"

I rush to throw my arm around her, guilt curdling in my stomach. This whole time, I wasn't even thinking about my mother or how worried she'd be. I assumed she wouldn't notice, or care. She nestles into me as she sobs, the dynamic all twisted. Jenna joins me and hugs us both tight. When I twist to catch her eye, I notice she's crying, too.

"I know I've been a terrible mother," Mum mutters, gasping for breath and wiping her eyes with her long nails. "I'm never here, always working and seeing people and – oh, Macey, I know I didn't show it, but it was *humiliating* when you found me with Doyle the other morning. You deserve stability, you both do. That's why I'm so grateful you have Tyler…"

Tyler.

Her voice trails off as I flush, glancing down sheepishly. If ever there was a good time to tell her about our breakup, it's now.

"Mum... Tyler and I broke up."

She glances up, eyes wide and mouth carved into a tiny "o" shape. I nod.

"You and Tyler..." She seems shocked, so I squeeze her gently and try to smile. "Oh, darling, are you okay? Why didn't you say anything to me?"

"It's no big deal. We weren't well-suited in the end."

"Oh." You can tell that surprises her. She doesn't understand how a good-looking, popular guy like Tyler could be anything *other* than "well-suited" for me. "So you're not upset about it, then?"

I shake my head.

There's nothing to be upset *about*.

"I'm so proud of you." She kisses me on the forehead, then detaches herself and stands to leave. "We all need some rest now, I think. You've had a very long day, driving all the way to Whitby and back! How about we get up early and make blueberry pancakes, like we used to?"

I don't want to tell her that I don't really like blueberries, that I'd prefer shop-bought chocolate chip pancakes with vanilla ice cream, but her face is so hopeful in the light of the TV. We nod at her, and she beams in delight.

"Wonderful! Night, girls."

We watch as she leaves, tying her robe and shutting the door behind her.

"Well..."

"Well."

Jenna and I traipse up a few minutes later. I dump my bag on my bedroom floor and collapse backwards onto my bed, clutching my phone tight to my chest and staring up at the ceiling. My pink sheets are smooth against my feet, heartrate loud.

It's over.

I'm back at school. Lexie has been cremated. Jenna won't ask any more questions about the camp. Tyler's gone. My friends don't suspect anything... but then maybe I've lost them, too. The other girl guides think Lexie's death was an accident; they probably feel partly to blame.

I'm completely and utterly off the hook.

Gone are the hours of worrying, the hours of thinking that someone will find something that'll link me back to Lexie's death. The days after she was found were the worst, spent waiting for the autopsy results and dreading their findings, my fingerprints and blood, sweat and tears highlighted in bright blue on every surface. I pictured my DNA intermingled with the river water filling her lungs, convinced that a part of me was locked inside Lexie's body and would come out during the investigation.

Even after no trace of my involvement was found, I worried still. I worried about myself more than anything. I didn't trust my mouth. I knew that somehow, I'd give something away.

Relief floods through now me as I picture Jenna's expression in the chippy, realising I wanted nothing more than to forget about the whole thing and move on with my life.

She won't mention it again, I know that much.

I can get on with my life now. I can make new friends, if I really have to, friends like Nima, even though she's a freak. If Rosie, Soraya and Jaye don't think I'm "fun" anymore, they can move on without me. Soraya can have Tyler, for all she wants. Maybe he'll be a better match for her, somehow, than he was for me.

I tap onto Instagram, just for something to do. I'm exhausted, yet hauling myself out of normal clothes and into pyjamas seems like such an *effort*. If my mind wasn't so active, I'd go to sleep there and then, bra and all. I refresh the page, eyes already closing, when a photo of Soraya pops up on my feed.

It's a selfie, heavily filtered to make her eyes huge and her skin seem silky smooth. She's smiling, lips pressed into a thick, pink line, brown eyes focused on the camera. It already has tons of comments – Soraya's pretty well-liked – and so I scroll through them, reading carefully, heart pulsing.

There, at the very bottom, is a comment from Tyler. He's changed his profile picture since we broke up, switching it from a soft sunset photo I always loved to a screenshot from one of his weight-lifting sessions. The comment reads, in very smug letters:

**oh you peng ting**

It's vile.

But I'm not surprised, which is perhaps why I'm not as upset as I should be. Soraya's gullible and Tyler's a douche, and there's no getting round that – it's not like they've *changed*.

I'm the one who's changed.

I throw my phone onto the floor beside me, not even bothering to plug it in. It's Tuesday morning now, a fresh day, only a week into my final year at Vibbington Secondary School and Sixth Form. It's the year we apply to university, get part-time jobs, focus hard on our studies...

It's a new day, and I'm so, so ready for it.

# 35

On Tuesday morning, I have maths first again. Our school works on a fortnightly rota, and my second week on the timetable is pretty maths heavy, which is just my luck. I debate cowering under the covers for all of five seconds, when a lump leaps over me and lands on top of my legs.

"Jenna!" I howl, as pain shoots through my shins. "Get off me!"

"I'm waking you up!" she exclaims, leaning back and grinning. "And giving you a lift."

I start to object, turning over and nestling further into my pillow, but she prods my arm – and then my face and my nose, and then my closed eyes.

"You're going to school, Mace. You need to show Tyler you're not affected by his lies!"

"But I *am* affected," I mumble, which causes her to leap from the bed and pull my duvet right off me. "Fine, fine, I'll go! I'm not affected, I'm not affected!"

"I'll meet you downstairs in half an hour." Then she disappears from the room in a haze of blood-scented perfume and morning breath.

I dress in nice clothes, forcing myself to look like the normal Macey Collins. Jenna's right. I can't let him think that he's hurt me, or it'll only boost his ego further. It's raining heavily, such a contrast from yesterday, so I pull out a turtleneck, denim skirt and tan Uggs. I'll show him who's *really* missing out from this.

Jenna's waiting in the kitchen with Mum's infamous blueberry pancakes, so I take the plate gratefully and smile at our mother. She's already dressed for a day at the office, but she's smiling, eyes bright, and passes the tub of yoghurt with a quick, "You look nice!"

"You do too," I say, and her smile grows even wider. I wolf down the pancakes at breakneck speed, and they're surprisingly good, even without my chocolate addition.

The school gates are crammed with milling students by the time we arrive. I'm buzzing with nerves. Jenna holds her thumbs up but it doesn't do much to stop me from panicking as I climb out of the car. My heart's in my mouth and I can't stop shaking, clutching at the inside of my sleeves.

It's the first time I've ever gone to school feeling like everybody hates me. I'm likeable, never involved in scandals or drama. It isn't like me to be spoken about, even – only when I first got with Tyler, and that wasn't exactly *bad*.

I pass the smokers, sat in their usual alcove just outside the gates. They don't know me – they're a couple years younger – yet I can feel their eyes on me, judging. I remember one of them from last week, a girl with clumpy false eyelashes who stared as I passed. She's there now, puffing away on her cigarette, filling her lungs with cancerous smoke in order to look cool. Her school skirt is too small and her tie hangs out of her pocket, and she's stood with her back against an older boy, watching me as I glide past, thinking she's too good for the likes of goody-two-shoes me.

We probably have more in common than she thinks.

The sixth form block is at the other end of the school. It's early still, but I know that's where my friends will be, gnawing at their bacon butties and discussing celebrities, scrolling through Rosie's Instagram and rating outfits. Tyler will be there. Rhys and Jed and Bob will be there – and Darcie Carlton.

Soraya will be there.

I swallow.

I need to do this.

My boots are heavy on the tarmac as I take long strides towards the building, arms swinging beside me like awkward gorilla paws. It feels like all eyes on me, even though I'm invisible.

The doors are wide open, so I don't need to use my card. It's like they're inviting me in – or warning me.

It's too easy.

Why am I doing this?

Rosie, Soraya and Jaye are sat right opposite the doors. They all turn to stare at me as I walk in. I catch Rosie's eye and she waves me over. Soraya glances away immediately.

"Macey!" my best friend calls. "Come on over!"

I know I'm being watched. I can feel Darcie and her table pointing, like poisonous frogs in the corner of the room. The common room has fallen silent, the serving hatch buzzing from the other end. My feet are loud on the floorboards.

"Hey," I say, dropping onto the sofa. "How are you all?"

They all reply amicably, nodding and smiling, but there's an edge to the atmosphere around us, something chilly. Tyler and his posse aren't here yet – they either went straight to maths, or decided to get Subway orders before class.

"And how are you?" Jaye asks. "You look exhausted."

"We were worried, you know." Rosie reaches to grasp my hand. "Really worried."

I smile, brushing off their concerns.

I'm fine. I *am* fine.

"I'm okay." A pause. "Yeah, I'm good."

"We don't believe Tyler, if it's any consolation."

I freeze, meeting Jaye's eyes again. I don't know why I assumed they'd take his side, but I never for one moment thought they'd believe *me*.

"You don't?" I echo. Rosie and Jaye exchange exasperated glances, before turning back to me with tiny smiles.

"Obviously," Rosie says. "As if Tyler would break up with *you*, Mace. You're far too good for him!"

Relief is pumping through my body as I squeeze Rosie's hand, eyes filling with tears. How daft was I? Of course they're on my side. They're my best friends.

Yet Soraya still isn't speaking, staring down at the half-eaten tuna baguette on her lap. The other two notice me watching her, and step in quickly.

"Soraya believes you too, Mace. She just knows Tyler better than us – it's a bit weird that he'd lie to her, though."

Oh, yes.

Totally bizarre.

"You're gonna have to tell us *everything*, though," Rosie cuts in, and it's back to normal. She's gazing at me with enthusiasm, eager to gossip and giggle, and Jaye seems exactly the same, asking six billion questions about the breakup and the party and where I got to yesterday, and why I did it in the first place.

I try to answer everything, managing to even make them laugh, taking a bite from Rosie's ketchup-soaked bacon butty. It feels like it did before the accident, like we're just four, normal friends, exchanging conversation and burbling with laughter as the common room dances around us, full and happy and *alive*.

Soraya doesn't say a word.

***

I was right – Tyler and his cronies went straight to maths. They're having extra tutoring as I walk in, struggling over an exam paper, our teacher sat before them with her legs wrapped round a chair.

Tyler catches my eye, but I glance away. I don't want to look at him.

Nima is already at her desk, highlighters and gel pens and even a tiny watercolour set placed beside a washi tape dispenser. Her kitten sticker sheet is poking out of her maths book, and she's wearing the tiniest matching polka-dot skirt and top.

"Morning," she says. She shifts to the left and begins to move some of the stationary out of my way, cheeks pink. "I didn't think you'd sit with me again, so…"

I'm equally embarrassed, and sit down without saying a word. The other students are filing in now, so there's no need.

All eyes are on me. It was bad enough in the common room, but now, in the tiny room with nowhere to hide, it feels like they're burning right into my skull. I focus on my book, copying down a list of questions from the board, scribbling as my mind distorts the numbers into figures twice their value. I feel like I'm going to throw up at any second.

The lesson seems to drag, which doesn't help matters. I can't seem to focus, mind spinning, vision blurring. The squares on the paper turn to circles, bubbles which overlap and froth and –

"Do you want me to explain?"

Nima is watching me, dark eyes kind. I don't take in her words at first, but she pulls my book towards her and extracts a blue gel pen from the pile, slowly beginning to guide me through the problems with careful annotations and her soft, gentle voice. I try to follow along, focusing on her finger, but it's fuzzy and the writing won't seem to stay still.

It's a relief when the teacher finally announces that we can pack up and leave, and I start pushing things into my bag, not caring when one of my worksheets rips and my pencil case squashes it into a crumpled mess. Nima stares at me, one eyebrow raised, as I try to leave as quickly as possible in order to just *get out*.

"Are you okay?" she asks, but I just nod, standing and trying to get past her. "Macey, you're so tense. What's up?"

I know they're not looking anymore, but I feel like the others are still staring at me, eyes narrowed and filled with disgust. I try to squeeze behind Nima again, but she won't budge.

"Macey? Is it Tyler?"

I nod again, though this time I feel even more nauseous than before. People are slowly leaving but Tyler is still sat at his desk, gnawing on his pencil and glaring down at his sheet.

"If it makes you feel any better, he was acting a lot better after you left yesterday – I think he realised he pushed it too far, and was trying to stop the other guys from following suit and being total dicks." Nima passes me my water, which I left on the desk without even realising. "I think he was just showing off. Everyone knows it wasn't as simple as he made out. He's just that kind of guy, and his mates are too dumb to argue."

I stop struggling for a second, pulling back to look at her. "Do you really mean that? Or are you just saying that because I freaked out and it scared you?"

"You don't scare me, Macey." Nima smiles to herself,

pushing her chair back further and standing to face me. I try my best not to look her in the eye. "You don't scare me at all. If anything, you intrigue me."

A shiver darts down my back as she says that.

I intrigue her. I interest her.

She somehow *sees* me.

"You're not as normal as you make out, are you?" Her dark eyes gaze into mine, curious. I gulp.

"No one's normal, really," I say. "Even if they might seem it."

"I think I'd like to spend more time with you, Macey Collins." She starts pushing her stationary back into her bag, a small smile tugging on her lips again. I go to help, picking up her exercise book and holding it out to her.

"I'm not very fun," I tell her. Because I'm not. If anything, I'm the opposite.

"I'm not looking for *fun*," Nima retorts, and there's a glint in her eye this time, as she hoists her rucksack over her shoulders and pushes in her chair. "You should eat lunch with me and my friends some time."

I hesitate, unsure of what to say.

After the common room this morning, I'm not so worried about my friends and I. Apart from Soraya, they all seem pretty firmly on my side.

Yet there's something about Nima, something different. She's not disloyal, focused on her image or popularity, staying cool. Honesty hangs around her like a cloud. You know what you're getting with her – no confusion.

"That sounds good." I make the first step to leave, and she stands back to let me pass. "Maybe I'll see you in the common room later?"

"Yeah," she says, grinning. It's a grin which lights up her

whole face and those almond brown eyes, gazing into mine. "Maybe you will, Macey."

# 36

I think I spoke too soon, assuming everything would be okay. Jenna was oblivious, I told myself, and my friends weren't asking questions. Everyone would just move on, forget that Lexie's death could ever have been more than just an *accident*.

That's why I was so shocked when I got the phone call.

"Is this Macey?" came a voice from down the line.

I was sat on my bed on Wednesday evening, feet tucked under my knees, heart pounding. I was working on my maths homework, and Nima was messaging me with help, though we kept breaking off to discuss Netflix shows instead of trigonometry. We actually have a lot more in common than judgemental Macey assumed; we love all the old American shows, *Friends* and *How I Met Your Mother*, and Nima has all this *Gilmore Girls* merch in her bedroom, which she sends me photos of and promises she'll show me one day.

I like her, weirdly.

I like her a lot more than I ever thought I would.

"Yes?" I answered, clutching the phone to my ear. "Macey Collins, speaking."

"It's Mrs McCoy, Lexie's mum."

Every muscle in my body froze.

"Hello," I replied, though my voice was awkward, stilted. "How are you?"

"Getting by, getting by."

Getting by wasn't good enough, I knew that. It was like

saying you were balancing the Eiffel Tower on your little finger, struggling to hold it up while paying attention to the rest of the world.

"I'm glad to hear it," was what I answered, despite her words filling me with guilt.

"You see, we were wondering… would you like to come for tea sometime this week? What with you being so close to her, we thought it'd be nice to give something back. I know she really respected you, Macey."

My heart was pounding, tongue thick. I hesitated for a second as the phone grew clammy in my hand.

"Macey?" Mrs McCoy repeated. "Feel free to say no if you have too much going on with your studies…"

"No, no, it's fine." I couldn't say *no*. It was like some awful wall inside of me, forcing me to please her. "I'd love to come round, Mrs McCoy. I'm sure it's what Lexie would've wanted."

"Excellent!" she said. "We'll see you at our place on Friday, around four? I'll text you the address."

She hung up.

That was two days ago. It's now Friday night, and I'm sat in front of my mirror, hair in a dinky bun and wearing one of my nicest dresses.

I don't want to go. No part of me wants to walk back into the house Lexie lived in, sit at the table she once sat at, with the family I stole her from.

I want to curl up and crawl back into bed, but I can't.

I have to do this. Mrs McCoy was right. It's what Lexie would've wanted.

A message from Rosie pings through at that moment, wishing me luck. Another from Nima arrives shortly afterwards. Over the last few days, I still haven't taken up her offer of sitting with her and her friends in the common room, but we have been growing closer amidst our bonding over TV shows and Disney films, and I'm not mad about that. Rosie and I seem to have gone back to normal, too, though Soraya still hasn't spoken to me. But that's not what tonight is about.

I grab my bag and sling it over my shoulder, gazing into the mirror. My blue eyes are bright, blonde hair straightened, skin smoothed. I look nice, normal, like I'm going on a date or dressing up nice for a girl's night out. I don't look like I'm going to the home of my first murder victim, to schmooze her family into liking me.

"Macey?" Mum yells up the stairs. "Macey, are you coming, love?"

*Deep breaths, Macey.*

The journey only takes five minutes or so, though we drive up and down the street several times to check we've gotten the right house. It's a tiny, suburban cul-de-sac, like the one Bob lives on, only smaller and more naff. The houses are squat, lit by bright orange lamps, and the front gardens are knotted with weeds and pebbles and broken bicycles. The cars on each drive are old and muddy, and peeling garage doors make way for tacky home gyms, compiled of three weights and an Argos treadmill.

Call me a snob, but we don't belong here. Mum's nose is upturned, expensive, lipsticked lips pressed together in a thin line. She pats my arm as we pull towards the house and stop, car groaning beneath us.

"Will you be okay if I leave you?"

I nod. I don't want her to come in with me; it'll only make things worse. I wonder if Mrs McCoy knows her brother-in-law has been sleeping with my mum since the funeral. Doyle was there only a few days ago, using our shower. I caught him coming out of the bathroom, a towel round his hairy waist. He always acts so awkward, embarrassed, which makes the situation ten times worse.

He's not like Mum's usual boyfriends, and has lasted a lot longer than her usual hook-ups. Which makes me wonder why Doyle McCoy is still here, still exists within the Collins' household. Why he's even *bothering*.

"You'll be fine," Mum adds, now. "Have a good time, love."

The pavement is slimy beneath my Converse, like someone has power-washed it moments before. It's green, and tufts of grass shoot up through the cracks.

I twist my head up towards the house.

It's small, semi-detached, clutching a neighbour tight to its side. The front door is made of that tacky fake-plastic stuff they use for window frames sometimes, filled with frosted glass panes. There's a plastic slide on the front patch of lawn, which has probably been there since the beginning of time. Greenery springs up around it.

I make my way up the drive to rap on the door, breath held. There are lights on in every window, including the one above, which has pink curtains and a gauzy feather-light suspended from the ceiling. The kitchen is right next to the front door, and I watch a shadow moving across the glass towards me.

Mrs McCoy pulls open the door. She's wearing a blue jumper and skinny jeans, blonde hair crimped, eyes tiny and twitchy behind her glasses.

"Macey!" she announces, smiling and going to hug me. "It's lovely to see you!"

I shrink back as her warm arms go around me, enveloping me in an embrace that smells of talc and vanilla. It's chilly outside, but the scent of roast lamb curls out of the house, like a sly welcome.

"Come on in!" she says, beaming and pulling back. "We've got tea on the go already, and Mike's got a batch of Yorkshire puddings on the go..."

I follow her into the house.

It's like I expected, I suppose. The rooms are cramped and the hallway sparse, shoes and coats lined up on racks and pegs. Lexie's things are still there, sharp jabs of pink amongst blues and greys and blacks. Mrs McCoy leads me into the kitchen with one hand in mine, and drops me onto a chair around the tiny table. There are photo magnets all over the fridge, along with colourful felt-tip drawings and hand-painted vases, three kiddie canvases filling the side among various bottles of cordial and wine. There's a family portrait in a frame, painted by someone who's been very generous with pink paint and sparse with the hair.

I never knew Lexie liked art.

"She painted that a few months ago," Mrs McCoy says, following my gaze. "She used to love drawing and creating things, so we bought her a set of acrylics for Christmas. That was her best piece yet; she worked on it for weeks after school, for her dad's birthday. We had it framed. We were so, so proud of her."

I smile, nodding, though there's a lump in my throat I can't suppress. So Lexie loved painting – and she was good at it. I try not to imagine what a few more years of practise could've done to her, or where it would've taken her.

"We were planning on buying her oil paints for Christmas," Mrs McCoy continues. "Imagine the mess! They don't come out of anything no matter how much bleach you use. But Lexie was adamant that that was all she wanted, poor love. Not more makeup, not more stationary… a set of proper artist's paints."

I smile again. It's becoming exhausting, slapping on this cheesy expression.

"My sister uses oil paints," I say. "Her carpet's been ruined since forever."

We both laugh, if only to fill the awkward silence.

I'm relieved when Mr McCoy trundles in from the garage, clutching a rolled-up newspaper and reading glasses. He smiles and waves upon seeing me, so I wiggle my fingers back and swallow. My throat's so, so dry.

"Macey!" he says, nodding jovially. "It's great to see you again. How've you been keeping?"

"I'm okay," I answer. Is it a lie? Who knows.

He sets about chopping vegetables for the meal while I make small talk with his wife. It's less weird now, and I'm almost growing used to the paintings and artefacts and photos glowing from every surface. It's kind of nice, kind of awful. She's dead, but her memory's kept alive by this house, this semi-detached shrine to the dear departed.

"Macey?" Mrs McCoy interrupts my thoughts. "Can I show you something?"

I follow her up the stairs, two at a time. The landing is even smaller than the hall downstairs, cluttered up by a drying rack and clothes bin, a basket of clean undies on the floor beside it. I step over it in order to traipse after Lexie's mother, as she pushes down on the handle of one of the doors and leads me into the bedroom at the very front of the house, the one with the pink curtains and feather lightshades.

"This was Lexie's room," she says, as she opens the door.

It's pink, very pink. The walls, bedding and rug are all shades of salmon, carpet barely visible beneath all of the furniture. It's a tiny room, compact, but it's just so *Lexie*.

"I thought you might want to see it," Mrs McCoy adds. I glance at her, only to find her blue eyes fixed on mine. She's watching me carefully for any kind of reaction, for the slightest change of face. "I thought it might... help."

Help what? I try to swallow again, but my throat is still dry and my tongue seems to have doubled in size, lolling lazily against my teeth like a big, red snake. It's dry, too, crusty, reptilian. Is there no liquid left in my body?

I remember the way she looked at me at Lexie's funeral, like she knew something about me, like she suspected something. She's gazing at me that same way now, eyes narrowed, set straight against me.

"Why did you invite me here?" I ask, though I'm not sure if I want to know the answer. The room is shrinking in on us, trapping us closer together in a tight, pink bubble.

"I told you why," she replies, though her expression is flat, unchanging. "You were Lexie's friend, and this is what she would have wanted. Can't you see that?"

I don't move a muscle. She's still staring at me, eyebrows slowly knitting into one.

"Don't worry, I don't suspect you." She smiles, though her eyes are still cold and her teeth don't show. "You're not in trouble. Nobody thinks you had anything to do with Lexie's death. You're in the clear."

I don't think I'm imagining the bitterness in her voice.

"Now, shall we go downstairs? Mike's made a lovely roast, and it'll be ready soon..." She moves aside for me to pass, but I still don't budge. My feet are glued to the pink rug, illuminated by the lamp shade of one hundred white feathers.

"I'm sorry for your loss, Mrs McCoy. I really wish I could've done something that night..."

But Mrs McCoy just clucks her tongue and shakes her head, turning to go. "I wish you hadn't done anything at all."

# 37

They sit me at the head of the table, opposite Mr McCoy. They don't need to tell me this was once Lexie's place. Daniel, her little brother, sits to one side of me. He hasn't said a word yet, but picks at his roast lamb and veggies like they're made of clay.

"Eat up, Danny boy," his dad says, prodding his arm with a fork. "You love your roast dinners!"

I take a mouthful. It tastes good, homely and warm, despite the gravy being made with granules and the slightly fatty lamb. We continue to eat without saying a word, a television playing in the living room to no audience.

When Daniel first came down the stairs, he stared at me with the reproachful eyes of someone who'd been betrayed. He got a glass of blackcurrant cordial and sat at the table with his little legs crossed, staring determinedly at his plate. Mrs McCoy introduced me as "Lexie's friend", to which his bottom lip trembled and his hand almost let go of the knife.

The silence was stilted, painful. Daniel wouldn't even look at me after he first walked in, watching his food and pushing it round and round with his knife and fork. I don't blame him, really. I wouldn't want to look at me either.

I shouldn't have come; that much is obvious. None of them want me here. They just want a confession.

I gulp, taking a sip from the glass of wine Mr McCoy poured me. It's dry, like sandpaper against my tongue, and cheap, as though they bought it on special offer in Lidl. The sound of knives and forks clinking against ceramics rings around the kitchen, and the oven buzzes in the corner.

"So, Macey," Mrs McCoy says, breaking the silence at last and placing down her fork to turn to me. "Are you still helping out at guides, or…"

It's a strange conversation starter, but I gulp and answer anyway.

"I am," I say. It was a decision I felt I had to make – I couldn't just stop going. It'd either look suspicious, or like I was giving up, and I don't know what would be worse. "It's not starting up again until October, though. Sharon felt it wouldn't be appropriate to get normal sessions going again so soon."

"I see." Mrs McCoy nods. "I see…"

We're silent for another few minutes, eating slowly, though none of us have much of an appetite. Daniel is cutting his meal up into very small pieces, sucking up his peas individually and chewing for far too long on each morsel of lamb. He lifts a carrot to his mouth and bites off the tiniest slice, barely visible on the stick of orange as he places it back down.

"Does she have any more special trips planned?" Mrs McCoy continues. "Any camps, perhaps? I've heard Sharon runs excellent ones – the food in particular is supposed to be fab. I remember cooking an open fire when I was a Brownie. It doesn't feel like two weeks ago, let alone twenty odd years!"

I force a smile. "No, there's nothing planned. A party at Christmas, like usual, but nothing special. You can come, if you'd like?"

The party is a yearly thing, and always has been. The girls

dress up and invite their school friends, and we use it as a sort of promotion session, persuading other kids to join the guiding community. There's food and tea and orange squash for the children, and we sing Christmas songs far too loud throughout the chapel, ending with a game of hide and seek among the pews. It's a big deal, the highlight of our year.

"Of course." Mrs McCoy nods again, eyes still fixed on me as she takes her next mouthful. "Though it's understandable why you haven't planned anything else. I suppose it'd hardly be fair, would it? Poor love, she would've loved more special adventures. That's one of the hardest parts about losing a child, you know, Macey. I keep thinking of how much she's missing out on, how many experiences she won't have because of… this."

I try to pull my best sympathetic face, but all the blood in my body is rushing to my head and I have to reach for the glass again. Mr McCoy offers me a refill and I hold it out for him gratefully.

"Of course, she was a shy girl, there's no doubt about that. She never fit in here. The other girls didn't seem to *get* her. I don't understand why." Mrs McCoy frowns, then glances back at me. "Do you know why she struggled so much, Macey? Why she never really made good friends?"

I shake my head. I don't know, not really. It's not as though Lexie ever did anything *wrong*.

"She never told me anything, you know. She tried to hide it from us. She acted like she loved guiding, like she loved school and all of her little friends. But I knew. I could tell there was something wrong, always."

"She was just different," I say, taking another Yorkshire pudding from the platter in the centre of the table. They're the frozen kind, a little too crispy. "She was lovely, but the other girls wanted her to be the same as them, I guess."

Mrs McCoy grimaces. "I'm sure." Then she adds, "Do you think that might've been the reason she died, Macey? Do you think... I don't know, maybe this is crazy, but do you think she could've died... deliberately?"

I almost choke on my roast potato. I reach for my wine to take another sip, and the McCoys watch me, unresponsive, as I try to get my breath back.

"The police ruled out suicide, didn't they?" I ask. "They said it was unlikely she'd have bothered going on the swing, not when the river was right there for her to jump."

"Perhaps she didn't want people to know it was suicide," Mrs McCoy presses. "Maybe she thought it would hurt us more if we knew the truth –"

"Love, calm down." Mr McCoy grasps his wife's hand and smiles at her, squeezing gently. "You don't need to agitate yourself."

"Agitate myself?" Mrs McCoy spins to face her husband, blue eyes wide and full of tears. "Agitate myself? When our daughter *died*, and this girl won't tell us anything? She's the key to unlocking it all, Mike!"

Daniel slides off his chair and disappears into the next room, little face trembling. They barely notice him leave. I swallow, putting down my cutlery. I'm only making things worse by being here. They want answers, and *I can't give them that.*

"I think I should go," I say, to which their heads swivel towards me like dolls. "It'd be best for us all if I just –"

"You're not going anywhere!" Mrs McCoy says, pointing a finger right at me. "You need to tell us what happened, Macey!"

"You know what happened!" I insist, though my cheeks

are colouring and my heart's racing. Mrs McCoy is shaking her teary face in mine, like she's never, ever going to believe me. "You know as much as I do!"

"I know that some way or another, you had something to do with her death." She stands, so that she's right in front of me. I can smell mint sauce on her breath. "You didn't prevent it, did you? My little girl was unhappy for months, and you did *nothing*!"

Tears are rolling down my own face now, hot and salty against my skin. I take a step back, hitting the radiator, and she leans so that her blue eyes are only millimetres from mine.

"You murdered my daughter," she whispers. The room is so silent now that I can hear the tap dripping above the sound of the oven, a light pattering of rain hitting the window behind me. "You murdered my daughter, and I'm going to find out how."

# 38

I run all the way home, feet smacking the wet pavement as I go. The sky is dark now, littered with clouds, and the moon gazes down from above the rooftops. It's raining down hard, tiny droplets of water which explode against my skin, chilling me to the bone. It's freezing, so freezing, and I flinch at every passing car in case it stops to check I'm okay.

"I'm fine!" I roar, against the quiet, suburban street. "I'm fucking *fine*!"

I'm not fine.

I'm

not

fine.

I want to go home and crawl back into bed, but I know I can't do that. I don't want to talk to my mum, I don't want to talk to Jenna, I don't want to answer my phone.

But there's no other option.

I pick up the pace, tears streaming down my cheeks as I race onto our street. A gang of teenage boys loitering on the corner shout crude remarks at my retreating figure, so I flip up my middle finger and continue to race, until the gates outside of our drive come into view and I career upwards. I still feel sick as I pull open the door and rush straight upstairs, practically throwing my shoes off at the front door. I hear Mum shout for me, but I can't seem to stop.

Once in my bedroom, I slam the door shut and collapse

on the middle of the floor with a sharp cry. My face is wet with tears and my hands shake as I claw at the carpet, fingers scrabbling desperately, burning with pain. I can't breathe, I can't breathe, I can't breathe –

*You murdered my daughter!*

I murdered her daughter.

I fucking *killed Lexie.*

I don't deserve this. I don't deserve this nice house, to visit Lexie's parents and eat their roast lamb in Lexie's chair, using Lexie's plate, next to Lexie's brother. I can't breathe, but maybe it's just because I don't want to – or because I don't have the right to.

Phlegm rising in my throat for one last time, I drag myself over to the wardrobe and tug open the door. My hand delves right down to the bottom and scrabbles about under loose tops and jeans and tucked-in socks until I find the thing I'm looking for.

I pull out Mr Sparkles, all matted pink fur, loose mouth and missing eye. He's warm since the radiator runs right by the back of the wardrobe, and his bedraggled mane is ratty. I hold him to me, breathing in his soft, talcum-powder scent, the same as that of Mrs McCoy, but all I can smell is Lexie.

I start to cry properly now, sobs that burst through my body and explode out of my mouth, harder and harder, faster and faster. I sob for Lexie, for the life I stole from her… and I sob for her family, for the daughter they lost because of me.

But on top of all that, I cry for myself.

I could've had everything. The boyfriend, the friends, the volunteering experience to lead me into a career in speech therapy, a life at university with two of my besties. I'm pretty, everyone says so. People like me. *Liked* me.

And now it's ruined. Lexie is ruined. My brain doesn't

seem to work the same, and my body barely functions at its normal pace. It's broken. *I'm* broken.

Mr Sparkles stares at me, all forlorn expression and sad eyes, scrunched up on my lap like a sad little child.

I ruined him, too. I took him from Lexie like a kid stealing candy from a baby, right out of the jaws of death with scarcely a look back.

I'm holding Mr Sparkles, stroking his funny little body, when there's a knock on the door. I freeze. It comes again, harder, before someone pushes down on the handle and enters.

"Mace?" It's Jenna. Her hands are covered in paint and her face is white without its usual makeup, nails stubby and bare. She frowns upon seeing me, closing the door carefully behind her. "I heard you crying, so I thought I'd check if you were okay…"

Then she stops. I try to hide Mr Sparkles from her but she spots him cowering behind me and points, finger trembling, at the lump.

"That's Lexie's teddy, isn't it?" she asks, eyes wide. "The one they couldn't find when they searched the river."

I don't move. We stare at each other, equally horrified, as the clock on the wall ticks.

"Macey, what the fuck are you doing with that? Do you have any idea how incriminating this is? They think she took it with her to the river that night, and now you have it, and you haven't told anyone –"

"Lexie didn't have it that night." My voice is colder than expected, and it causes Jenna to lean back against the door for support. She lowers herself until she's sat opposite me, back to the frame.

"What do you mean?" she asks, eyebrows knitted. "You

were in your tent that night, Mace. How do you know what Lexie took to the river?"

The clock continues to tick, like the timer of a bomb.

I smile. It hurts my face.

"I was with her," I say, trying not to let my voice crack. "I was with her when she died, Jen."

"Macey..." She's shaking her head, not getting what I'm saying, visibly confused. "Mace, what are you saying?"

I take a deep breath.

There's no holding back now – nowhere to hide.

"I'm saying that I killed her, Jen. I killed Lexie."

# 39

Lexie was the only thing on my mind as I crawled back into my tent on the second evening of camp. Her pale face as she refused to go on the tyre swing, stark white in my mind, those grey eyes staring right at me.

"It's just too dangerous, it'd be stupid to go at night..." she'd whispered, but the other girls had just laughed.

I was glad she hadn't agreed to use the tyre swing, of course – it really was too dangerous, and most likely would have ended in disaster. Yet part of me just couldn't see why she'd refused. Did she want to be a laughingstock, mocked mercilessly by Chloe and her cronies, forever an outsider and afraid to take chances?

If she wanted to fit in, she had to at least *try*.

I turned onto my side, the tent sagging above my head. I didn't dare glance at my phone again, terrified that there'd be a message from Rosie, another selfie with Tyler's hand lingering on Soraya's body, snuggled beneath the covers. They'd all gone home by now, of course, but the thought still haunted me. I squeezed my eyes shut in an attempt to get some sleep.

Wind waged war on the forest as I tried to get comfortable, tossing and turning, hot and sweaty in my sleeping bag. It ripped through the trees and howled into the black night, screaming itself hoarse until the noise was indistinguishable from a banshee's squeal, electrifying as it flew through the darkness.

Somewhere, through the back copse and bracken, cried the river. It was swirling, pulsing, alive with a sullen intensity that seemed to grow as I lay there, listening, ears pricked. Water bashed the rocks and lapped the edges of the decking, sending spray hurtling up the trunks and covering them in weeds and slime. My heart surged in time with the rhythmic crashing, over and over again, like a melody or a drum's beat.

Then I heard it.

A softer sound, closer to home, the gentle tearing of material. It almost sounded like a rip, enough to turn my skin cold and stop the breath in my throat, a knife sliding through the tent above me.

It wasn't a knife, however. It was just the zip, slowly pulling upwards to open the door.

"Macey?" came a tiny, forlorn voice. A torch flashed across my face, bright white and blinding, and I held my hand up to block it from my sight. "Macey, I need your help."

There was a slight rustling and the sound of wellies being pulled off as Lexie emerged through the flap, all big eyes and luminous cheeks. She placed her torch on the ground so that the space was lit by a scattering of light and we could see each other properly.

A breeze rushed in through the open door, and I shivered beneath my sleeping back. Lexie just sat there, staring, waiting for me to respond.

"What are you doing?" I asked, reaching for my hoody and tugging it on as I sat up. "It's late. You should be asleep!"

"I need you to come with me," she hissed back. "Chloe was right, I am a wimp. I need to use the tyre swing, Macey – I need to show them I'm not pathetic!"

The tyre swing? She couldn't be serious. It was pitch black

outside and the wind was horrendous, and the river could be heard from here, swirling and tumbling and growling. But Lexie's face was insistent, mouth set in a firm, determined line as she watched my expression, breath held.

She was *definitely* serious.

"Please, Macey," she whispered. "I need to do this, and I'll need some help…"

"Why can't we use it tomorrow?" I replied, eyes narrowed. "When it's light, and Sharon can help you!"

"Because I'll lose face then, with everyone watching me!" She could sense how hesitant I was, and pushed further, adding, "It'll give me so much more confidence in myself, and with you there, you can prove that I did it and that I'm really not a baby…"

"But if Sharon finds out, I'll be in big trouble," I cut in. "We both will, Lexie. This isn't just about Chloe and the others, it's about *us* – I'm not putting you in danger just because of a bit of name calling, it's not worth it!"

"It's completely safe, you said so yourself!"

She had me there. It was what I'd been insisting all weekend, that it was approved by health and safety and so there'd be no issues whatsoever. There was a harness, ropes, weight tests… and so there was no way it could go wrong, not really.

But something didn't feel right.

"We can't, Lex," I told her. "It's dark, so we can't see things as well, and we're not supposed to be out of bed. Go tomorrow, just you and Sharon, while we're taking down the tents. I'm sure no one would notice!"

"They would," she said. "You know they would. Please, Macey."

I still don't know why I couldn't say no.

\*\*\*

We crossed the field in our wellies, shivering in the night-time air, darkness enveloping our hoody-clad bodies. Lexie had the torch and flashed it ahead to check we hadn't reached the trees yet, dodging the fire and table, almost walking straight into the log shed.

"Stick close to me," she instructed, to which I rolled my eyes and took a step closer. The roles had reversed and Lexie was now in charge, tugging me towards the river and into dangerous territory.

As we stumbled into the undergrowth, nettles and bracken scratched at my leggings and branches seared my arms. I raised one hand to block myself from them as I bent to Lexie's height and scurried after her, heart pounding in my throat and filling my ears. This was ridiculous – *ridiculous*. Without the torchlight it was impossible to see a thing, and the ground and trees were slick with a splattering of raindrops, making it even harder to walk without slipping right over.

Through the trees, still quite a way off, the river churned. It was loud and insistent, yelling at us to hurry up, that it was hungry, that it wanted its tea.

"Hurry!" Lexie hissed. "I don't want anyone to notice we're gone, and I think I forgot to close my tent flap…"

So we'd left a trace – typical. I almost turned around then, so close to backing out and leaving Lexie safe and sound in her warm, dry tent, tucked up with Mr Sparkles. Yet that wasn't what would've happened. Lexie would've continued without me, no matter what.

We could feel the river's spray on our cheeks before we

saw it. The familiar body of water rose out of the woods like a pool of oil, jet-black and bubbling, resembling slime. It lapped at the decking with its thick tongue as we approached, wellies smacking the wooden planks. Lexie's eyes were wide as she turned to me, face pale in the torchlight, to ask what we should do next.

"Are you sure about this?" I asked, to which she nodded. Spinning round, she made her way over to where the tyre squatted and raised her hand to it, nodding once more.

"Shall I wear a lifejacket?" That's how I knew she was nervous.

"I think so." I rummaged in the shelter for one, pulling out a yellowed, shrivelled thing that was still soaked from the morning's kayak adventure. Maybe it wouldn't be much use, I wasn't sure, but it was something to calm our nerves. "And Sharon must *never* find out about this, okay? If you want to prove yourself to the other girls, just make sure they stay completely silent, or we'll both be in huge trouble."

"I'm not stupid." Lexie took the lifejacket off me and pulled it on, sticking out her stomach so that I could do up the buckles. I made sure it was tight, protecting her little body the best it could, then let her go and gazed over at the tyre.

It was attached to a rope system, which needed to be clipped to the pulley. The clip itself was easy to navigate and locked in tight, metal to metal, secure when I tugged on it. The tyre sat against the decking like a slightly squashed doughnut, smiling at us, luring us in.

Lexie was holding the harness. It was one of those that goes between the legs, round the waist and over the shoulders, locking you into place with six hundred different clips and bits of rope. It was tricky to get each piece correct, but Lexie angled the torch the best she could, until we knew it was safe enough that it wouldn't come undone.

"And now," I said, "we clip you to the tyre."

Lexie couldn't get the torch to shine directly on the part which secured her harness to the rope of the tyre, but hopped atop the wheel so that it was as easy as possible. Straddling it and clutching the rope, she passed me the clip on the end of her harness, and I reached up, waiting and hoping blindly to hear a clank of metal which would mean I'd attached it correctly.

The clip seemed to hit something, and the sound rung out into the night. I couldn't tell if it had attached, or if it was clutching the right thing. All I could do was hope.

"Are you ready?" I asked her. She still seemed pretty petrified, clutching it with her tiny white hands and gazing at me with those grey eyes. "Shall I hoist you up, Lex?"

She nodded in determination, and whacked the edge of the tyre with her hand.

"Yes," she said. "I'm ready, Macey."

# 40

I tugged on the rope, watching as Lexie rose away from me. She was still clutching the torch and so her face was illuminated as the tyre was pulled into the sky, higher and higher.

Beneath her, the river watched on. It was crashing and tumbling, wind whipping through the clearing and rustling the surrounding leaves, and Lexie's tyre twisted and wobbled as it was attacked from all angles.

"It's so cold!" she yelled, voice only just distinguishable above the sound of the rushing water. "The wind's awful up here, Macey, I don't know if it's safe!"

"You're all clipped in!" I called back, though it was making me feel queasy just watching her. "It's safe, I promise!"

"I don't know if I want to do this!" she shouted, and I could hear blatant terror in her voice. "It's too high and too windy – what if I fall?"

"Just hold on tight!" I insisted. It was easier than telling the truth – that now she was up there, it was impossible for Lexie to get down unless I swung her to safety.

"I can't do this!" she said, shaking her head so that the torchlight flickered. "Macey, get me down!"

"I'm sorry, Lex, you've just got to hold on tight and wait for it to be over. It'll be fun! Wait until you tell all of the others what you've done…"

"I don't care about the others, this is a stupid idea!" She was kicking her legs back and forth now, causing her to wobble and the metal of the clips to clink-clank like an old chain. "Macey, I can't do this –"

"Yes you can!" I yelled – and then I let go.

She was soaring, the tyre whipping through the sky as it swung towards me and back up into the trees. Her screams were disguised by the wind as she flew through the air, faster and faster, arms flailing behind her, not holding onto the rope as I'd told her to, torch clutched in her hand and illuminating her hair like a solitary white flag –

She seemed to fall in slow motion.

One minute, she was a bird in the black night, wings outstretched and ready to take off into the sky without me, without us. Then she was a pebble, dropping from a great height with the torch spinning away from her, hoody billowing and long, drawn-out screech echoing through the forest above the river's cry.

"Help me!"

There was a loud splash, the sound of something heavy hitting the water, her lifejacket smacking into the surface and dipping under. Heart pounding, I rushed to the edge. The river surged, waves hitting my legs as ripples extended from her landing spot, bubbles marking the spot.

"Lexie!" I cried, leaning forward and straining my eyes. I could barely breathe, scouring the surface desperately, hands outstretched. "*Lexie!*"

Something moved under the surface, a splash of yellow and the white of a still-on torch spinning under the fast current. The lump was moving away, caught up in the river, rising towards the night-time air as it was pushed further away from me.

A hand reached out of the water, pale blue and tiny. And then two shoulders. A pink welly. Her head.

"Help!" Lexie spluttered, scrabbling at one of the rocks. She tried to grasp at a tuft of grass but it broke off in her hand, scattering the surface. Her face was white and her mouth was swollen, eyes wide and full of terror as she tried to speak, river water burbling at her lips. "Macey, help me!"

I tried to grab her hand but it wasn't strong enough, so clutched at the harness's rope instead. Its clip was ice-cold beneath my fingers and too slippery to hold onto, and I lost my grip and she went spinning away, the yellow of her lifejacket stuck to my eyeballs. The current was too strong, water tripping over the rocks and splashing against me as she cried out once more, a strangled yell thick with water.

"Lexie!" I screamed again, but she was moving away too fast now, unresponsive as she lolled onto her back, limp body moving through the trees and away from me. "Lexie!"

It was too dark to see where she'd gone, and I didn't have another torch. I wasn't stupid – if I tried to go in after her, the river would swallow me whole. The kayaks were padlocked and the decking ended a little way off, giving way to slippery riverbanks and algae-covered rocks.

Yet I couldn't just *give up*.

Heart in my mouth and body wracked with cold guilt, I dashed forward, clambering over the embankment and watching the river for any sign of life. Moonlight shone through a hole in the canopy and I just spotted a flash of yellow before it was tugged away again, lost under the water's black body, pulsing against her.

I continued to run, unable to stop myself. I was faster now, wellies hitting the ground as I ran, keeping up with the river's current just enough to see her again, now veering to my side of the riverbank…

*Please let her be alive, please let her be alive –*

Her lifejacket snagged on a rock and I took my chance, splashing into the shallows to find her, moonlight just showing enough of her face to stop me in my tracks.

She was blue, completely blue, those grey eyes open wide and staring upwards. There was no life in her expression, just plain terror, mouth twisted into an ugly grimace. I watched, choking on my own saliva, as the river grabbed hold of her again and threw her body into its depths.

"Lexie!" I cried out, one last time, tears filling my eyes as I dropped to the ground. "*Lexie!*"

But she was gone.

\*\*\*

I cried until my throat was hoarse, dry-retching into my hands, stomach clenched and eyes closed. I was freezing cold, shivering in my hoody and leggings, water in my wellies and hands dripping with the ice-cold river's spittle.

*You killed her, you killed her, you killed her –*

I could barely breathe for that one line flying round my head, screaming against the sound of the river crashing against the rocks, spraying my face and trembling fingers. I killed Lexie. *I killed Lexie.*

If only I'd clipped the harness on properly, made sure she couldn't fall. She was still secured into those ropes when she fell, but the ropes weren't clipped to the tyre, which was no doubt still swinging back and forth above the water. Lexie would still be alive if I'd given it a proper tug to make sure it was safe, instead of just hearing the noise and hoping for the best…

I debated finding Sharon, just for a moment. Looking back, maybe it would have helped – maybe if the truth had come out then, I wouldn't be living in fear now. Yet having people know the truth about what happened to Lexie seemed somehow so much worse.

She was gone. Dead. I knew that. I'd seen it in her eyes. Sharon could do nothing to help. Nobody could, now.

My legs were wobbly as I made my way back along the river to the decking, tears still streaming down my face. The ground was wet against my wellies, slippery and loose, and I almost tumbled into a rock in my haste, just catching myself at the last moment. There it was, the tyre swing, suspended over the river on its rope.

It looked like a noose.

I stumbled over my feet, tripping over bracken and bits of broken logs and branches, shaking my head and stopping every now and then to clutch the tree trunks for support. *Don't be sick, don't be sick, don't be sick – no one can know you were ever here.*

I soon found the stone path that led back to the campsite, and tried to be as quiet as possible as my wellies crunched over the pebbles, towards the forest's opening. The wind was howling and the trees made a racket as they rustled. I knew the others were all tucked away in bed, but I didn't dare risk drawing attention to myself.

I passed Lexie's tent on the way to my own, and that's when I saw it. She'd left the flap open and her sleeping back was soaking wet, laid across the entrance and half on the grass in a soggy, pink mess. Mr Sparkles was sat atop it, staring at me beseechingly, one eye wide.

I don't know why I felt the need to take him, but something about leaving him there just felt… *wrong.*

We shut the door tight behind us, Mr Sparkles and I. In my own tent, with the flap zipped firmly shut and the night roaring around me, I felt almost... *safe*, in the worst way possible.

"I'm sorry," I whispered weakly, into Mr Sparkles' bedraggled ear. "I'm so, so sorry..."

What had I done?

# 41

I don't know how I managed to sleep that night. I tossed and turned as rain drizzled outside my tent, the dark sky turned murky with clouds and fog. Despite the fact it was summer, true Yorkshire weather shone through the sunshine, drenching the camp and wiping any evidence of my involvement clean from the deck. My fingerprints slid away in a haze of spray from the river and the slow downpour, hairs and spittle lost in the wind.

I was hot. Far too hot.

My body felt clammy and wet, palms sticky, forehead covered in beads of sweat. I tossed and turned, sleeping bag stuck to my skin like clingfilm. I couldn't get comfortable. My camping mat felt every lump and bump in the earth, every rock and clump of grass. They poked my back, taunting, never letting go –

All the while, Lexie's body lay in the river some way away, lifeless, cold. I tried not to think about it. I tried not to think about her staring eyes, grey and unmoving in her white skull. I tried not to think about those pink wellies, probably now loose in the water, drifting downstream. The thought still haunted me, impossible to escape.

*You killed her*.

It was Sharon who came to me first, crawling into my head, wiggling a finger in my face and shaking it so vigorously that her arms wobbled. She had that disapproving look on her face, the one grownups wear when you've done something really, really wrong, and was mumbling under her breath. I didn't want to listen, but her words were just *there*, seeping into my mind like tickling fingers. I couldn't block them out.

"I can't believe you'd do it, Macey. I just can't believe you'd do it…"

Next up were the girls, all four of them, screaming obscenities as I tried to bury my head in my pillow and ignore them, hair sticking to my face. Lucy, Kayleigh, Orla. And Chloe. Lots of Chloe. They wouldn't leave me alone, taunting and teasing, blaming, accusing me.

"You killed her!" they called. "She was our friend, and you killed her! It's all your fault!"

"It was your fault, too!" I wanted to yell back. "She only used the tyre swing because she wanted to prove herself to you!"

But it wasn't their fault, not really. It was mine, mine, mine. I was their leader, seventeen-years-old and incapable of stopping childish bullying, of carrying out a health and safety check, of looking after a child in my care.

Kids make mistakes, but adults *live* by them.

Rosie, Soraya and Jaye hurried towards me then, frowning and cocking their heads. They were taking photos on their iPhones, photos of the murderer, the girl who once walked among them but now stood alone. I watched as the comments came rolling in around their heads, lime green vomit emojis and knives.

**could always tell she was dodgy, what a vile human.
and to kill a kid like that, can't believe we let her into
our school!**

**ewww don't poison my eyeballs, she's so gross –**

**what a freak. murdering scum!**

The list went on and on.

As the rain poured and the night dragged, I howled until the fabric was wet and my cheeks were puffy, throat hoarse. I cried tears of guilt, like a cold hand that had wrapped itself around my throat and was pulling tight; tears of sorrow, sorrow for those I'd hurt, those like Lexie's family and those who'd loved her.

But mostly, I cried for Lexie.

I cried for the life she'd never lead, the boys she'd never kiss, the jobs she'd never have, the universities she'd never attend. I cried for her little brother, the family holidays she'd be absent from, the exams she wouldn't sit.

I cried for the pain. The cold water, rushing through her lungs and filling her mouth, choking her, burbling at those blue lips. The rush of rocks against her body, the current whipping her down the river too fast, clashing her head against the embankment. Those hands, scrabbling at the grass, tearing it away, scattering it across the water –

I couldn't tell anyone what had happened. I *couldn't*. No one could ever know that I'd not clipped her on right, causing her to drop to her death. They wouldn't see it as an accident – it would be murder, pure and simple.

Even if it *was* seen as an accident, not everyone would agree. I couldn't bear the disapproval, the shaking heads and pointing, the turned backs and stilted conversations. Losing my friends, the respects of those I loved, those who loved me.

Lexie was dead. Nothing could change that. Not me 'fessing up, revealing what really happened that night. Not me waking Sharon up now, causing more trauma and stress.

It wouldn't change the fact her body was laid in a bath of icy cold, swimming in murky brown water, face covered in a thick layer of algae and sludge. It wouldn't help anyone to know that without my input, Lexie might still be alive.

But would she? Would she have attempted the tyre swing by herself? It was impossible, physically impossible, but I wouldn't put it past her. She was determined, always, even in death.

I'd never know. I'd never know if I could've saved her, if my refusal would've made a difference. I'd never know the difference one clip could've made.

"Shit," I hissed, blinded by the tears. "*Shit.*"

Mr Sparkles seemed to agree with me. He'd turned stiff in my arms, like a rock, fur matted and cold. He'd died, just like Lexie, and his body hung against me like a constant reminder. I'd killed him too.

"I'm sorry," I repeated, though I wasn't sure who I was apologising to at this point. "I'm so, so *sorry.*"

# 42

Jenna sits opposite me, back against my door, eyes wide. I'm still clutching Mr Sparkles on my lap. The room is cold and the air is tense as we stare at each other blankly, unsure of what to say next.

"You killed her?" she echoes. "It was you who helped Lexie use the tyre swing? I always thought it was weird that she'd manage it by herself, but... the clip, not managing to do it up right. That was you?"

"It was all me," I say, though my throat is thick with unshed tears and my chest is tight. "All of it, right from the beginning, when I first met Lexie. I didn't stop the bullying, I didn't try to help her when she started changing herself to fit in, I didn't stick up for her when she needed me. I was useless, and now she's dead."

"But... I don't understand why you didn't just go to the police, Macey, straight away. It was an accident, but you've left it so long now that there's no evidence that it *wasn't* deliberate."

As if I don't know that already.

"We have to tell someone," she says, standing and grabbing the door handle. "Mace, her parents are going mad with suspicion and worry, and if you don't tell them it was you, you'll be in even more trouble when the truth comes out –"

But I can't let her do it. I jump to my feet, eyes watering

and hand outstretched to stop her, and shake my head.

"No, Jen, you can't tell anyone!" My voice sounds hard and cold even in my own head. It terrifies me, the urgency of my feelings. The extent I'll go to in order to cover my tracks. "Jen, they'll send me to a juvenile centre somewhere, or to a real prison soon – I'm almost eighteen! It's manslaughter, Jen, even if it's not murder! I'll lose everything. Uni, my friends, my A-levels…"

"It was an accident," she repeats, though she doesn't seem so sure now. Her eyes are filled with worry and her breathing is short, stilted. "You're a good kid, get good grades, you're focused in school. They won't send you anywhere, Mace, not if you just own up!"

But we don't *know* that. It's speculation, wishful thinking.

"I can't risk it," I insist. "If I tell them, they might think it's my guilty conscience talking –"

"What's more important?" Jenna is glaring at me, arms crossed, one hand still on the handle. "You getting away with this, or Lexie's mum and dad never knowing whether their little girl *killed herself* or not?"

I don't have an answer, awful as that may seem.

"Macey, you've got to tell them. I can't do that for you – I'm not a complete bitch – but I can tell you it's the only option here. You can't get away with this, it's *wrong*."

I nod, though my mind is spinning faster and faster. I don't notice dropping Mr Sparkles, but he lies on my rug now, flopped over and dejected. There's no life in him, no reason to cling on.

"Just promise me you'll think about it," she adds, and I nod again.

That's an easy promise to keep; I think about little else.

She sits down on the rug opposite me then, back still

facing the door. Reaching for Mr Sparkles, she tugs him onto her lap and sits, cross-legged, with him perched against her. He's stiff, sad. Cold. A shell, just like Lexie was.

"You need to finish the story, Mace," she says. "What happened after you went back to the tent? How did you not spill what happened when everyone woke the next morning?"

I grimace, the ghost of a laugh tickling my throat.

"That was the easiest part."

I was awoken by an urgent rustling at my tent door the next morning. I don't know how I managed to get a wink of sleep that night, but my eyes were puffy and I could barely open them as light shone through the flap and Sharon's head appeared, eyes wide.

"Macey!" she hissed, gesturing for me to stand. "Put something warm on and come outside, right now!"

I immediately thought the worst and my heart began to pound, but her expression was more worried than angry. I shoved Mr Sparkles further under my sleeping bag and crawled into my hoody, shivering. Sharon was clutching a saucepan. She began beating it violently with a spoon as I followed her into the sunlight.

Lexie's tent squatted next to mine, pink sleeping bag soaked and covered in mud. Her pillow hung by the door beside it.

"Girls!" Sharon yelled, going *bang, bang, bang* with the saucepan and spoon. "Girls, get up at once!"

Four sleepy heads emerged from their tents, bleary-eyed and snotty-nosed. They looked bewildered, clearly with no idea about what was happening, but their faces registered shock as they noticed Lexie's tent.

"Where's Lexie?" Lucy asked, voice trembling. "Has she gone home early?"

"That's what I'm trying to discover," Sharon replied,

though her face was set and her eyes narrowed. "Do any of you know where she's got to? Did you hear anything last night, or did anything happen after I went to bed?"

I couldn't stop my cheeks from flushing, but no one was looking at me. They were glancing at each other in confusion, shaking their heads back and forth.

"No," Chloe piped up. "Nothing. We played some games, then Lexie went into her tent. Nothing else happened. We went to sleep pretty much straight away."

"And you, Macey?" Sharon turned to me, voice more urgent now. "You heard nothing either?"

"Not a peep," I said. "I sent them to bed when it turned dark, and made sure they were all in their separate tents.

The lie slipped right off my tongue.

"We'll have to search the camp, then," Orla stated. "Make sure nothing bad happened to her…"

I'm pretty sure Sharon and I were both thinking the same thing. That if anything bad had happened to Lexie, the last thing we wanted was for the girls to find out first.

"You four get on with breakfast," Sharon instructed, frowning. "Macey and I will go look. When we find her, it'll be a nice surprise to come back to some nice warm food…"

We set off around opposite sides of the site, Sharon over to the toilet block and garage, me into the back forest. My wellies were still soaked from last night and so I'd tugged on my trainers, water seeping through the toes as I hurried along the path. I felt dizzy, heart pounding in my chest and hands clammy.

I hit the deck in a matter of minutes, though I knew she wouldn't be there. My feet pounded along the embankment, slipping and sliding, clutching at tree trunks and rocks in an attempt to stay upright. I followed the river right up until the edge of the site, where a fence sliced through the bank, the water beside me slow-flowing and empty.

It was clear, like glass, the pebbled ground untouched. I stared until my vision blurred.

"Shit," I murmured, craning my neck to try and see the rest of the river, my eyes following it until it veered around a corner and out of sight. "Oh *shit*."

Sharon was back at the camp already, helping the girls fry bacon and eggs in two large frying pans as Lucy and Orla sliced bread buns. Her face dropped as she saw me returning and ran out to greet me.

"Nothing?" she asked.

"Nothing."

So Lexie wasn't on the site. She hadn't just gone for an early morning walk. It was impossible for us to find her now, I knew that. She was probably halfway down the river in her yellow lifejacket.

The other girls had fallen silent, flipping the eggs and bacon and serving them up without saying a word, little hands trembling. Sharon's whole face was white. She wrung her hands as she paced the ground, one foot before the other, in some sort of routine.

"Right," she said, between gulps. "Right."

Our next port of call was to ring Mr and Mrs McCoy. We knew Lexie had been feeling homesick and that her parents would do anything to make her happy, so it seemed possible that she could've been picked up during the night. I watched, trying not to retch, as Sharon typed in the number from Lexie's consent form and watched as the screen flashed green.

"Hello?" came a voice down the line. "This is Tracey McCoy speaking. How may I help you?"

"It's Sharon. I don't want to panic you, but did you come

by here last night to pick Lexie up?"

Silence.

We waited, breaths held, for her to speak again.

"No." Then, in a more frantic tone, "Mike? Mike, come here, something's happened to Lexie!"

"As I said, I don't mean to alarm you, she's probably on the site still. But her tent was empty this morning, so we just thought –"

"We'll be right over to look for her," Mrs McCoy interrupted, and I could hear the nod in her voice. "Mike's just getting the car ready, so we'll be there in about half an hour."

"Like I said, try not to worry –"

But Mrs McCoy had already hung up.

I tried to eat one of the bacon sandwiches as we waited. It tasted like cardboard in my mouth. The bread was too thick, too stodgy, and the bacon was strong with smoke. Every part of my body screamed *guilty*, even if they had no idea.

Sharon suggested we started to take down the tents as we waited, and it was a relief to shut Mr Sparkles away in my bag. It was already pretty obvious that we'd have to call the police, though the others still hoped she was on the site somewhere. Once they realised she wasn't hiding in the woods or in a toilet cubicle, there'd be no other option.

We pulled down Lexie's tent, and I packed her bag. Her clothes and toiletries were scattered across the tent's innards, and water drizzled in through a channel in the tarpaulin floor. I pushed t-shirts, shorts, her swimming costume and hoodies away, shivering, then finally reached the empty bag she'd kept for her wellies, folding it and tucking it into the side of her rucksack. They'd be found soon, no doubt.

We all heard Lexie's car pull up. Mr and Mrs McCoy burst

out of it, faces red and tear-streaked, dressed loosely in pyjamas and coats and big boots. They'd clearly left the house in a hurry and thundered across the field towards us, clutching their phones, eyes wide.

"Have you found her?" Mr McCoy interrupted, eyes darting round at us all. Guilt ripped through me just watching him, distress abstract on his face. "Lexie? *Lexie?*"

"We think she went missing some time during the night," Sharon cut in, though her cheeks were pink and she looked like she was going to burst straight into tears. "We've searched the site, I don't see how we could've missed anything, but we're not qualified to search beyond that and we can't leave the girls on their own... I think we need to call the police."

Mrs McCoy's jaw was unhinged, hanging below her nose in abject horror. "The police? This is my little girl we're talking about, my Lexie –"

She began to sob again, body crumpling as she wept into her hands, body jiggling up and down. Mr McCoy slipped a paw around her but was looking pretty distraught himself, and swallowed heavily before speaking.

"That sounds like the next best step, Sharon," he said. "Let's get them in."

The phone seemed to ring for an age. We stood, scarcely breathing, bodies poised in suspense.

"Emergency. Which service?"

"The police," Sharon said, then gulped. "And... and maybe an ambulance."

The girls and I were told to wait by the fire. Even Chloe was silent, face white and eyes staring into the flames. They didn't know what had happened, but I could tell they knew enough – that it was somehow their fault, that their teasing must have something to do with Lexie's disappearance. That knowledge hung heavily on their twelve-year-old shoulders, set deep in their worry, a red flashing light.

I was silent. I don't know if that was more suspicious than not – no one seemed to have noticed. Mr and Mrs McCoy hadn't hedged their suspicions yet and Sharon was blaming herself, pacing up and down as she wondered why she hadn't heard anything, why she'd gone to bed so early and left us to entertain ourselves. I watched her saggy arms wobble as she walked up and down, up and down, up and around, up and down.

The police didn't use sirens, didn't use their flashing lights. It wasn't an emergency; I knew that better than most. Whether they found her in a day, a week, three months… it wouldn't make a difference. She was already gone. This part was just procedure.

"I'm Officer Joy." A policewomen stepped forward, eyes narrowed and hands clasped before her. She had a head of dark brown curls and deep-set eyes, like Chloe's, on her heart-shaped face. "Has anything changed since your last call?"

"No," Sharon informed her, shaking her head. "No, nothing. We've searched the site and found nothing. These are her parents, Mr and Mrs McCoy."

Officer Joy nodded, gesturing to two of her colleagues, who were climbing out of the car. "Okay. We'll need a description of the missing girl, and an item of her clothing for the dog to sniff. Are these her bags here?"

She was pointing to an unoccupied collection of bags, bright pink and labelled with sparkly stickers. Mrs McCoy nodded as the officer proceeded to remove a pair of Lexie's used undies from the bag, holding them out to the dog.

"We've been told to search for the next hour, and if we don't find her, we'll draft in other officers."

Mr and Mrs McCoy looked horrified at the prospect of having to wait another hour to find her, but could only agree.

"You'll stay here, in case she comes back. Make yourself something warm to eat and drink, perhaps some breakfast – it looks as though you left in a hurry. We'll be back before you know it."

Those famous last words.

## 44

Officer Joy arrived back at camp just thirty minutes later, dogs and other officers in tow. Her face was grave, a greyish tone covering her cheerful brown.

"The dogs picked up no scent," she said, to which Mr and Mrs McCoy clutched each other and shook their heads, expressions filling with horror. "I wouldn't worry – it's not uncommon, especially after heavy rainfall. But we found no trace of her on the site, no ripped clothing or missing items, and that's a great sign she's okay."

"Why?" Mr McCoy spat. There were tears in his eyes and he was trembling, either with rage or with fear, fists clenched. "She could be lying in a ditch somewhere *off* the site – have you considered that?"

"We're considering every possibility," Officer Joy said, though there was something uneasy about her now, jittery and self-aware. "We'll call in more officers next, off course – and, if we're lucky, the helicopter."

At that, Mrs McCoy let out a strangled scream and dropped to the ground. I watched, frozen, as her heels sunk into the grass and she collapsed over them, eyes closed and face all screwed up, hands on her eyelids and the most awful noise leaking from her mouth.

"Lexie!" was the only thing she seemed to be able to say, shrieking it over and over and over, as Mr McCoy attempted to comfort her and the other girls backed away in fear. "Lexie,

Lexie, *Lexie*!"

"Girls, I'm going to call your parents to pick you up early," Sharon said, turning to us in an attempt to shield us from Mrs McCoy's convulsion. "And Macey, it's up to you as to whether you want to stay here and help, or go home for some proper food."

I didn't know what to say. Hadn't I done enough already?

"Macey?" she echoed, bringing me back to my senses. "I can ring your mum now, if your phone's out of charge?"

"It's okay," I said. "I'll stay and help."

The other parents arrived in no time, speeding up the track and into the little car park. They ran over the grass in their Sunday morning attire and scooped up the girls, white faced and shaking, patting Mrs McCoy like she was some sort of animal. They were all thinking the same thing. That they were just so glad it was Lexie who'd gone missing, not one of their own.

"I'm sure they'll find her soon, Tracey," Lucy's mum said, forever the diplomat. "Try not to worry yourself."

The McCoys, however, couldn't do anything but nod and agree. They didn't believe her. They had a feeling.

They knew they'd lost her.

"Maybe she ran away?" Chloe's mum suggested. She was dressed in a trouser-suit, the most put-together of all the mums, hair straightened and eyes lined. "Was she unhappy in any way?"

Oh, the irony of it. Chloe shifted beside her while the other girls pretended to not know what she was on about, shrugging and clinging to their own parents, faces white with worry and guilt.

Officer Joy hadn't left her vehicle for at least half an hour now, sat with the dog and other two officers, scouring a screen and speaking into the radio with a set expression. They were calling in reinforcements, no doubt, and perhaps sending notices to other officers in the area. I didn't know how to feel about that. I was so conflicted, mind twisting and turning, heart pounding, feet tip-tapping against the grass, eyes unfocused…

I wanted them to find her, to just get it over with.

But at the same time, finding her would mean realising what had happened to her, perhaps uncovering the truth about what I did that night, me and Lexie. The very thought of it made my stomach turn.

*Don't think about it*, I told myself, squeezing my fists closed. *You can't change what happened.*

When I glanced up again, Mrs McCoy was watching me. Her gaze was steady, blue eyes placid against her red, pulsing skin. She just stared, not saying a word, still hunched over on the floor. Hands pressed against the earth and heels set behind her, she looked ready to launch herself at me, like some kind of monkey.

She noticed the clenching of my fists, the tightness of my voice, the panic in my eyes.

She noticed, because she was Lexie's mum, and that was her job.

In that moment, I swear she knew what had happened that night, knew that it was all my fault. I shrivelled under those watery blue eyes, like little aqua gemstones or raspberry bonbons, too clear, too transparent, too –

"The rest of the lads are on their way," Officer Joy announced. We all turned to her, hearts pounding. The other mums were still stood around by their daughters and Sharon, and everyone was silent, tense. "There's a helicopter coming, too, which is very lucky. I know it feels scary right now, and it'll be tempting to want to help with the search, but the best thing you can do right now is take your children home until we find Lexie. You'll be kept updated, I can assure you of that."

Sharon looked faintly green, but nodded along with Officer Joy and turned back to us, mouth set in a firm, straight line. "I agree, ladies. It'd be better if you took the girls home, to stop them worrying and keep them out of the way. I've got your numbers. You'll be notified as soon as she's found."

That just left me. Mrs McCoy's eyes were fixed on me as Sharon took my hand and squeezed it, asking for one last time whether I wanted her to ring my mum.

I didn't. I needed to be here, for Lexie, for myself. I needed to be here when they found her. I couldn't explain why – I just *needed* to be.

"You too, Tracey," Sharon added, turning to Mrs McCoy. "You need to go home, or at least get back in the car, where it's warm. I'll call you as soon as we find her."

I wasn't expecting her to take the advice, but the pair soon had returned to their car and were driving away to buy a coffee, perhaps just to take their minds off it all. We watched as they left, that sick feeling still churning inside of me. There was a McDonald's up the road, but they were gone much longer than just that. I think they knew that there was no point waiting around; they'd come back once there was news.

The helicopter was heard above us before the extra cars arrived, flying overhead and causing a racket. We shielded our eyes from the early morning sun and watched it soar overhead, propellors slicing through the air as it flew across the sky in a streak of vibrant colour. There were three cars provided for the search, each with four officers and at least five dogs. Huge, hefty beasts, with gnashing jaws and beady eyes. I held my breath as they leapt out and organised themselves into lines, hurrying past us and into the forest, eyebrows knitted.

They knew what they were doing. They'd find her.

There was no doubt about that now.

It was one o'clock by the time we heard anything. Officer Joy, who was waiting by the car with a clipboard of paperwork and files to catch up on, heard the radio buzz in and leaned to listen. Sharon and I sat by the smouldering fire in our camp chairs, silent, hands knotted on our laps, watching her like hawks.

Her body tensed. She froze. We watched as she let go of the radio and stepped back, slowly, turning to face us.

"A body's been found," she said, just like that. "She'll need to be identified, but she's wearing one of the lifejackets you have in the store, with a girl guiding logo on the breast. They're pretty certain it's Lexie."

# 45

I still can't remember how I reacted to the news that Lexie's body had been found.

Officer Joy sprung into action, scurrying around the car and carrying out all of the necessary procedures, answering the radio and tip-tapping away on her laptop. The dogs and men had been away for quite a while now, and we weren't in a position to leave until they arrived back to their cars to talk to us again. Lexie's body was being transferred by helicopter to the main hospital in town, where she'd have to be formally identified.

Sharon and I still hadn't said a word. I don't think I could've spoken, anyway. My voice would've given something away, I just know it. Sharon's face was white and she was clutching the arms of her camp chair tight, knuckles stretching through her skin.

I just sat there, hands clutched on my lap, heart pounding. I can't remember what I was thinking, if anything. Maybe I just felt numb.

It was Sharon who had to ring Mr and Mrs McCoy. They'd have to identify her, of course, stare into those stone grey eyes and decide whether it truly was their twelve-year-old daughter lying dead in the morgue. Even thinking about that felt wrong, disjointed. That wasn't how things were supposed to go.

"Hello?" she said, speaking weakly into her phone.

"Tracey, it's Sharon."

"Sharon?" came Mrs McCoy's voice, thick with urgency. "Have you found her? Have you found Lexie?"

"Tracey…" Sharon closed her eyes and leaned back against the chair, shaking her head over and over and over, like a wind-up doll. "Tracey, I'm so sorry. They found a body."

The other end of the line was silent. I could sense Officer Joy watching us, expression dour.

"I'm so sorry, Tracey. They want you to identify her at the hospital in town. It might not be Lexie, but –"

The beeping coming from her phone signalled that she'd already hung up.

We waited until the officers came pounding through the woods again before beginning to pack our things into Sharon's boot, squashing the tents and bags and assorted food and cutlery into a mismatched bundle. The men behind us were quiet, subdued, speaking in hushed tones and patting each other on the back in some kind of weird camaraderie. One even tried to shake hands with Sharon and apologise, though what he was apologising *for*, I don't know. They were going to have to interview us at some point, but it just felt wrong now – Lexie was dead, a twelve-year-old life cut short so suddenly, and as far as everyone knew, it was *just an accident.*

I pushed my rucksack deep into the boot, behind Sharon's sleeping mat and tent. Mr Sparkles, my sopping wellies and phone were all in there, evidence of… everything. I shivered, covering the edge with someone's limp coat, as if it'd make a difference.

The sun wasn't so hot today, the sky a sad shade of watery grey, like waxy skin. I had goosebumps, though that probably wasn't due to the cold. The forest watched us as we prepared to leave, mocking, waving its greenery in our sour faces. *We got her in the end*, it lisped, the sound of running water still singing through the trunks. *We got her, we got her, we got her!*

I sucked in a breath, rubbing my arms.

I'd led her right into the river's jaws. I'd led her there to be eaten, completely oblivious to its dangers. It was my fault.

Footsteps sounded behind us then, big boots against gravel.

"Sharon?" came a voice, startling me. "Macey? We have a few questions to ask, if that's okay with you – and then we'll let you go home."

I turned. A short, tubby officer was watching me with watery blue eyes, clutching a pocketbook and holding one hand to his belly. He was balding and wizened, like a pecan, and reached out his free hand to greet us.

"I'm Officer Pudrow," he explained, shaking our hands in turn. "I understand this must be a very traumatic time for both of you, but if you don't mind, we need to get the basics down before we can get on with the case."

Sharon nodded, but I could barely maintain eye contact with the man, shifting from foot to foot.

"How long did you know Lexie?" he asked, pulling out a pen to start taking notes. "She was a girl guide in your care, am I right?"

"That's right," Sharon said. She was unsmiling, brows knitted as she watched his pen scribble back and forth, back and forth, against the paper. "She's been with us for about two years."

"And you?" He turned to me, smiling, as though to appear friendly. It didn't seem friendly at all – more like a grimace. "How long have you been volunteering?"

"About three years." It sounded like such a long time,

saying it like that. It only felt like yesterday that Lexie had first walked in through the door, clutching Mr Sparkles tight to her chest and filled with the hope that somewhere in that room, she'd find her new best friends.

I swallowed.

"We found the body in a yellow lifejacket," Officer Pudrow continued, turning back to Sharon. "We think she was using the tyre swing, the one by the river – it appears to have been left out overnight, hanging right over the water, like it's been recently used. Did anyone give permission for the tyre swing to be in use? And were the girls allowed to use it without your supervision?"

"Of course not!" Sharon said. "It was a dangerous piece of equipment, requiring different harnesses and ropes to be in the correct place. I have training, but the girls are just *kids*. There's no way Lexie would've tried to use it on her own."

Officer Pudrow frowned at that, pointedly marking something on his paper. "So you don't believe it's likely that Lexie was there alone that night?"

We could see what he was getting at. My heart was racing and my hands were latched together tight, but it took everything I had to bark out, "She was dared, earlier on in the evening, to use the tyre swing. The other girls were bullying her. It wouldn't surprise me if she tried to use it herself to… prove herself."

That satisfied him. He nodded, scribbling away again, then glanced back up again with those watery blue eyes. "I know this might be a difficult question, but… when was the last time you saw Lexie alive?"

That was when Sharon flushed.

Of course. She'd gone to bed early, leaving me in charge. That looked suspicious all around. It made it seem like it was her fault, like leaving a minor in control of the girls was what had caused disaster.

"I wasn't too well, so I went to bed early." Her voice was stilted, nervous, as though *she* was confessing. "I know I should've stayed up with them, but I trusted Macey. She's good with the girls. She made sure they all got to bed."

Officer Pudrow was watching me again, so I was forced to nod.

"Right," I said. "They played some truth or dare and chatted around the fire, then I made sure they all went to sleep. I watched Lexie go into her tent and zip it up. That was the last time I saw her. It never crossed my mind that she'd try to use the tyre swing, or I would've stopped her!"

The lie dripped off my tongue like honey, and they lapped it right up.

"Okay." Officer Pudrow nodded, for what felt like the six hundredth time. "Okay. That'll be all for now. We know it's been a traumatic day for both of you – though we may have to get in touch again, with time, depending on the coroner's report."

I smiled, thanking him. I didn't *want* to thank him, not really – I just wanted him to leave. I wasn't sure how much longer I could keep up the pretence.

"My condolences," he added, before spinning and waddling back to his car.

My heart was still pounding, fists clenched, as I watched his retreating body. Sharon was frozen. The air around us whistled, chilly against my goosebumped arms and ankles. In the distance, the forest moaned. We stared at the car park's edge as the first car left, pulling out of the field and onto the main road. We didn't move until it was gone.

"Well," Sharon said, breaking the silence and shivering.

"Shall we set off?"

We climbed into the front seats together, doors clanking. The radio started as soon as the key hit the ignition. It was a love song, upbeat and chirpy, and I slammed down on the 'OFF' button just as soon as it begun.

Now that I was alone with Sharon, it seemed so much easier to just… exist. I knotted my hands together once more and stared ahead, tears filling my eyes, as we watched in the same position before pulling slowly into reverse.

"Oh God," I whispered, shaking my head as I felt something slip down my cheek, salty and warm. "*God.*"

There was nothing else to say. Even Sharon knew that.

Lexie was gone.

Gone.

# 46

So that's it. My story. Jenna knows the rest – how I arrived home freezing cold and grimy, and dropped straight into bed and slept for the entire day, only getting up when Mum served dumplings and beef stew for tea. I belched half of it up straight afterwards, then slept again, completely out of it, curled up under the covers as though nothing could wake me.

Until the police had knocked on our door the next morning, asking if they could speak to a Macey Collins residing here.

"Macey?" Mum hissed, poking her head around the door. "Macey, the police are here to see you. Get up, sweetheart, and put some decent clothes on!"

I pulled on leggings and a hoody, throwing my hair into a bun, then tiptoed downstairs in fluffy socks. Officer Pudrow and Officer Joy were sat at the breakfast bar, chewing on some dried mango Mum had left out, smiling at me.

"Macey!" Pudrow announced, like we were old friends. "It's great to see you again!"

Jenna watched the whole thing from the sofa in the corner of the kitchen, hunched over her breakfast with earphones plugged into silence. She knows how fervently I stuck to my story, emphasised the fact that Lexie was determined and headstrong, had been bullied since joining the group two years ago. She nodded along, backing me up from behind the lies. She was there when Officer Joy asked about Mr Sparkles, who they'd never found by the river or within it, and whether I knew where he might have got to.

"Sorry," I replied, shrugging nonchalantly. "I have no idea."

She's staring at me now, across my bedroom, Mr Sparkles clutched to her chest. Her eyes are narrowed. Now she knows everything – now she knows what happened to Lexie, and why I could never tell. Now she knows why it doesn't matter who knows about Lexie's death. It won't change a thing.

"Bloody hell," she whispers, shaking her head. "You've been hiding all that for the last month?"

It sounds like such a short amount of time, though it feels like years. I nod, tears filling my eyes, and slump into myself as they drip down my cheeks and over my fingers. Jenna crawls towards me. I hear the sound of her jeans rustling over the floorboards as she reaches me.

"Oh, Macey!"

I feel my sister's arms slip around me, warm and soft and BO-smelling, as she holds me close. It's done. Her sleeve catches my tears as I sob, sob myself raw, into her jumper and bony shoulders beyond. It all just comes out, slip-slopping over her in a wave of truth and realisation, the knowledge that I did, in fact, kill Lexie, my twelve-year-old friend and little sister, the girl I should've protected but didn't.

I can feel Jenna's body heaving up and down, up and down, as she appears to cry beneath me. Perhaps that hurts even more; the fact that my sister is so affected by this whole thing, too, when it's nothing to do with her or anybody else.

I pull away, sniffling and wiping my nose with my hand, as she stares at me with puffy eyes. I search her face for any sign of fear, dislike. Her lips are dry and trembling, and she slips her fingers through mine.

"I'm so sorry," she says, shaking her head. "I had no idea how hard this was for you, Mace – I can't imagine how you must still be feeling."

"I just want it to be over," I whisper. "I just want everyone to stop asking about it, to stop prying, trying to work out what did or didn't happen that night…"

"Then you need to tell the truth!" Jenna insists. "We need to ring up that nice Officer Joy – she seemed nice, anyway – or Sharon, or Mum, anyone! You need to confess, Mace. It was an accident, and I'll support you all the way –"

"But it won't bring Lexie back," I cut in, while she rolls her eyes.

"No, it won't." She squeezes my hands and cocks her head to one side, hair tipping over her face. "But it'll bring justice, Mace. Her family will know what happened to their daughter, and you won't have to live in fear anymore. You can give the unicorn back, and we can start *moving on*. Get your A-levels, go to university, meet someone new… You can't do any of that with this *thing* hanging over you."

"But I can't," I whisper. "I'll lose *everything*."

It's all flooding through my mind now, images of my friends and Sharon and the girl guides; my dad and his new little family, shaking their heads at me; Tyler and the boys; my mum, refusing to look me in the eyes again; Lexie's family. I can't let them find out what I did – I just *can't*.

Jenna doesn't say anything for a moment, watching me. "Okay. I can't force you to. But you know what I think, Mace. Just… consider it, okay?"

I nod, though we both know that I've already made my mind up.

We sit there, watching each other, hands linked, clock ticking. There's nothing more to say now, no more secrets hanging in the air. The room is still cold but there's sweat on my upper lip, face hot, red and sore like a blister. I swallow, and Jenna smiles at me. There's understanding in that smile. Honesty, and trust.

It feels good – I can't deny that. It feels good to finally be free of the truth, the thing that's haunted me so heavily these past few months.

"Would you like a drink?" I say, beginning to stand. "I think Mum still has some prosecco in the fridge from that work do she had, and she won't mind us using some of her fancy glasses – "

That's when I notice the door handle move.

It's a subtle gesture, the softest creak of metal against wood. Jenna follows my startled gaze and we watch it in unison as it tilts again, just a little, barely noticeable and yet accompanied by that same, ancient *creeeeaaaaak*.

"Mum?" Jenna calls, voice hesitant. "Is that you?"

Silence. Neither of us dare move a muscle. The handle stays still, just a chunk of gold-tarnished metal, quiet as the grave. There's no sound coming from downstairs, not a whisper from Mum, no running water or the television playing. I find my balance, placing one foot forward in an attempt to move closer to the door, heart pounding in my chest and rising slowly up to my mouth.

"Mum?" I echo, holding out my arm to open the door. The corridor is silent, still. Behind me, Jenna tenses. I'm cautious, nervous, fingers clutching the metal before pushing down. "Mum, what are you –"

But it's not Mum.

There, in the hall, is Doyle.

"Can we help you?" Jenna speaks up first, standing and crossing the floor to join me. The man doesn't say anything.

He's wearing a dressing gown, those pale feet sticking out from beneath it, wearing Mum's flip-flops.

I've only seen him a few times since Lexie's funeral, wandering about the house or tucked under Mum's covers, but I've heard *plenty* of their activities, and can only assume where he's just appeared from.

"Does Mum want something?" I ask.

Doyle stares right at me. "No," he replies, shaking his head. His eyes are clear, like gemstones, spheres perfectly white. I gulp, and he smiles. "No, your mum doesn't want anything. But Lexie's mum does. She's my sister-in-law, Tracey."

My stomach drops.

Something about this whole exchange makes me feel uneasy, on edge.

"You're Mr McCoy's brother – and Lexie's uncle," I repeat, though I knew that already, didn't need to clarify. Doyle. Doyle McCoy. I feel faintly sick now, mind spinning guiltily as we lock eyes. "Her Uncle Doyle."

I'm tongue-tied. Jenna holds me tight as we watch him, unsure of what to say next, an odd tension hung in the air between us.

I *want* to believe he's here for Mum. They have been sleeping together, after all; it wouldn't be hard to believe. Maybe he took a wrong turn coming out of her bedroom and accidentally ended up outside my bedroom, bare calves and all.

Yet I don't believe that. I don't.

I know he's here for me.

"Your mum is a lovely lady," he says, though there's something off about the way he says it, something robotic. "We hit it off at the funeral, as you can tell. I hope you don't mind me coming round. I'd hate to invade."

We don't say anything. I don't know what he's trying to get at yet, but it certainly isn't an apology for dating our mum.

"The thing is…" His face twists into a smile, but it's a cold, emotionless beam, stark against his pale skin. "I'm not here because of Lisa. I'm here because of you, Macey. I'm here to find out what really happened to Lexie."

That's when I know.

He heard. He heard it *all*. The confession to Jenna, how I lied to the police, how it's my fault Lexie ended up dead in the river that night. He knows I have Mr Sparkles, can see him behind me on the rug, and he knows that I've been keeping this from everyone, that I don't plan on telling.

The look on his face screams triumph.

"See, my sister-in-law noticed there was something odd about you from the beginning," he continues. "When Lexie disappeared, you didn't *want* to find her. It seemed like you already knew, had a guilty conscience, wanted to hide something from us all. She knew it was your fault, and she needed to find out how. *We* needed to find out how."

He glances behind him then, as though checking to see if anybody's listening.

When he turns back, there's a grin on his face.

"So I used the business card your mother gave me, when she spilt all that juice. It wasn't planned. The opportunity just fell into my lap. It gave me the perfect opportunity to come here, Macey – to come here and to watch you."

The clock ticks on behind us, loud and insistent, like a heartbeat. I don't dare open my mouth. Doyle's eyes don't move from me for a second as he watches, hands in his dressing gown pockets.

"We heard you coming back from Tracey's. Your mother thinks I've left, but I hid in the shower. Then when Jenna came to check on you, I decided to listen in. Oh, Macey..." He shakes his head back and forth, then takes a step towards us, eyes still locked on mine. "Haven't you been a bad girl?"

I gulp, stepping backwards into Jenna, heart pounding faster and faster by the minute. Doyle pulls his hand out of his pocket, and it only takes a minute for me to realise what he's holding.

"One phone call," he says. "That's all it would take, Macey, and you'd be locked up, where you belong. You should've been arrested weeks ago, but you decided to keep schtum, is that it? That makes it even more suspicious, like it was... I don't know, deliberate?"

"It wasn't deliberate," Jenna scoffs, pulling me closer and standing her ground. "You know that – you heard what Macey said. She only helped Lexie because she was scared she'd try to use the swing herself, and it was dark, she couldn't help not clipping the tyre on correctly –"

"But will anyone else believe that?" Doyle's eyes glisten. "Will the police believe you? Your friends? Or even Lisa?"

"It won't come to that," Jenna cuts in, though she doesn't look so sure. "We're not telling anybody until Macey's ready, okay? This is her decision. Let her confess, don't do it for her. You know how that will look –"

"Exactly. It'll look like you murdered my niece, Macey, which is the truth of the matter. You murdered Lexie."

As if in slow motion, he lifts a long, white finger. The phone is on, the screen lit up with a keypad of tiny green numbers. His finger hovers over the nine. I can scarcely breathe.

Nine.

Nine.

Nine.

The phone begins to ring.

"You dick," Jenna whispers, eyes wide. "You big –"

"Emergency. Which service?"

Doyle's face remains calm as he announces his business, insisting on speaking to the police officer in charge of the Lexie McCoy case. It only takes a few minutes to get through to them, and when Officer Joy answers, a smile breaks out over his pale face.

"I have information for you," he says, eyes still locked on me as he speaks. "Information about what really happened to Lexie that night."

Jenna instinctively reaches out to claw at him, but I tug her away. It's too late now – the damage has already been done.

"It was Macey Collins," he continues, voice raising a notch. "She killed Lexie. I overheard her confessing to her sister just now. She wasn't planning on coming forward, so I had to ring you myself. She was there when Lexie died, helped her onto the tyre swing, deliberately didn't clip her onto it properly. It's all her fault."

I feel sick.

Doyle's expression is elated, blue eyes round and piercing, sharp against my own. They stab my vision, painful and pointed, but I can't look away.

"She's a murderer," he adds, shaking his head as though in disgust. "All this time we've been sympathising with poor damaged Macey, and she murdered Lexie!"

Jenna and I can't hear what Officer Joy is saying; she's just a muffled murmur in the backs of our ears. Doyle's smile grows wider and wider, however, as she continues to speak.

"That's fine, Officer," he says, nodding. "I'll bring her to the station for questioning right now –"

I don't realise I'm running until I'm out of the door.

# 47

I dash down the stairs, Doyle's flip-flops clicking behind me, heart in my mouth. Along the corridor and to the front door, I pull it open with a crash and hurry onto the street, bare feet cold against the gravel and aching as it digs in.

"Macey!" comes that horrible, snarling voice, right at me. "Macey, get back here!"

Then there's a squeal, like something has grasped him from behind and is tugging him inside again. The sky is dark and the air is icy, and I hide my body under the shelter of some bushes, shivering in the half-light as I try to catch a glimpse of the porch, pushing leaves away in order to spy Doyle and my sister.

The door swings closed, however, and the front of the house emerges into darkness. I just stare at it for a moment, unsure of what to do next, hands trembling.

I can't go back, not now. Officer Joy will be looking for me, thinking I killed her deliberately, like Doyle said, and that that's why I never came forward with the truth. There's no escape from the truth, not now that it's out. Someone will find me, somehow. And I'll have to pay.

My phone buzzes in my pocket, lighting up through the fabric. I pull it out, wincing. My legs are cold and the dress barely covers my shoulders, and the icy glass is painful against my fingers, like a cut.

**don't come back yet – go see a friend, I'll speak to the officers and get this sorted. love you xo**

I stare at the words, head spinning. Don't go back? Where am I supposed to go? Jaye and Rosie live in a village a few miles out of Vibbington, and I can hardly turn up at Soraya's parents' home with bare feet and a puffy face, especially not now that she's with Tyler.

That only leaves one person.

I remember back to when I first met Nima, when she helped me pick up my books and smuggle me out of that dreaded maths lesson. She'd known Tyler for a while, she said – because they're *next door neighbours*.

Tyler lives on a wealthy street towards the centre of town, where the houses are semi-detached and Victorian, each three or four floors high and with metal rails around their front gardens, decorated with old oil-lamps the council never wanted to take down. It's Vibbington's only "tourist" attraction. One of the houses is now a converted museum, and all cars and modern décor have to be kept well out of site in the garages at the back, true to its period.

If Nima really lives there, it's my only option. It's freezing cold now and my phone reads five degrees, despite it being September. I rub my arms desperately, glancing back at the house one more time, but I know this is my only choice.

I take the back streets, straying away from the main roads, anything that Doyle could drive through and spot me. I dodge into alleyways and bushes the minute a car passes, aware that girls in short dresses and no shoes are prime targets to lurking creeps, even if a passer-by just wants to help. The roads are mainly empty now, the odd cat slinking under a car's body and rushing out in front of me, a fox sidling up to a dustbin at the back of a restaurant in search of its midnight snack.

My feet hurt. The pavements are covered in gravel and grit, the odd swipe of dog poo clinging to my toes. I daren't walk on the grass for fear of thorns and litter, but I manage to step on something sharp anyway, letting out a yelp and leaping into the air.

"Thanks a lot, Jenna," I whisper, but I don't really mean it. I know I couldn't have gone back to the house, not with Doyle there and Officer Joy on the lookout. I don't know how I can ever go back, even once Jenna has had a chance to plead my case – but I can't think about that, not yet.

Nima's street grows closer and the air feels warmer, less forbidding. Hot air drifts from restaurants and shop doors as I wander along the roads which join with Main Street, tiny streets filled with cafés and bistros, most of which have closed for the night yet are still steaming away. There are takeaway shops selling kebabs and pizza, and the scent of hot, greasy food wafts towards me, warming my chilly arms and frozen lungs.

I finally turn off onto Victoria Avenue, the old oil-lamps glowing all along the street, houses large and imposing. Two or three have their gates wide open while others are padlocked shut. It's a known spot for burglars, as most of the homes belonging to doctors and solicitors, people with fancy TVs and iPads in every room of the house.

Tyler's is the fifth house along. A red-brick property with a green door, the house leading right up to a fourth floor, which is where he sleeps in the attic room – where I once slept, too. There are two houses either side, one of which is semi-detached and all aglow, the other separated by an alley which no doubt leads to the garages behind. I pick the one attached to Tyler's, a similar red-brick property, and swallow the mountain of fear building inside my mouth.

If her parents answer, I can always just turn around and run, or ask to speak to Nima, who might be able to help. I think back to her kind brown eyes and welcoming smile, and a hint of confidence creeps back in, just enough to keep to push me up the path and onto her doorstep.

Three knocks. That's all it takes for the door to swing open, and a tousled head to poke out.

My stomach flips.

Nima's eyes are wide and circled in blue liner, but she breaks into a grin upon seeing me stood there, freezing cold, and tugs the door back to reveal herself.

"Macey!" she exclaims, beckoning to me. "Come in!"

Relief floods through my body and a weak smile takes over my face.

I'm safe.

I'm *safe*.

She doesn't seem to notice my bare feet or shivering body, and if she does, she doesn't ask, simply holding the door back for me to enter. The house is warm, carpet soft against my sore feet, every surface decorated in cream and marble. I breathe in, out. Nima passes me a chocolate button from the packet she's holding.

"To what do I owe this pleasure?"

She's smiling, properly smiling, like it's made her day to see me stood here in her hall. Her brown eyes are all crinkled and her nose is scrunched up, like a bunny rabbit, as she passes me another chocolate button.

"I was just passing," I say. It's pretty obvious that there's more to my story than that, but she doesn't pry, looking at me with genuine curiosity. I swallow. "I thought I'd pop in to say hi, but if it's not a good time…"

"It's a great time!" she cuts in. "My parents are staying over in Manchester for work, so I have the house to myself. I'm just watching a Disney movie – *Lilo & Stitch*, would you believe – but how about I show you my room? Would you like a drink?"

And just like that, I'm in.

She pours me a lemonade in the kitchen, sprinkling some sort of pink glitter into it, then leads me up the stairs. Her house is just like her in the sense that it's absolutely *perfect*, not a hair or fleck of paint out of place, each colour complimented by furniture and ornaments, carpet vacuumed to within an inch of its life. She's wearing a checked skirt and black tights with a woollen jumper and expensive sliders, and dances up the steps above me to the very top floor.

Her door is pink, contrasting with the sleek, modern house around it. She has a floor to herself, a strip of landing with a chest of drawers perched beneath the window, which overlooks the alleyway and a pitch black sky. It's identical to Tyler's, just flipped. She passes me the lemonade before pushing down on the handle and gesturing for me to follow.

"My room," she says, grinning. "Or should I say, *ma boudoir*."

It's like walking inside the world of a Disney princess. The walls are pink, a subtle shade that almost matches her door, and rose bushes climb right up to the roof. I almost assume they're real, but as I get closer I notice they're painted right onto the wall, each and every one of them, and turn to Nima with wide eyes.

"They took *hours*," she says, by way of explanation.

Her bed sits in the centre of the room. It's a double, covered in a fancy duvet and frilly pillows, a fluffy pink throw spread across the end, tiny plush fairies cuddled up between the cushions. There's a lava lamp on her bedside table and little glass animals dance along her window ledge, origami birds hung above the blinds, which are baby blue and covered in clouds. Photos hang on string, polaroids taken with her geeky friends. Mike and Steph... and three others I don't know.

"Your room is awesome," I whisper, though my voice is still hoarse from crying and cold. I drop onto the edge of the bed, careful not to let my grimy feet anywhere near the throw or soft white sheets, and she perches beside me with a smile. "Did you decorate it yourself?"

"Mostly." She adjusts herself, pulling her own feet under her so that she's cross-legged. "But enough about me! How are *you*, Macey? How's your day been?"

"Fine." I answer too quickly, and she raises an eyebrow, mouth twitching.

"Fine?" she echoes. "Are you sure? I'm a good listener."

I know I could tell her – I know I could tell her everything. She wouldn't judge, but would just listen, nodding along as I explained everything that had happened.

But I can't. She's one of the last people who actually *likes* me, and I don't want to ruin that.

"I had an argument with my mum," I tell her instead. The lie slips off my tongue, quick and easy, no questions asked. "I ran out – that's why I have no shoes on."

"So you walked *all the way here* with no shoes on?" She looks more shocked than suspicious, so I nod, trying for a smile.

"It wasn't that far, but it was pretty dumb, I know."

"Just a bit!" She glances round her room, eyes narrowed. "Have you eaten anything today? I have something in my cupboard, let me go check. I've been saving them for a special occasion…"

I want to say no – this isn't a special occasion, and I don't want her to waste whatever it is on me – but it's been hours since I left the McCoy house. It feels like even longer.

Nima slips away from me and crosses the floor to her wardrobe, which is white and edged in fancy wooden swirls. There's a mirror inside the door and an abundance of brightly coloured clothes decorate the rail, above boxes of pastel green, blue and pink. Inside one of them, she plucks out a ruby-red box of chocolates.

"They're from Belgium," she explains, carrying them over to us. "My dad often works there."

It feels like I'm dreaming; there's no way this can be true. A couple of hours ago, I was sat at Lexie's table, eating a roast with her family… and now I'm here, barefoot on Nima's bed, a coffee liqueur chocolate in my hand and warm breath on my neck.

It doesn't feel right. I'm avoiding the problem, skirting around the fact that Lexie's gone and I'm about to be punished, badly. I'm forced to swallow, as Nima's gazing at me expectantly, brown eyes fixed onto mine, heart-shaped face insistent. I place the chocolate in my mouth. It's gooey, strong with coffee and rich with cream, sliding over my tongue like a long, sweet slug.

"Nice?" Nima asks, eyes still fixed on me.

I nod.

Then she leans forward and kisses me.

# 48

Nima's lips are soft, moist, like pillows of soft pink on her face. I haven't closed my eyes – I don't know why – and so I'm gazing right at her eyelashes, which are long and black and splayed right across her cheeks, like the wings of a bird.

It feels nice, though. I can't explain the sensation, but it's... simple. *Right*. Like all I need in this moment is Nima and her pink bedroom, her soft hands against my neck, fringe tickling my forehead and lips pressing harder and harder against mine, more urgent now, desperate for more –

I pull away, heart racing. She still has her eyes closed. Slowly, almost not at all, I shuffle backwards across the bed and lean away, so that I can't smell her floral perfume or chocolate-scented breath.

Am I dreaming?

"I'm sorry," she whispers, shaking her head, eyes still squeezed shut. "I shouldn't have done that..."

"It's okay," I mutter instinctively – and that's when I realise. It is okay. The kiss was more than okay. It's okay that I'm here, in this moment, kissing Nima in her fairy-tale hideaway of a bedroom. Although it feels strange, so unlike the Macey Collins I always thought I was, something about Nima makes me feel safe, secure, like I'm wrapped in a blanket and hidden away from the rest of the world.

I think part of me already knew that, though.

"You probably want to leave now," she says, allowing her

head to drop into her hands. "Oh, this is so embarrassing! I really am sorry, I overstepped the mark –"

"I don't want to leave."

Time seems to stop in Nima's bedroom, her boudoir. She glances up at me, cheeks flushed pink and eyes wide. My hands are shaking so much I have to clamp them beneath me.

"You didn't overstep the mark."

Neither of us dare breathe as we gaze at each other, hearts pounding, loud against my eardrums. All the blood in my body seems to have rushed to my head.

I lean closer, lips parted, and she does the same.

When we collide, it's like fireworks are exploding all over my body. Nima is gentle and fierce all at one, a fiery warrior trapped in the body of a princess, hands sliding over my neck and down my back as we kiss, mouths joint in a mismatched jumble of teeth and tongue and flesh. She tastes of chocolate and spice, of lemonade and happiness, of excitement and security all at once… and of safety.

We fall onto the covers in union, her skinny body arched over mine, skirt riding up her legs as she leans into me. I'm on my back, dress all awry, slipping off one shoulder as she presses against me. Her lips are light as they move from my mouth and across my cheek, leaving a trail, making their way to the hollow between my jaw and neck, applying pressure as slowly as possible, then harder, more desperate.

She feels so fragile, so bird-like beneath my arms. Her body is thin, delicate, legs and arms short but perfectly crafted. Her straight hair dips towards me and brushes my face, like a feather.

"Is this okay?" she checks. "Tell me if it's not…"

But I shake my head and wrap my arms further around her back, so that her spine is digging into my arms and I can feel her shoulder blades beneath my fingers, like two wings about to sprout from her jumper.

"It's not too much," I whisper. How could it ever be?

She leans back into me, closer this time, lips grazing my chest and the line of which my collarbone falls. Her hand is on my leg – quiet, anti-social Nima, the girl I always underrated – and her fingers are circling my thigh, just lightly, a marshmallow-like motion which sends shivers across my body. I lie there, holding her, as her hand inches further and further up my leg, hot against my skin.

"Can I…" she murmurs, and I can't do anything but nod. It's like I'm hypnotised, part of some dreamlike state, locked with Nima inside her fairy-tale kingdom. Was I at the McCoy house earlier, sat at Lexie's table, talking to her family? Was the interaction with Doyle even real?

Nima's hands are gentle as she tugs at my dress, pulling it off and over my head. I can scarcely breathe. The room is warm and yet I'm covered in goosebumps, laid there in my underwear on her princess bed, that tiny, perfect body held against me like a glove.

Then she pulls back all of a sudden, eyes wide.

"I've never done this before," she says, out of nowhere. "I've only kissed two people, and one of them was a guy. I've never been… *close* to a girl."

Her face is pink, like she's embarrassed by the fact. I don't know what to say. I can't seem to string together coherent thoughts, mind spinning at a rate of knots, body swarming with heat.

"Neither," I say, eventually. "Just Tyler."

"I like you," she says, eyes never moving from my face. "I like you a lot, Macey."

"I like you too."

Because I do.

I really, really do.

We fall back into one another, less tentative this time, more at ease, reassured. Nima kisses me like this isn't her first real time being close to someone, like she's used to it, like she's in control.

And I… I let her lead. I'm too weak, too tired, too lost in her to take charge. Every bone in my body is immersed in the bliss, the joy of it all, eyes closed and heart thumping.

That's when my phone chimes.

Nima sits up at once, peering around for the culprit, face flushed and hands shaking. It seems to have shocked us from our dream and back into reality, and I rustle around in my crumpled dress to try and find the pocket.

Pulling out my phone, I turn it on with trembling fingers.

**I tried talking to Officer Joy, but there's just no evidence to help you, Mace – the fact that you didn't come forward yourself suggests you're guilty. I tried, but you need to come home and talk to them yourself. Then they'll get your side of the story. love you xo**

Shit. Once again, that sick feeling returns, the one I've gotten so used to. Nima's watching me, concerned, brown eyes wide and imploring.

"Is everything okay?" she asks, reaching to squeeze my hand. "You look like you've seen a –"

"I have to go." I leap from the bed, grabbing my dress and tugging it over my head and shoulders. I'm still clutching my phone and push it into my pocket, feeling it clunk as it reaches the bottom.

"Go?" she echoes. "What do you mean?"

"Thank you for tonight," I say, ignoring her query. I'm

trying to remain calm as I cross the floor to the door, but my legs wobble, like they're made of paper.

Where do I go now? What do I do?

"Did I do something wrong?" Nima repeats, brow furrowed.

"No!" I reply, but it's so sudden that it comes out almost like a bark. "You didn't do anything wrong. I just need to leave – there are things I need to do."

"Like what?" she presses. "What's going on, Macey?"

But I'm out of the door and down the stairs before I have the chance to reply.

The street is silent as I make my way outside, shivering and wincing as my feet hit the cold pavement. I hear the door open behind me and Nima shout something, but I can't stop to reevaluate. I need to leave. I race down the road and around the corner, once again determined to stick to the back roads and avoid any place I could be spotted. My heart's pounding in my mouth and I'm too anxious to stop and think.

I can't go home – there's no chance now, not when they know what I've done and will most likely send me away, ruining my chance of a future. I have no other friends to go to, not that I'd want to bother them with my problems, or for them to find out what I did that night. There's no other option, no way out. I've hit the brick wall I've so long been running from.

That only leaves one thing. Something that's been on my mind this whole time, creeping round the corners.

My feet are slow as I jog towards the other end of town, feet slapping the pavements and screaming in gravel-induced pain. My eyes are filled with tears. Yet something inside of me screams that I'm doing the right thing. Something I should've done weeks ago.

I can't remember when I last came here; it feels like years, when in reality it was weeks, days, even, since I stood on the slimy bridge and gazed down into the stream. I'd just slept with Tyler at Bob's party, and that event had almost tipped me over the edge. Almost.

My feet burn as I run through the woods on the outskirts of town, heart pounding, body heavy. I feel sick. Someone, somewhere, has been smoking weed, and the smell is pungent and earthy as it hangs all around me.

There's a wind picking up, the beginnings of a storm. It's cold, wet, the forest floor slimy beneath my toes. Pebbles and leaves and sharp twigs prod my toes. I push aside branches as I race, feeling them against my skin, my hair.

Why me? Why me? *Why?*

The bridge is up ahead, gazing at me through the trees. It only goes over a tiny break of water, hardly the river Lexie drowned in, but it's shallow enough for you to break your neck, that I'm sure of. The planks are green with algae and a breeze rushes towards me as I clasp the rail, gazing down into the darkness, the current caught in the moonlight. I watch as it flies across the pebbles, faster and faster, ice cold, calling me down.

Like I said, I've been here before – we both know that.

Only last time wasn't the first.

The first time I came here I was ten years old, the same age Lexie was when I first spied her across the chapel. I was gap-toothed and straggly-haired, skinny and pale, a lost sheep on a moor of thousands. My dad had left, my mum was a mess, and my older sister – my best friend – was going off the rails right before my eyes.

The first time I came here, I wasn't happy. I was desperate

to blend in, to disappear, but that made me even more obvious.

The first time I came here, I was just like Lexie.

"Macey! Macey, the bus is coming! Come on, Macey, open your mouth – it needs to drive through the gap in your teeth!"

It was September, the beginning of autumn, and a cool breeze trickled through the forest. I was running, patent black shoes hitting the path hard. There were a few girls behind me – three or four, if I remember rightly – with sticks and miniature vehicles stolen from the year one classroom, designed to scare me, to make me run faster, further.

"Hey, Macey! This car's in a rush – it needs its tunnel!"

I tried to block out their words, to focus on running, on getting away. I couldn't veer from the path – Mum would kill me if I got lost and was late home – and so I continued to run through the trees, heart pounding. The ground was studded with jewel-bright litter, packets of Wotsits no one had bothered to bin after their picnics, jelly pots discarded from a child's pushchair. Cigarette butts littered the ground, and something which looked like a clear, popped balloon had been speared on a nearby branch.

The sky was grey but the forest was dark, just a sparse smattering of light poking through where the canopy was most dense. I was cold, far too cold. But I couldn't turn back now.

I could sense the bridge coming up ahead, a short way up the path, over the stream. I could hear the water, too, though it was nothing more than a tinkle, a light scattering of droplets against the pebbles below. We weren't supposed to go past the bridge. The land beyond was privately owned by a nearby toff, and we'd all heard horror stories about him catching trespassers in rabbit snares. I stopped short as my shoes hit the planks, almost toppling over, and grasped the railing with trembling hands. Glancing backwards, I could just make out my assailants through the trees, dappled grey light pouring over them.

Darcie Carlton was in the centre, the shortest of the lot, stood with her hands on her hips as she flew to a stop before me. Despite her height, she was by far the most imposing. Fully-developed, even though she was only ten or eleven, and with fiery red hair her common-as-muck mother had no doubt helped her dye.

I inhaled sharply as she stared at me, a malicious grin spreading over that pretty face of hers. Her eyes gleamed.

"Macey," she repeated, taking a step forward. "Why aren't you running from us?"

I couldn't speak, the words stuck in my throat. She was gazing at me with such intensity, such hatred, face mocking me with its perfection. The gap in my teeth felt more obvious than ever, skin pale and goose-bumped, legs matchstick-thin beneath my school skirt.

"Are you scared of crossing the bridge?" she pressed, eyes narrowed. "Is that why you've stopped? You're scared Giles will trap you, because he thinks you're a pest?"

I shook my head, heart pounding, but she'd already burst into sharp peals of laughter.

"You're so pathetic, Macey. No wonder your dad left. I bet he didn't want to be associated with such messed-up kids. Isn't your sister some sort of goth now? My sister's in her maths class at the secondary school, and apparently all the boys think she's a freak. Your whole family's full of freaks, Macey, and you're the biggest of them all!"

I tried to step backwards but the railing stopped me, spine digging into the rotting wood. It didn't feel solid, just enough to save me from plummeting to the ground.

"You need to face up to it, Macey!" she continued. "You're a freak! It's no wonder you have no friends, no boyfriend, no dad. No one will ever love you. You should just go die – no one would even miss you!"

I felt the wood beneath my fingers, slimy and cold. I pressed one foot onto the railing, hoisting myself up, so that my bum was flat against it and my feet were off the ground.

Behind me, the stream rattled on. It was only three or four metres away, tumbling over a scattering of pebbles, filled with weeds and greenery, bits of leaves and rogue forest. I glanced over my shoulder, watching as it rushed away from me, the water screaming as it hurried along.

"Is she okay?" one of Darcie's cronies muttered, in a slightly mocking tone. "Is she going to fall?"

They watched as I hoisted myself over the railing, so that my body was latched onto the other side. I wasn't going to jump, of course – I was only trying to scare them – yet their faces spoke abject terror.

It was surprisingly peaceful, clinging to the rail above the stream like that. Weirdly calming. I sucked in a breath, body trembling as my fingers clutched the wood, slick with algae beneath their tips.

"You said I should just go die," I echoed, finally finding my voice. "If that's what you want…"

They glanced at each other, finally taking a step backwards.

"We didn't *mean* it, dumbo," Darcie said. "Just… just get down, Macey, you're being stupid."

I didn't move, still hanging over the river with my feet and hands clinging on tight.

I was trying not to show how cold I was, how numb my fingers were growing, how much I wanted to burst into tears and tell them all to leave.

I needed to scare them, to get them off my case. It was my only chance.

"If you don't want me to jump," I said, loosening my grip for them to see, "then stop. Stop making fun of my teeth, my family, my sister. You've been warned, Darcie!"

She shook her head, cheeks colouring, and linked arms with the girls around her.

"Fine," she replied, scowling. "Have it your way. But you're still a freak, Macey Collins – this just proves it."

I watched as they ran away through the trees, leaving me stranded on the wrong side of the bridge, trembling with what felt like *triumph*.

Four years of bullying, over in a heartbeat. Four years of name-calling, of being the odd-one-out, of having no friends, of sitting alone in the school canteen and being partnerless in PE lessons… gone. Just like that.

As I clambered back over the railing, feeling my feet hit solid ground, I swallowed heavily and smoothed down my skirt. Only one thing was clear in my mind, stark red against the fearful blue of my thoughts.

I was never, ever going to be called a freak again.

# 50

Watching somebody getting bullied is completely different once you've been on the receiving end. While I sympathised with Lexie, the real reason I never stepped in and helped is because it didn't affect me, not anymore. I was once that girl, targeted and teased, left out of all the jokes, the fun. I worked hard to pull myself from that spot. This wasn't my problem.

When the bullying stopped, I transformed. The Macey who once was is now just a memory, tucked out of sight in my mind, locked away. I got braces the following year, though no one had pointed out the gap in a while – and as I grew older, I realised it wasn't all too noticeable, anyway.

Then Rosie arrived.

I was eleven when she first strutted into the classroom, straight from South Africa, a polka-dot headband pushing back her curls, face studded with gem-like freckles. I wanted to be her friend – *needed* to be her friend. She was the answer to all my prayers.

It's easy to blend in once you're not a target. You can wear what they wear without someone pointing it out; you can buy makeup, nail polish, cool clothes; you can eat the same food, frequent class parties, talk to boys. Rosie and I started secondary school together, intent on making an impression, where we met Soraya and Jaye, our partners in crime. I became an acquaintance of Darcie Carlton, the girl who'd been my enemy for so many years. I might have even been more popular than her, at one point. I was certainly more *liked*.

I got good grades, had a pretty face, fit into the masses. People respected me. I distanced my image from that of my family, made sure as few people as possible knew I was related to Jenna Collins. I kissed boys, had my first proper snog at a party in year ten, just to get it over with. I didn't sleep with anyone until Tyler, but I let this sleazy guy touch me up after the year eleven prom – it gave me something to talk about during truth or dare, so that I was no longer the innocent one, the girl with the least experience.

I worked hard to be liked. It becomes an effort, building your reputation, staying out of scandals, trying to blend in. I'd mastered the art.

And now it's ruined.

Everyone will find out what I did to Lexie. They'll have to – you can't go into a centre for young offenders without everyone knowing. I won't finish my A-levels, or progress to university, like I always hoped.

I won't be well-liked, respected, the girl who stays out of all scandal. I'll be targeted. I won't get another boyfriend, new friends, a new life. People will despise me. They'll rub my nose in it when Tyler and Soraya become official, leave endless sleazy comments on my Facebook page, my Instagram, try to add me on Snapchat just to send hate. They'll ruin my life, the way I ruined Lexie's.

It's dark and cold, and I'm trapped within the forest in my bare feet, wind blowing up my dress, hair still coiled tightly above my head. The bridge is slimy beneath me, enshrouded in pitch black air. I take my phone, first, pulling it out of my pocket and cradling it in my hands.

**I'm so sorry.**

Just three words, yet meaning so much. I add everyone to its recipients… Jenna, Mum, Rosie, Soraya, Jaye, Tyler, Nima, Sharon. My dad, even his new girlfriend. The head of sixth form, Mr Roberts. Mrs McCoy – Lexie's mum.

I hit send, before hurtling my phone up into the air and watching it land with a splash in the stream up ahead. The rushing water brings it back down towards me, before it disappears under the bridge in a haze of blue light and vanishes from sight.

Now me.

I just want it to be over… all of it. I want to go the way Lexie went, feel the cold water fill my lungs and burble at my lips, spilling blood and tears into the stream. I want to feel my limbs succumb to the cold, feel my breath drift away into my cool night, evaporate into a pool of nothingness.

I want to die.

I lift my foot onto the wet railing, almost slipping, and carefully clamber onto the top. It's the third time in my short life that I've threatened to jump from here, and you know what they say about the third time holding luck. The rail is slug-like beneath my fingers, green and living with tiny organisms, crying out for me to toss myself over and onto the ground below.

I angle my body so that my head will hit first. I don't know if that's what I should be doing. I've never done this before, obviously. It's not deep enough to drown me, so breaking my neck feels like the next best option. I take a deep breath, clutching the railing with my toes and fingernails, eyes open wide against the cold air. Nothing has ever felt so *right*.

I've tried to live with the guilt, but it's just not fair, not on anyone. It's not fair that Lexie's dead while I live on. It wasn't fair to burden Jenna with my story. It wouldn't be fair for those who love me to continue to love a *murderer*.

"I'm so sorry," I repeat, this time out loud.

I let go of the railing.

And I fall.

Dear diary,

I've been thinking about death a lot lately. Dying, being dead. Wondering how you can go from being alive to being somewhere other than here, on earth. Wondering how someone so complex, with thoughts and connections and emotions and skills, can cease to exist in the blink of an eye.

Lexie was smart. Beautiful. Artistic. She had a family who loved her, a life full of colour and paint and fun, a life she should've continued well into the future, where she could have had her own children, a husband, friends, all the things girls like Chloe Alice would find so easy.

I can't tell anyone I've been thinking about death. Not Jenna, Nima, Rosie. They'd worry, look too deep into it, assume me thinking about death would lead to the dreaded s-word. It won't. It won't.

No one knows what happened to Lexie, so I don't need to think about that yet.

It's interesting, though. And bleak. The idea that no matter what you achieve in life, it's all for nothing. All the legends of our time... those who built our landscapes, who invented the things we can no longer live without. What was it for? To pave the way for future generations, who will achieve the same depressing end? To make life easier for children, grandchildren, who'll fall from tyre swings in a cruel twist of fate on a cold summer night? To create a world which will eventually implode?

It's pointless, life. So, so pointless.

Why do we bother?

Why do I bother?

# acknowledgements

These might be the most sparse acknowledgements you ever read. Self-publishing a book means there's nobody to thank for the cover design, formatting, editing... I had to do it all myself, on my very well-used laptop at my desk at uni. So firstly, thank you to my laptop, for listening to the thousands of words I've poured into you and for not giving up on me yet. And for Microsoft Word. You've helped me write every manuscript ever, and to format this hellish book ready to self-publish. It's been a journey, to say the least.

First and foremost, thank you to my Wattpad family. Five long years of writing and posting my work online. Five years of comments and criticism, of feedback and support, of creating and deleting books. 'Guided' was the third book I actually completed on there, and the one which gave me faith in my writing. Ten thousand reads later, Macey's story is here, as a paperback novel, for you all to buy and place on your bookshelf. It's been a lot of hard work, time and effort (obviously) but I wouldn't have done it without you. A sane person wouldn't sing to an empty audience, just as I wouldn't write to if I didn't have such an incredible group of people to devour each chapter.

So to Sana, Bridget, Isobel, Ada, Christina, Hannah, Hannah, Martha-May and more... I fully believe you deserve the dedication at the start of this book, because you're the main reason it exists. Your weekly (daily!) comments, votes and messages made writing this book a pleasure and a joy. You're such incredible writers yourselves and deserve all the success in the world with your own books, and I'm so excited to support you when the time comes!

Next, to Holly Hamilton, a fellow writer of young adult fiction. Your advice and mentorship has been invaluable over the years, and I'll be forever grateful for your support. Thank you. To Lydia Smith, for listening to my rants about nothing in particular and for not minding too much when I plan my books in lectures instead of actually making notes.

To Driffield Secondary School and Sixth Form, for inspiring this book in many, many ways, for better or for worse. To my family, for not realising how much time I spent writing 'Guided' instead of revising for my A-levels. To my mum, for pointing out my stupid mistakes and missing punctuation, for reading and (hopefully) enjoying my book's first draft.

To my best friends and favourite people in the world... Esther, Molly, Catherine, Charlie. Just because. Because you exist, and because I wanted your name to be printed here. Because you make me so happy, and I can only write when I'm happy.

Thank you, the reader, for purchasing this book for whatever reason. I hope you got something positive from it, and that it made you feel. Thank you for the support, and for appreciating my work (even if you absolutely hated it).

And finally, to Emma Smith, for being an absolute legend and writing this thing. I assume, if you're reading this, that I actually found the courage to get 'Guided' printed. You're pretty epic.

NORMAL, RIGHT?

# MID-NIGHT SHER-BET

## EMMA SMITH

YOUNG LOVE NEVER LASTS...

BUT FRIENDSHIP MEANS FOREVER.

SHE KNOWS...

# WASTED

## BOOK TWO

## EMMA SMITH

TWO MEN ARE DEAD... AND NOW
ONE OF THE GIRLS IS, TOO.

# EMMA SMITH

is a young adult author from Yorkshire, England. She wrote and illustrated her first "book" when she was seven years old and hasn't stopped writing since. When she's not walking on the beach or drinking an iced coffee with a crumpet and some chocolate, you'll probably find her reading something dark and mysterious… and most certainly YA.

**@themmasmith on Instagram**

**emmasmithbooks.com**

Printed in Great Britain
by Amazon